ALICE'S NI

WONDERLAND

Alice's Nightmare in Wonderland is a curious sort of a book. In fact, it is a portal to another world, the dream-world of Wonderland. As well as the book itself, you will need two dice (or a standard pack of playing cards), a pencil and an eraser. Using these tools, and a simple set of game rules contained within the book, you will guide the eponymous heroine of Lewis Carroll's *Alice's Adventure in Wonderland* on a new and perilous quest as she finds herself called upon to save the world of playing cards and talking animals from the increasingly deranged Queen of Hearts.

Have you ever wondered what would have happened if Alice had not drunk from the bottle labelled 'Drink Me', or if she had not joined the Hatter, the March Hare, and the Dormouse for tea? Well now you can find out. In *Alice's Nightmare in Wonderland*, YOU decide which route Alice should take, which perils to risk, and which of Wonderland's strange denizens to fight. But be warned – whether Alice succeeds in her quest or meets a dire end as the nightmare escalates will be down to the choices YOU make.

Are you ready to go back down the rabbit-hole?

Proudly Published by Snowbooks in 2015

Snowbooks Ltd.
email: info@snowbooks.com
www.snowbooks.com

British Library Cataloguing in Publication Data
A catalogue record for this book is available from the
British Library.

Hardcover 9781909679818
Paperback 9781909679597
Ebook 9781909679740

With special thanks to the Dodo play-testers, Amy
Winchester, Antony McGarry-Thickitt, Colin Oaten,
Don Alsafi, Fabrice Gatille, Flip Espinoza, James A
Hirons, James Aukett, Keith Phillips, 林立人 Lin Liren,
Mark Myers, Mill Goble, Nicki Gray, Paul Windmill,
Raj, Stephen R Dutton, Steve Dean, Steven Pannell,
Tiago Vieira Perretto, Xymon "Awesome" Owain.

ALICE'S NIGHTMARE IN WONDERLAND

BY JONATHAN GREEN

SNOWBOOKS

Also by Jonathan Green

Snowbooks
You Are the Hero – A History of Fighting Fantasy Gamebooks
Christmas Explained – Robins, Kings and Brussel Sprouts
Sharkpunk (short story anthology edited by Jonathan Green)
Game Over (short story anthology edited by Jonathan Green)

Fighting Fantasy Gamebooks
Spellbreaker
Knights of Doom
Curse of the Mummy
Bloodbones
Howl of the Werewolf
Stormslayer
Night of the Necromancer

Sonic the Hedgehog Adventure Gamebooks
Theme Park Panic (with Marc Gascoigne)
Stormin' Sonic (with Marc Gascoigne)

Doctor Who – Decide Your Destiny
The Horror of Howling Hill
Star Wars: The Clone Wars – Decide Your Destiny
Crisis on Coruscant

Gamebook Adventures
Temple of the Spider God

Warlock's Bounty
Revenge of the Sorcerer

Path to Victory
Herald of Oblivion
Shadows Over Sylvania

For Clare, Jake and Mattie.

Contents

WELCOME TO WONDERLAND

"WHAT A STRANGE WORLD WE LIVE IN."

Introduction

The book you hold in your hands is a gateway to another world, the dream-world of Wonderland. Once inside its pages and you will find yourself falling down the rabbit-hole to embark upon a thrilling adventure.

You see, this is no ordinary book. Rather than reading it from cover to cover, you will discover that at the end of each narrative section you will be presented with a series of choices which allow you to control the course of the story.

In *Alice's Nightmare in Wonderland* you guide the eponymous heroine of *Alice's Adventures in Wonderland*, by Lewis Carroll, through a nightmarish dreamscape to the conclusion of her quest. You decide which path to take, which risks to brave, and even which of the weird inhabitants of Wonderland you will meet along the way to engage in battle.

Success is by no means certain and you may well fail to complete the adventure at your first attempt. However, with experience, skill, and maybe even a little luck, each new attempt should bring you closer to your ultimate goal.

In addition to the book itself, you will need two six-sided dice, or a conventional pack of 52 playing cards, a pencil, an eraser, and a copy of Alice's Adventure Sheet (there are extras at the end of this book).

"It was a very difficult game indeed."

Playing the Game

There are three ways to play through *Alice's Nightmare in Wonderland*. The first is to use two conventional six-sided dice. The second is to use a conventional pack of 52 playing cards. The third is to ignore the rules altogether and just read through the book, making choices as appropriate, but ignoring any combat or attribute tests, always assuming you win every battle and pass every skill test. (Even if you play the adventure this way, there is still no guarantee that you will complete it at your first attempt.)

If you are opting to play through *Alice's Nightmare in Wonderland* using the game rules, you first need to determine Alice's strengths and weaknesses.

"WE'RE ALL MAD HERE!"

Alice's Attributes

Alice has five attributes you will need to keep track of during the course of the adventure, using Alice's Adventure Sheet. Some of these will change frequently, some less so, but it is important that you keep an accurate record of the current level for all of them.

> *Agility* – This is a measure of how athletic and agile Alice is. If she needs to leap across a chasm or dodge a deadly projectile, this is the attribute that will be employed.

> *Logic* – This is a measure of how clever and knowledgeable Alice is, and will be tested if Alice ever has to think her way out of a tricky situation or solve a mind-bending puzzle.

> *Insanity* – The deeper Alice plunges into the nightmare that is besetting Wonderland, the more her sanity will be put at risk. Rest assured

that you should do all you can to prevent Alice from losing her marbles altogether during the course of the adventure.

Combat – This is a measure of how skilful Alice is at fighting, whether it be in pugilist fashion with her fists, or wielding a keen-edged blade in battle.

Endurance – This is a measure of how physically tough Alice is and how much strength she has left. This attribute will vary more than any other during the course of Alice's adventure.

Unlike some adventure gamebooks, in *Alice's Nightmare in Wonderland* Alice's strengths and weaknesses are not determined randomly. Instead, you get to decide what she is good at and, conversely, what she might not be so good at.

Alice's *Insanity* score always starts at zero. Her *Endurance* score always starts at 20.

Alice's remaining attributes – *Agility*, *Logic* and *Combat* – start at a base level of 6. You then have a pool of 10 extra points to share out between *Agility*, *Logic*, *Combat* and *Endurance* as you see fit, but you can only add up to 5 points to each attribute. So the maximum starting score for *Agility*, *Logic*, and *Combat* is 11, and the maximum starting score for *Endurance* is 25. (You must apportion all 10 points one way or another, and cannot leave any unused.)

For example, you might choose to add 2 points to Alice's *Agility* score, 4 to her *Logic* score, 2 points to her *Combat* score, and add the remaining 2 points to her *Endurance* score, which would give Alice the following starting profile for the game:

Agility = 8, *Logic* = 10, *Insanity* = 0, *Combat* = 8, *Endurance* = 22.

Alternatively you might want to add 4 points to her *Agility* score, nothing to her *Logic* score, add 1 point to her *Combat* score, and spend the remaining 5 points bolstering Alice's *Endurance* score, which would give her this starting profile:

Agility = 10, *Logic* = 6, *Insanity* = 0, *Combat* = 7, *Endurance* = 25.

If you wanted to make her more of an all-rounder, you could raise Alice's *Agility*, *Logic* and *Combat* scores by 3 points each, and use up the last point on her *Endurance* score, which would give Alice this starting profile:

Agility = 9, *Logic* = 9, *Insanity* = 0, *Combat* = 9, *Endurance* = 21.

Having determined where Alice's strengths and weaknesses lie, record the value of each attribute in the appropriate box on Alice's Adventure Sheet in pencil, and make sure you have an eraser to hand, as they will doubtless all change at some point as you play through the adventure (and some more than others).

Although there are limits on how high each of Alice's attributes can be at the start of the adventure, there is no limit as to how high any of Alice's attributes can be raised during the course of the adventure, dependent upon bonus points Alice may be awarded. However, should

Alice's *Endurance* score ever drop to zero, or below, then her adventure is over and you should stop reading immediately; if you want to tackle the quest again, you will have to start from the beginning, determining Alice's attributes anew, and then starting the story from section 1 once more.

"ĐO YOU PLAY CROQUET?"

Testing Alice's Attributes

At various times during the adventure, you will be asked to test one or other of Alice's attributes.

If it is Alice's *Agility*, *Logic* or *Combat* that is being tested, simply roll two dice. If the total rolled is equal to or less than the particular attribute being tested, Alice has passed the test; if the total rolled is greater than the attribute in question, then Alice has failed the test.

If it is Alice's *Endurance* score that is being tested, roll four dice in total. If the combined score of all four dice is equal to or less than Alice's *Endurance* score, then she has passed the test, but if it is greater, then what is being asked of her is beyond what she is capable of and she has failed the test.

If it is Alice's *Insanity* score that is being tested, roll two dice, and in this case, if the total rolled is less than her *Insanity* score, Alice has failed the test. However, if the total rolled is equal to or greater than her *Insanity* score, then Alice has passed the test.

"It's Always Tea-time."

Restoring Alice's Attributes

There are various ways that Alice can restore lost attribute points, or be granted bonuses that take her attributes beyond their starting scores, and these will be described in the text.

However, an easy way to restore lost *Endurance* points is to find things for Alice to eat and drink. Sometimes Alice may find enough food that she can make herself some provisions to take with her for later on in the adventure.

Make sure that if Alice does find any supplies of this nature that you record them on Alice's Adventure Sheet, along with any information about exactly how many attribute points they will restore when consumed.

"Curiouser And Curiouser!"

Alice's Special Abilities

In addition to her five basic attributes, Alice also has two special abilities that she can employ at critical moments during her journey through the nightmarish Wonderland.

> *Curiouser and Curiouser* – If Alice finds herself in a tight spot she can use this ability to change the nature of the dream world around her, although this might result in her actually making things worse rather than better.

The Pen is Mightier – This ability allows Alice to avoid coming to blows with an enemy, by altering the narrative of the encounter and thereby enabling her to get away unscathed.

These very special abilities can only be used three times each during the course of the adventure. Each time Alice's calls on one of them, you must cross off a box on Alice's Adventure Sheet under the appropriate special ability.

"OFF WITH HER HEAD!"

Combat

Alice will repeatedly be called upon to defend herself against the bizarre and malevolent denizens of the nightmarish realm that Wonderland has become since her last visit. Sometimes she may even choose to attack these horrors herself. After all, as they say, the best form of defence is attack.

When this happens, start by filling in Alice's opponent's *Combat* and *Endurance* scores in the first available Nightmare Encounter Box on Alice's Adventure Sheet.

Whenever Alice engages in combat, you will be told in the text whether Alice or her enemy has the initiative; in other words, who has the advantage and gets to attack first.

1.   Roll two dice and add Alice's *Combat* score. The resulting total is Alice's *Combat Rating*.

2. Roll two dice and add Alice's opponent's *Combat Score*. The resulting total is her opponent's *Combat Rating*.

3. For each Combat Round, add a temporary 1 point bonus to the *Combat Rating* of whichever of the combatants has the initiative for the duration of that round.

4. If Alice's *Combat Rating* is higher than her opponent's she has wounded her enemy; deduct 2 points from her opponent's *Endurance* score, and move on to step 7.

5. If Alice's opponent's *Combat Rating* is higher, then Alice has been wounded; deduct 2 points from Alice's *Endurance* score, and move on to step 8.

6. If Alice's *Combat Rating* and her opponent's *Combat Rating* are the same, roll one die. If the number rolled is odd, Alice and her opponent deflect each other's attacks; go to step 10. If the number rolled is even, go to step 9.

7. If Alice's opponent's *Endurance* score has been reduced to zero or below, Alice has won; the battle is over and she can continue on her way through Wonderland. If her opponent is not yet dead, go to step 10.

8. If Alice's *Endurance* score has been reduced to zero or below, Alice's opponent has won the battle. If you want to continue your adventure

you will have to start again from the beginning, determining Alice's attributes all over again, and starting from section 1 once more. If Alice is still alive, go to step 10.

9. Alice and her opponent have both managed to injure each other; deduct 1 point from their respective *Endurance* scores. If Alice's *Endurance* score has been reduced to zero or below, Alice's adventure is over; if you want to play again you will have to determine Alice's attributes anew, and start again from section 1. If Alice is still alive but her enemy's *Endurance* has been reduced to zero or below, Alice has won; the battle is over and she can continue on her way through Wonderland. If neither Alice nor her opponent are dead, go to step 10.

10. If Alice won the Combat Round, she will have the initiative in the next Combat Round. If her opponent won the Combat Round, they will have the initiative. If neither of them won the Combat Round, neither of them will gain the initiative bonus for the next Combat Round. Go back to step 1 and work through the sequence again until either Alice, or her opponent, is defeated.

Occasionally Alice may find herself having to fight more than one opponent at once. Such battles are conducted in the same way as above, using the ten step process, except that you will have to work out the *Combat Ratings* of all those involved. As long as Alice has a higher rating than an opponent she will injure them, no matter how many opponents she is taking on at the same time. However, equally, any opponent with a *Combat Rating* higher than Alice's will be able to injure her too.

"YOU'RE NOTHING BUT A PACK OF CARDS!"

An Alternative to Dice

Since *Alice's Nightmare in Wonderland* is inspired by *Alice's Adventures in Wonderland*, rather than dice rolls you may prefer to determine random numbers during the game using a pack of playing cards.

To do this, when you are called upon to roll dice, simply shuffle a standard 52-card deck (having removed the jokers) and draw a single card. (If you are asked to roll four dice, draw two cards.) Number cards are worth the number shown on the card. Jacks, Queens and Kings are all worth 11, and if you draw an Ace, it counts as being worth 12 (for example, if Alice is engaged in Combat), and is an automatic pass if she is testing an attribute – any attribute.

"SHOES, AND SHIPS, AND SEALING WAX."

Equipment

Alice starts her adventure with nothing but the clothes she stands up in, including a pinafore she wears over her dress which, fortunately, comes with a deep pocket at the front. This is where Alice stores anything she picks up during the course of her adventure.

Anything that she collects should be recorded on Alice's Adventure Sheet, including any clues or passwords, as well as weapons, provisions, and other miscellaneous unusual items.

"BEGIN AT THE BEGINNING."

Hints on Play

There is more than one path that Alice can follow through Wonderland to reach her ultimate goal, but it may take you several attempts to actually complete the adventure. Make notes and draw a map as you explore. This map will doubtless prove invaluable during future attempts at completing the quest, and will allow you to progress more speedily in order to reach unexplored regions of the nightmarish realm.

Keep a careful eye on all of Alice's attributes and her *Insanity* score in particular. Beware of traps and of sending Alice on too many wild goose chases. However, it would be wise to collect useful items along the way that may aid her further on in her quest.

"GO ON TILL YOU COME TO THE END: THEN STOP."

Ending the Game

There are several ways that Alice's adventure can end. If her *Endurance* score ever drops to zero or below, her trials in Wonderland have exhausted and overcome her. If this happens, stop reading at once. There may also be occasions where Alice is prevented from progressing any further through the adventure thanks to the choices you have made for her, or she meets a sudden and untimely end. In all of these cases, if you want to have another crack at completing the adventure you will have to start again with a new Alice's Adventure Sheet and begin the story afresh from section 1.

There is of course one other reason for Alice's adventure coming to an end, and that is if she successfully completes her quest, the very same quest that awaits her now…

ALICE'S ADVENTURE SHEET

AGILITY

LOGIC

INSANITY

COMBAT

THE PEN IS MIGHTIER

CURIOUSER AND CURIOUSER

ENDURANCE

EQUIPMENT

NIGHTMARE
ENCOUNTER BOXES

COMBAT=

ENDURANCE=

COMBAT=

ENDURANCE=

COMBAT=

ENDURANCE=

COMBAT=

ENDURANCE=

COMBAT=

ENDURANCE=

COMBAT=

ENDURANCE=

COMBAT=

ENDURANCE=

COMBAT=

ENDURANCE=

COMBAT=

ENDURANCE=

COMBAT=

ENDURANCE=

DOWN THE RABBIT-HOLE

"You're late! Wake up!"

Alice wakes with a start and sits up, blinking in surprise and looking about her in bewilderment. It is a balmy summer's afternoon and she is sitting beside a river, the long grass that has formed her bed dotted with daisies. The waters gurgle softly as they pass by on their way downstream.

Something about the scene seems very familiar.

"Don't just sit there! Get up! You're late!" comes the shrill voice again.

The hot weather making her feel sleepy and dull-witted, Alice follows the sound to its source. There, standing in the shade of a chestnut tree, is a white rabbit.

But this isn't just any white rabbit. This particular rabbit is dressed in the manner of an English gentleman – jacket, waistcoat and all. The rabbit's ears are a little threadbare, the stuffing poking out through holes worn in the skin, and as it tilts its head to one side to observe her with its glassy pink eyes, Alice thinks she hears a grating of gears.

Alice jumps to her feet as it flashes through her mind that, once upon a time, on some previous occasion, she saw something like this rabbit wearing a waistcoat and carrying a pocket-watch. But there is no timepiece clutched in the rabbit's paws this time.

"Who are you to say I'm late when you are not even carrying a pocket-watch?" Alice asks, not one to be outdone by an animal that looks like nothing more than a taxidermist's test subject.

The rabbit says nothing, but simply unbuttons its waistcoat, and Alice gasps as her former cockiness is consumed by gut-wrenching terror. Where the rabbit's stomach should be, a huge watch ticks – a clock large enough to fill the cavity from ribcage to pelvis – raw and ragged scrags of meat poking between the wire stitches that bind watch and rabbit together.

"How can I be late," Alice asks the rabbit, "when I don't even know what it is I'm late for?"

She is suddenly aware of the wind having picked up, as scuds of cloud race each other across the sky, a sky which has changed from sapphire blue to a seething, bloody claret.

"You are needed in Wonderland," the White Rabbit informs her, the twitching of its nose accompanied by a mechanical whirring sound.

"Wonderland?" There is something familiar about that name, Alice is sure of it, but she can't quite put her finger on what it is.

"It's the Queen of Hearts. The whole realm has suffered the ravages of her tyrannical reign, and if you thought things were bad before, they are considerably worse now. It's a miracle I managed to escape her Tick-Tock Men."

"Before?" Alice whispers in a daze. "Tick-Tock Men?"

"Yes, Tick-Tock Men! How else do you think I ended up like this?" the rabbit says, looking down at his stomach and the ticking timepiece embedded within what little flesh remains there.

Alice stares at the creature in dumbfounded amazement before finally finding her voice again. "Why are you telling me this? What do you expect me to do about it?"

"Why?" gasps the rabbit, in incredulity. "We need you, Alice. Wonderland *needs* you."

"But what do you need me to do?"

"We need you to kill the Queen, of course."

"Kill the Queen?" Alice echoes. "But why me?"

The White Rabbit gives an exasperated sigh and takes a deep breath, in an attempt to compose itself, before speaking again.

"Because it's your nightmare!"

Now turn to **1**.

1

Alice stares at the rabbit unsure what to say, a dozen questions crowding her mind. Who is the Queen of Hearts? Who turned the White Rabbit into a walking timepiece? And how does he expect her to kill anyone? After all, she's only eleven years-old. But before she can give voice to even one of the questions, the White Rabbit speaks again.

"Come on, there's not a moment to lose. The clock is ticking!" he says, looks pointedly at his clock-filled stomach cavity. And with that, he turns tail and scampers off across the meadow, through the long, wind-tugged grass.

If you think Alice should set off in pursuit, turn to **20**. If you think that following half-clockwork talking rabbits could never be considered wise, turn to **39**.

2

Following the gravel path to its end, Alice stops before the front door of the neat little house. The brass plate has the name '*W. Rabbit*' engraved upon it and above the door, on a lacquered piece of wood, someone has painted the words '*The Burrow*'.

"Well, there will be no prizes for guessing who lives here," Alice says to herself.

Alice has been brought up to mind her manners and knows that she should never enter a room without knocking first, and that goes double for entering people's

kevcrossley 2·15

houses. However, there are many things in this strange land that do not follow the usual order of things, so perhaps she should enter first and knock second.

If you want Alice to knock on the door, turn to **10**. If you want her to try opening the door instead of knocking, turn to **483**.

3

Alice opens the box. Inside is a dainty cake in a paper case, on which the words 'EAT ME' have been painstakingly marked out in currants. It looks delicious. If you think Alice should take a bite, turn to **77**. If not, what should she do next? Keep trying the doors around the hall (turn to **339**), or drink the contents of the bottle (turn to **387**).

4

Heading west Alice soon comes to a dead-end. She is just about to turn back when she notices the entrance to a rabbit-hole underneath the hedge.

"I wonder where this one leads?" she says to herself, recalling what happened the last time she crawled into a rabbit's burrow.

If you think Alice should crawl into the rabbit-hole, regardless of what might happen to her dress, turn to **14**. If not, she will have to retrace her steps – turn to **180**.

5

Alice can tell from the way they move that the Tick-Tock Men mean her harm and so the best thing to do would be to try to escape their clockwork clutches. Picking up the skirts of her dress, she sprints towards them and then at the last possible moment feints right before throwing herself left.

Take an Agility test. If Alice passes the test, turn to **25**. If she fails the test, turn to **42**.

6

And so, Alice finds herself at the entrance to a magnificent maze. If she stands on tiptoe she can just see the turrets and heart-carved crenulations of a high-walled palace beyond the towering yew hedges. It is quite apparent to Alice that the only way to reach the palace is to negotiate the leafy labyrinth.

Taking a deep breath, she steps forward into its shaded pathways, and promptly comes to a junction. Laid out on the ground in coloured gravel is an ornate compass rose, with a large red heart at its centre. Left is north and right is south, so which way should Alice go?

North?   Turn to **38**.

South?   Turn to **90**.

7

Alice looks at the picture she managed to take from the wall. It appears to be a rather ugly portrait of an even uglier woman. She is sitting on a stool, beside the range in a smoky kitchen, holding a baby wrapped in a shawl. Alice can't shake the feeling that she should know who the woman and the baby in the picture are.

As she continues to tumble down the well she passes through pools of light cast by lamps and lanterns that hang from its walls. It is as she passes through one of these pools of light that she sees the image in front of her change before her very eyes.

The screaming baby's features melt and morph until Alice is no longer looking at a human child but a squealing piglet. Shocked by the unnatural metamorphosis, Alice hurls the picture at the wall, where it snags on a nail, tearing the canvas.

Add 1 to Alice's *Insanity* score and turn to **82**.

8

"They may have bodies made of Christmas pudding and heads doused in burning brandy, but if they are anything like other insects," Alice says to herself, "then they probably have a fondness for sweet things. But then again, I am sure that dousing their flames would send them packing too."

If you want, Alice could try dousing the Snap-dragon-flies' flames with the remaining tot of Shrinking Potion from the 'Drink Me' bottle (turn to **450**). Alternatively, if Alice has a piece of cake she could try offering that up to the insects, in the hope that such an action will help her get past unharmed (turn to **92**). If you don't think Alice should waste such precious resources on her strange assailants, she will have to prepare for the worst (turn to **112**).

9

"Thank goodness!" exclaims the Caterpillar, sounding genuinely concerned, the spiracles along its body opening and closing in agitation. "I was starting to think I had lost you to a higher state of being, for you never to return."

Alice's encounter with the Paper Tiger was all in her mind. Restore her *Endurance* score to what it was before she fought the imagined threat.

"Return to where?" Alice asks, still feeling as if body and mind are not quite one.

"Why *here* of course," says the Caterpillar. "Wonderland! I only wish we were meeting again under better circumstances."

"So what circumstances are we meeting under?" says the child.

"It's the Queen of Hearts. She's even madder than she was before."

"We're all mad here," Alice mutters under her breath.

"Her lunacy has infected this reality, turning the dreamscape of Wonderland into a nightmarish realm of imagined horrors and manifest phobias. Do you see?" says the Caterpillar. "That is why the Queen must die."

Alice doesn't understand half the words the Caterpillar has been using, but she understands that everyone she meets in Wonderland seems dead set on her doing away with the monarch of mayhem and madness.

"Do you have any questions before you set off on your way again?"

"Yes, I do," says the child, after pondering the question for a moment. "If we've met before, and you were a caterpillar then, why aren't you a butterfly now?"

"Old Father William says I have a bad case of neoteny. Now, if you want one last piece of advice, steer clear of the Duchess's madhouse. The Nightmare has already well and truly taken hold there. Make for the Palace instead and remember, keep moving forwards, never turn back. Now, be on your way."

Record the word 'Metamorphosis' on Alice's Adventure Sheet and then turn to **316**.

Alice raps on the door with her knuckles and then waits. She doesn't have to wait long before she hears pattering footsteps from the other side of the door and then a small voice squeak, "Who is it?"

"Now that is a good question," Alice says to herself. "I think I'm Alice. Yesterday things went on just as usual, as far as I can recall, but so many queer things have happened today I wonder if I've been changed in the night. Let me think: was I the same when I got up this morning? I almost think I can remember feeling a little different. But if I'm not the same, the next question is, who in the world am I? Ah, that's the great puzzle!"

"Alice?" she says out loud at last, if a little uncertainly.

"It's 'er alright," comes a second voice, gruffer than the first. "Best let 'er in."

The front door opens and Alice finds herself staring at a Lizard wearing the cap and clothes of a gardener, and a Mouse dressed very smartly indeed, in the manner of a bank clerk.

"This way," says the Mouse. "And you can come too, Mr Bixby," he adds, addressing this to the Lizard.

The Mouse leads Alice from a tiled hall, into a room filled with glass cases containing displays of stuffed birds, animals and fish, and from there into a snug study. Waiting for her behind a green leather-topped writing desk is the master of the house – the White Rabbit.

"Ah, there you are," the Rabbit says, giving an exasperated sigh.

Turn to **135**.

11

"White to win in eleven moves!" Alice says triumphantly, moving the White pawn to Red's side of the board. (Add 1 to Alice's *Logic* score.)

Alice has spent long enough in the library; it's time she was on her way again – turn to **454**.

12

As the dresser disappears again above her, Alice reaches a section of the well shaft adorned with framed maps and pictures hanging from hooks. If you want Alice to try to grab one of these, turn to **33**. If not, turn to **82**.

13

A trumpeted fanfare suddenly sounds from somewhere to the south, strident horns reverberating across the maze.

"The Queen!" one of the gardeners shouts. "A summons from the Queen!"

Ignoring Alice entirely now, the three gardeners down tools and hurry off westwards, clearly more in fear of failing to heed the Queen's summons than making sure Alice doesn't get away.

Turn to **36**.

14

Ignoring the worms and woodlice and other creep-crawlies that tickle the back of her neck as she crawls along the rabbit-dug tunnel, Alice keeps shuffling forward, using her knees and elbows to help her on her way.

The tunnel twists and turns, but fortunately does not suddenly become the vertical shaft of a well, and then Alice sees a circle of daylight up ahead. The sight giving her the motivation to keep going, and it is not long before the child pulls herself from the tunnel to find that she is still inside the maze, only she is not sure exactly where.

The only way onward is a path leading east, but, if you prefer, Alice could crawl back along the burrow to where she first entered the rabbit-hole.

To send Alice back down the rabbit-hole, turn to **34**. If you want Alice to continue by heading east into the maze, turn to **360**.

15

Just as she is wondering which way to go, Alice catches sight of a broad grin, floating two feet above the path that leads east away from the fur-thatched cottage. Her curiosity piqued, she sets off along the path, even as the smile vanishes into thin air again, leaving behind it the rumour of a chuckle in the air.

Turn to **6**.

16

Incredibly, the White Rabbit still appears to be alive, but then he was already dead when Alice first met him beside the river bank, nothing but stuffing and clockwork. Although that might be considered a form of life.

"Alice, you must go, the Queen is onto us," the Rabbit's head says.

For a moment Alice is paralysed by shock, taking in the devastation in appalled horror, from the Rabbit's decapitated body behind the desk, to the Mouse's crushed skull, to the Lizard barely conscious in the corner of the room.

There's clearly nothing she can do for the Mouse but she might yet be able to save Bill the Lizard, or even the White Rabbit.

If you want Alice to help the Rabbit, turn to **168**. If you want Alice to help the Lizard, turn to **98**. If you would rather Alice flee the scene as quickly as she can, turn to **179**.

17

Putting any aspirations of climbing up to the nest behind her, Alice commences her wary descent of the crags, watching out for any loose scree that might send her tumbling down the side of the peak, or uneven rocks that might have her going over on her ankle.

Eventually, her descent is done and Alice finds herself re-entering the tulgey wood, although now she can see the battlements of the ruined fortress beyond the tops of the unhealthy-looking trees.

Turn to **512**.

18

Is Alice wielding a Croquet Mallet? If so, turn to **68**. If not, turn to **97**.

19

"I wonder what they live on," Alice muses. "Frumenty and mince pie, I expect, and they probably nest in Christmas boxes."

Such musings are all well and good, but they are not going to save Alice from the angry Snap-dragon-flies. Turn to **112**.

20

Burning with curiosity, Alice runs off across the field after the rabbit. Just as she is starting to feel that she might actually be catching up with it, the creature disappears down a large rabbit-hole under a hedge.

Stumbling to a halt, Alice peers down into the earthy darkness. This is all looking very familiar, but she can't quite remember why.

If she pulls away some of the turf from around the entrance, she should be able to squeeze inside the burrow, but such activity will doubtless make a mess of her dress, and what would Nurse say? At her back, the wind continues to rise.

If you think Alice should follow the White Rabbit underground, turn to **57**. If you think that crawling down rabbit-holes is not behaviour befitting a young lady, turn to **64**.

21

Warily, Alice breaks off a piece of the mushroom and, putting it her mouth, gives it a desultory chew before swallowing it as quickly as she can, so foul-tasting is the fungus. Almost immediately her vision starts to swim and unsettling hallucinations warp the world around her…

Blinking, Alice finds herself in a room, not unlike the Hall of Doors she found at the bottom of the rabbit-hole.

In fact, looking around her, she is quite sure that it *is* the same hall.

Before her are three doors. Carved into the wood of the first door is an image of a labyrinth. The second door bears the image of a palace, while the third door has nothing carved into it at all. Alice is quite sure that she needs to open one of these doors, but which one?

The labyrinth door? Turn to **40**.

The palace door? Turn to **61**.

The unmarked door? Turn to **389**.

22

Alice follows the path as it becomes steeper and steeper, climbing higher and higher into the range of crags that rise above the tulgey wood, eventually passing the limit of the treeline.

Soon Alice is high enough to look down upon the forest. On the other side of the crags she can see the crumbling ruins of a white stone keep, while beyond the limits of the forest she can see the sea. She is on an island!

Continuing on her way through these uplands, Alice catches sight of an untidy nest higher up the side of a particularly precipitous crag, that is little more than a ramshackle collection of branches, and her curiosity is piqued at once. What could have made a nest so large and so high up on the island?

If you want Alice to climb up to the nest to investigate further, turn to **32**. If you think she should leave well enough alone and make for the castle beyond the crags, turn to **17**.

23

Alice soon starts to tire as she battles the waves to reach the shore. Hoping that if she stops to rest for a minute she might recover enough energy to see her safely to the beach, she stops swimming and starts treading water again.

She suddenly becomes aware of movement beneath her, and fearing that it may be the Crocodile returning from the briny depths, she takes a deep breath and ducks her head under the water. But it isn't the Crocodile.

Rising from the seemingly bottomless ocean, with powerful strokes of its paddle-like flippers, is a hideous creature. Its body is that of a huge sea turtle, but its head is that of a calf. Alice can even see the stitches where the head has been attached to the body.

The calf's head is screaming with insane fury, bubbles streaming from its mouth, while Alice's heart is racing in fear. (Add 1 to Alice's *Insanity* score.) Despite being terrified, Alice realises that she must either fight the creature or flee from it, but does she have the strength to do either?

If you think Alice should attempt to escape from the monster, turn to **45**. If you think she should prepare to fight the horror, turn to **59**. If you would rather she use *The Pen is Mightier* ability, turn to **89**.

24

Alice finds herself back at the entrance to the maze with its distinctive compass rose marked out in coloured gravel on the ground.

"After all my efforts I'm still just as far from the palace as when I first entered this interminable labyrinth!" cries Alice. "Why it's enough to send one mad!"

Add 1 to Alice's *Insanity* score.

There's no point exiting the maze at the entrance, so which way should she go now?

To go north, turn to **38**, and to go south, turn to **90**.

25

Her plan works. The Tick-Tock Men reach for where they think she is going to be, only to grab hold of thin air with their metal claws when she slides past the other way.

The Tick-Tock Men immediately turn around and start to come after her again. Alice has to find a way out of the hall and fast!

Running to one of the doors she tries it, only to find that it is locked. So is the next. And the next. If you think Alice should keep trying the doors, turn to **296**. If you think she should turn and prepare to face the sinister guardians of this place, turn to **169**.

26

Ducking and diving between the rose-bushes, Alice is able to ensure that she only has to fight the gardeners two at a time.

Fight the first two on the list first, and as soon as one of them is dead the third joins the fray. As soon as Alice has defeated a second opponent, the third gardener turns tails and runs away in fear of her. (Alice has the initiative.)

	COMBAT	ENDURANCE
TWO OF SPADES	7	7
FIVE OF SPADES	7	6
SEVEN OF SPADES	6	6

Once the gardeners have been dealt with, turn to **36**.

As the Grandfather Clock bears down on her, Alice readies herself for battle once again. (Alice has the initiative.)

GRANDFATHER CLOCK   COMBAT 8   ENDURANCE 9

If the Grandfather Clock makes a successful hit against Alice roll one die (or pick a playing card). If the number rolled is odd (or the card picked is red) the elder Tick-Tock Man cuts her with its scissor-like clock-hand fingers, causing Alice 2 *Endurance* points of damage. However, if the number rolled is even (or the card picked is black) then the mechanical horror hits her with its swinging pendulum, causing her 3 *Endurance* points of damage.

If Alice survives her epic battle with the Grandfather Clock, turn to **16**.

The Spinebacks are driven by an insane, animalistic bloodlust – a bloodlust that can only be sated by the taste of raw flesh.

If you want Alice to use the *Curiouser and Curiouser* ability to change the story at this awkward time, turn to **18**. If you want her to use *The Pen is Mightier* ability instead, turn to **87**. If you want Alice to prepare to fight the mutated humanoid hedgehogs, turn to **78**.

29

Hearing a great beating of wings, Alice looks up to see the Gryphon swooping down towards the monster. The Alice-Jabberwock gives a roar of defiance, and tries to knock Alice's saviour from the air with one huge claw. But the eagle-lion is too fast. It banks and soars over the monster's back, raking one wing with its outstretched claws.

Make a note of the fact that the Alice-Jabberwock has suffered one attack already and turn to **79**.

30

"Tweedle-dum and Tweedle-dee, I think you're afraid of me," laughs the Ogre's right-hand head.

"Tweedle-dee and Tweedle-dum, I'll chew your bones, one by one," snarls the left-hand head.

What can Alice do to defend herself against the hungry Ogre now?

If you want Alice to put *The Pen is Mightier* ability to good use (if she can), turn to **176**. If not, turn to **192**.

31

Passing a bed of buttercups and a crumbling brick wall drenched in honeysuckle – real butter and honey dripping from their flowers – Alice reaches a crossroads where four gravel paths meet.

To her left is an ornate wrought-iron gate, which stands ajar, beyond which lies a very grand house indeed. To her right, beyond carefully trimmed box hedges she can see the fountain. Ahead of her she can see a tree growing at the north-east corner of the garden.

To go through the gate to the left, turn to **319**. To head for the tree to the east, turn to **80**. To approach the fountain, turn to **51**.

32

Taking her courage in both hands, putting her trust in her ability to negotiate the near-sheer cliff safely, Alice commences her climb.

Take an Agility test. If Alice passes it, turn to **422**. If she fails the test, turn to **52**.

33

Reaching out with both hands, Alice plucks the nearest picture from the wall.

Roll one die (or pick a card). If the number rolled is odd (or the card is red), turn to **53**. If the number rolled is even (or the card is black), turn to **7**.

34

Alice encounters scuttling centipedes and plump, white squirming grubs as she crawls along the tunnel through the earth. Just as her eyes are becoming accustomed to the gloom she sees an exit from the rabbit-hole up ahead.

Pulling herself out of the hole in the ground Alice discovers that she is at another dead-end in the maze, the only way onwards a hedge-lined path heading east. As Alice picks the soil from her hair, she considers which way to go.

If you want Alice to follow the hedge-lined path east, turn to **180**. If you want her to head back down the rabbit-hole, turn to **14**.

35

As the insects move towards her on their humming holly-leaves, Alice ponders what it must be like to be effectively festive fare on wings.

Take a Logic test. If Alice passes, turn to **8**, but if she fails, turn to **19**.

36

The only thing left behind by the gardeners that might be of interest to Alice is the red paint they were using to re-colour the white roses. If you want her to take the Tin of Red Paint with her, add it to Alice's Adventure Sheet.

Leaving the rose garden, which way should Alice go? East (turn to **490**) or west (turn to **272**)?

37

As the Grandfather Clock bears down on her its steps become slow and lumbering, and its unnatural body stiffens, until finally it comes to a complete halt.

"Must have forgotten to wind the clock this morning," the White Rabbit's head says from where it landed on the writing desk, its eyelids shuttering open and closed independently of one another.

Turn to **16**.

38

Alice follows the gravel path, hemmed in by the clipped yew hedge walls, until she comes upon the lichen-covered statue of a flamingo that has been placed at a turn in the trail. Which way should Alice go now?

East?	Turn to **58**.
South?	Turn to **24**.

"Talking rabbits," Alice says to herself. "Whatever next – frog footmen?"

She turns and starts to walk away from the riverbank towards the path that she decides she must have followed to get here in the first place, even though she doesn't remember doing so. But the rising wind has now become a gale, tugging at Alice's hair and clothes, whipping her hair about her face, and the child fancies she can hear the rumble of thunder far off beyond the horizon.

If you think Alice should chase after the rabbit after all, turn to **20**. If not, turn to **64**.

The handle turns and Alice steps through the door to find herself in a maze formed of high yew hedges. Running along the gravel path before her she turns a corner and finds herself at the heart of the labyrinth.

Sitting at the edge of a heart-shaped pool is a girl of about her age, with tangled blonde hair and wearing a blue pinafore dress.

"Why, it *is* me!" Alice exclaims.

The other Alice doesn't react but continues to gaze into the limpid waters of the pool.

Unsettled by this curious state of affairs, Alice runs on through the maze, turning this way and that, until she finds herself standing before an ornate gate, decorated with wrought iron flowers and ivy leaves. The gate is locked, by not one but six separate locks.

But now her other self is here too and Alice watches as she turns the locks, each one in turn, until the hands of each at are right angles, creating a rectangular shape around the gate.

As the other Alice sets the final lock to the right position, there is a rattling of cogs and gears and the gate swings open. Beyond it is a tunnel that passes through the thick yew hedges. Her other self darts along the tunnel and the gate closes again behind her.

"Alice, you must come back now," comes the voice of the Caterpillar from somewhere beyond the towering hedges. "Come back…"

Turn to **108**.

41

Screeching like a banshee, the glamour that hid her true face the first time Alice and the Red Queen met dispelled, the vampire throws herself as the child, determined to rip her still beating heart from her chest.

If you want Alice to use the *Curiouser and Curiouser* ability in the hope of helping herself now, turn to **500**. If you want her to use *The Pen is Mightier* ability to resolve her struggle against the Red Queen, turn to **60**. If you would rather Alice trust her fate to the keen edge of the Vorpal Sword, turn to **72**.

42

Alice is fast, but the clockwork-driven Tick-Tock Men are faster. As Alice ducks left, one of them strikes her with the metal claws of an outstretched hand, sending her tumbling to the ground and opening three long scratches across her right arm.

Lose 2 *Endurance* points and turn to **209**.

43

"I know what you're thinking about," says the head on the left; "but it isn't so, nohow."

"Contrariwise," continues the head on the right, "if it was so, it might be; and if it were so, it would be; but as it isn't, it ain't. That's logic."

"I was thinking," Alice said politely, "which is the best way out of this wood: it's getting so dark. Would you tell me, please?"

"But you 'aven't won your challenge yet," returns the left-hand head.

"Haven't I?" says Alice, all innocence, sweetness and light.

"No!" replies the right-hand head. "So go on then."

"Let's see how clever you think you really are," says the head on the left.

"Very well," says Alice, drawing herself up to her full height. "I once dreamt that in a forest there lay a castle, and in that castle a king lay sleeping, dreaming of a child, dreaming of a forest. So let us consider who it was that dreamed it all. It must have been either me or the king. He was part of my dream, of course – but then I was part of his dream, too! Was it the king, or was it me?"

"Well it was you," says the left-hand head, "'cos you was dreaming of the king."

"Contrariwise, he was dreaming of you, so it was the king who dreamed it," counters the right-hand head.

"Don't be stupid!" his brother retaliates. "How could he be dreaming her when she was dreaming him?"

"But contrariwise he was dreaming her so it couldn't've been her what was dreaming it all, nohow!" persists the other.

With the two heads fully embroiled in their argument now, Alice tiptoes away from the entrance to the cave and, when she is sure she is out of sight of the Ogre, as soon as she reaches the safety of the treeline again, she sets off again at a run.

As she hears the sounds of blows being exchanged, as the battle of words becomes a battle of pugiling fists, Alice sees the battlements of a ruined fortress appear over the tops of the twisted trees away ahead of her.

Turn to **512**.

44

Alice soon comes to a dead-end. She is about to turn back, and retrace her steps to the last junction, when she spies the entrance to another rabbit-hole under a hedge. Where could this one lead?

If you think Alice should enter the rabbit-hole, turn to **34**. If not, she will have to go east, back the way she has just come – turn to **360**.

45

Drawing on reserves of energy she did not even know she had, Alice swims away from the monster as quickly as she can. But the creature, with its sea turtle body, is designed for swimming through the ocean and quickly catches up with her, catching her leg in its mouth. (Lose 2 *Endurance* points.)

Letting go of Alice's leg again, the creature circles the child once before moving in for the kill. Turn to **59**.

46

Alice turns tail and runs for it, heading west as the gardeners give pursuit. Pelting down the paths of the maze she turns a corner and abruptly comes to a set of tall gates. Beyond the gates and a drawbridge over a wide moat, lies the barbican gatehouse of a vast palace.

However, standing in front of the gates are two burly brutes wearing ill-fitting tabards that make them look like playing cards – the Six and Seven of Clubs in this instance.

"Halt! Who goes there?" demands one of the guards.

It is then that the gardeners round the corner, still hot on Alice's heels, and the guards assume an aggressive stance.

"You're coming with us!" the guard declares gruffly.

With two burly guards in front of her and three angry gardeners behind her, Alice realises that to resist arrest would be to invite certain death. And so she allows the playing card guards to grab hold of her, one on either side, and march her through the gates, over the drawbridge, and into the palace beyond.

Turn to **386**.

47

The Grandfather Clock lands between Alice and the door, blocking her escape route from the study. It begins to dawn on her that this could all have been a trap, set by the Queen of Hearts to eliminate her enemy, before she even knew she *was* her enemy. But Alice might escape the mad Queen's trap yet.

If you want Alice to use *The Pen is Mightier* ability to save herself, turn to **37**. If not, she will have to prepare for battle (turn to **27**).

48

As Alice sets the last clock-lock to the right position, there is a rattling of cogs and gears and the gate swings open at last. Beyond is revealed a tunnel through the yew hedge. Alice makes her way through the twilight-emerald darkness to where it ends before a wall of greenery.

Hearing a clanking of gears a second time, Alice turns in startled surprise as the gate begins to swing shut behind her. But her fears are soon allayed; as the gate closes, the hedge before her parts, letting her through into a different part of the maze.

Alice steps through quickly and the gap in the yew hedge closes again behind her.

Turn to **470**.

Alice is standing on a chequer-tiled floor that looks like a huge chessboard. The poker she was holding is gone, having become the Vorpal Sword once more.

Beyond the edge of the chessboard the ground has broken away and beyond that Alice can see nothing but darkness, although it is a darkness through which circle rotating broken mirror shards. As Alice's gaze falls on the shards she catches glimpses of other places through the looking-glass fragments: gardens of clipped topiary; a palatial house under a threatening, gun-metal grey sky; a forest of towering fungi; a grim island; a crumbling ivory tower.

Standing in front of her, on the opposite side of the chessboard, is a girl. She appears to be about eleven years of age, with tangled blonde hair and a determined scowl on her face.

"And so we meet at last," the girl says.

"But…" Alice struggles to find the words as she realises that she is looking at a mirror image of herself, albeit one with a cruel expression more akin to that of the Red Queen on her face. "You're me."

"Not yet, but that is the plan," replies the other.

"Now I really must be dreaming," Alice gasps in disbelief.

"But of course you are, foolish girl. You've been dreaming ever since you met my minion on the riverbank. This has *all* been a dream. But that doesn't make it any less real."

"Your minion?"

"Of course! He didn't know he was, but that makes no odds in the end."

So, Alice knows the truth at last. "This has all been a trap to lure me here? But to what end?"

"Conquest, of course. To seize power, to usurp control."

"Conquest? Of Wonderland?"

"No, you imbecile! Of you! Of your physical form! I plan to take over your body!" Alice's alter-ego shrieks, suddenly sounding a lot like a crazed queen Alice once met at a croquet match. "When you entered the Looking-Glass House the first time, I entered your world in return, and had a taste of the delights it had to offer. But when you woke from your dream I was dragged back here, to this unreality, this pale shadow realm of insubstantial hopes and fears given transient form, to brood and scheme. For it was worse being back here, having seen what the waking world had to offer, than it was to be lost within your unconscious id in the first place. Having had a taste I wanted more, and for that to happen I had to take control. And now here you are, ensnared within my trap, my plan of acquisition coming to fruition at long last. Why, today must be my birthday."

"Well, it's not my birthday!" Alice says crossly. "And if you're me then it can't be your birthday either."

"Why not?" challenges the Other Alice.

"Because that's simple logic."

"Then it must be my unbirthday," the Other Alice gloats.

"A Looking-Glass Alice taking over my body from inside a dream? Why that's impossible!" says Alice, her well-reasoned logical argument helping her gain a foothold in this unreal reality, some of her old confidence and resourcefulness resurfacing.

"Impossible? Why, sometimes I've believed as many as six impossible things before breakfast," counters the Other.

"And to think I was once very fond of pretending to be two people," says Alice, weary of all this verbal sparring. "But it's no use now to pretend to be two people! Why, there's hardly enough of me left to make one respectable person!"

"And that person will be *me*!" hisses the Other.

"And how do you reason that?" asks Alice.

"Simple," says the Other, "all I have to do is kill you. If you die here, when your body awakens, it will no longer be you looking out of your eyes. It will be me!"

"And how do you propose to do that?" Alice challenges her black-hearted doppelgänger. "You are no bigger than I am, even in this unreality. We are the same, except that I am the bearer of the Vorpal Sword."

"Imagination is the only weapon in the war against reality," the Other Alice mocks her, and with that begins to transform.

The Other Alice's neck begins to elongate, writhing like a serpent as it does so. At the same time, her body starts to swell, bursting free of her pinafore dress, her skin blackening as it becomes hard and scaly. A huge pair of wings burst from her back and unfurl to stretch across the width of the chessboard. Her feet become gigantic dragon-like talons, her fingers steel-hard curling black claws. And looming above it all, atop the twisting serpentine neck, is the mirror image of Alice's own face.

"Your move," laughs the Alice-Jabberwock.

How can the real Alice hope to conquer the Other Alice's monstrous alter ego, even if she is armed with the Vorpal Sword? If only she didn't have to face the Jabberwock alone.

If Alice has a Golden Feather, turn to **29**. If not, turn to **79**.

50

Turning on her heels, Alice sets off at a sprint along the gravel paths.

Take an Endurance Test. If Alice passes the test, turn to **472**. If she fails the test, turn to **461**.

51

Alice takes a moment to stand before the fountain pool, enjoying the cooling shower of moisture upon her face, watching rainbows form between the sparkling sprays of water, and listening to the ceaseless splash and gurgle of the cascading fountainhead.

"It is traditional to throw a coin into a fountain and make a wish," Alice says to herself.

If you think it appropriate for her to maintain that particular tradition, turn to **95**. If not, turn to **241**.

52

Alice is halfway up the cliff-face when she misjudges a hand-hold and, unbalanced, her feet slip beneath her. With all her weight suddenly hanging from one hand, she can hold on no longer.

She lands at the bottom of the cliff in a heap, whimpering in pain, her hand immediately going to her ankle. Just as she feared, she has sprained it badly.

Lose 3 *Endurance* points, reduce Alice's *Agility* score by 2 points and her *Combat* score by 1 point. If Alice is still able to go on, turn to **17**.

53

Still dropping like a stone down the well shaft, the petticoats of her dress ballooning about her like a parachute, Alice looks at the picture she managed to grab. Only it isn't a picture, it's a map.

The map is of an island. It shows a swamp, and beyond that a path that branches left and right before a large, gnarled tree in the middle of a forest. The right-hand path leads to craggy uplands, while the left-hand path passes a cave. Both paths eventually lead to a white stone keep that reminds Alice of a Rook chess piece.

As Alice continues to fall, the wind whips the map out of her hands again.

Turn to **82**.

54

Alice takes a swig of the crimson potion and carefully places the bottle back on the table. No sooner has she done so than she feels the world about her start to spin.

"What is happening to me?" she gasps. "Am I growing bigger or am I shrinking?"

Abruptly the world stops spinning and Alice looks about her. She is just the same size as she was before she drank the potion but her surroundings have changed.

She is standing next to a white-painted arbour that is strung with wisteria. Resting upon a table inside the arbour is a glass bottle containing a bright blue liquid. A path leads away east through the maze.

If you want Alice to drink from the bottle, turn to **74**. If not, she must follow the path east (turn to **270**).

55

"There must be some way to resolve this unhappy situation," Alice thinks as the creature composed of china and silver-plated steel comes closer with every jerking step.

Take a Logic test. If Alice passes, turn to **281**. If she fails, turn to **271**.

56

The snapping blades nick Alice's arm, drawing blood, as she tries to turn to avoid the mechanical menace's violent assault.

Lose 2 *Endurance* points and turn to **47**.

57

Squeezing along the tunnel, Alice drags herself through the loamy dark, unable to see more than a foot in front of her face. There is no sign of the White Rabbit now.

The further Alice wriggles along the tunnel, between probing roots and writhing worms, dangling from the roof of the burrow, the more opaque the gloom becomes.

Without any warning the tunnel dips suddenly downwards, so suddenly, in fact, that Alice doesn't have a moment to think about stopping herself before she is plunging headfirst down the damp throat of what is clearly a very deep well.

But as she falls, and her eyes become accustomed to the darkness, Alice realises that the sides of the well are lined with cupboards and bookshelves. Looking down she can see no end to the well-shaft in sight.

However, she is coming up on another cupboard. If you think Alice should try to find out what it holds as she passes, turn to **109**. If not, turn to **156**.

58

Alice soon comes to another branching of the ways in the yew-hedge maze, but which way should she go?

North?	Turn to **70**.
East?	Turn to **465**.
West?	Turn to **38**.

59

As the bizarre vivisect-hybrid bears down on her Alice realises that rather than screaming it is singing, its howls distorted by their passage through the water. "Will you, won't you, will you, won't you, will you join the dance?"

Alice has no choice but to fight the Mock Turtle (which has the initiative).

MOCK TURTLE   COMBAT 7   ENDURANCE 7

If Alice survives her encounter with the mad Mock Turtle, turn to **118**.

60

Now is not the time for Alice to start to doubt her own ability to complete the quest and slay the monster that is the Red Queen. Reduce Alice's *Combat* score by 1 point and then turn to **72**.

61

Alice steps through the door to find herself standing in a gloomy castle corridor.

As she is taking in her surroundings, another Alice runs past her and then stops at an iron-bound oak door. Taking a large iron key from a hook on the wall, she unlocks the door and peers inside…

"Alice, you must come back now," the voice of the Caterpillar echoes from somewhere deeper within the chill corridors of the palace. "Come back…"

Turn to **108**.

62

Just when Alice thinks she can't possibly fall any further, ground appears at the bottom of the well and she lands in a pile of dry leaves which, miraculously, break her fall. Unhurt, she is on her feet in a moment.

Turn to **114**.

63

The Caterpillar told Alice what the secret password was, but can you remember what it was? If you can, turn the word into numbers using the code A=1, B=2… Z=26, add them up and turn to the paragraph with the same number as the total.

If you cannot remember the password, or the section you turn to makes no sense, turn to **113** instead and try an alternative.

64

An arm up in front of her face to shield her eyes from the force of the wind, Alice determinedly strides into the teeth of the rising gale as leaves and twigs whirl about her. A thorny branch suddenly whips past, catching her, leaving a deep gouge in the flesh of her exposed fore-arm, causing Alice to gasp in pain and surprise. (Take 1 point from Alice's *Endurance* score.)

The rumble of thunder comes again, closer now and louder, only it's not thunder, it is the sound of booming laughter. Looking up at the storm-wracked sky, Alice can see a hideous face forming amidst the clouds. It is that of an ugly woman, with a large pointed nose, wobbly double chins, and wearing a crown. And its glowering storm-cloud eyes are fixed on Alice. (Add 1 to Alice's *Insanity* score.)

The wind is getting stronger all the time. Glancing after the White Rabbit, Alice sees it vanish down a rabbit-hole at the edge of the field. There is no other shelter within sight.

If you think Alice should seek shelter inside the rabbit-hole, turn to **96**. If you think she should stand strong in the face of the growing storm, turn to **85**.

Alice darts left and right, trying to confuse the Snap-dragon-flies, hoping that she will be able to dodge past them at any moment. However, all Alice's manages to achieve is to aggravate the insects which dart it with their thorny stings bared, both delivering painful jabs.

Lose 3 *Endurance* points and, if Alice is able to continue with her adventure, turn to **112**.

Raising the Spade as if it were a weapon rather than a digging implement, Alice prepares to defend herself against the gardeners. The three curiously-dressed labourers immediately drop their tools, a look of horror on their faces.

"The Ace of Spades!" one of them shouts, his eyes fixed on the blade of the Spade held above Alice's head. "A higher card!"

And with that, all three turn tail and flee into the leafy pathways of the maze.

Turn to **36**.

67

Her shoes slipping in the sand, her breath coming in desperate, ragged gasps, Alice flees from the Walrus's angry charge. But the animal is built for an aquatic life, making it slow and ungainly on land.

Alice soon outpaces the Walrus and deciding that it will be even harder for the creature to follow her into the dunes than along the beach, she heads into the marram grass topped hills.

Turn to **312**.

68

Hefting the Mallet in both hands, raising it over her shoulder, ready to bring it down hard on the heads of the horrific hedgehogs, Alice is surprised when the wooden club gives a raucous squawk and is suddenly a wooden club no more.

Kicking its spindly legs and flapping its wings furiously, the mallet-turned-flamingo frees itself from Alice's grasp and takes to the air, squawking angrily, eventually disappearing over the hedge-tops of the maze.

Strike the Mallet from Alice's Adventure Sheet and turn to **78**.

69

The scissoring blades snap shut and a lock of Alice's hair tumbles to the floor. She has escaped serious injury by only a hair's breadth. Turn to **47**.

70

It is not long before Alice reaches another right-angled turn in the maze. Should she go south (turn to **58**) or west (turn to **84**)?

71

Cupping her hands together, Alice catches some of the water as it spurts from the tip of the knight's spear and then, trying to do so in as lady-like a manner as she can manage, drinks deeply.

The water is as refreshing as Alice had hoped, but better than that it actually has a reenergising effect upon her body. (Add up to 8 *Endurance* points and add 1 point to both Alice's *Agility* score and her *Combat* score.)

Now it's time to explore somewhere new – turn to **380**.

Alice is ready for the Red Queen this time. Hefting the Vorpal Sword in her hands once more she prepares to do away with the vampire-queen who now haunts this place, once and for all. (Alice has the initiative in this battle.)

VAMPIRESS   COMBAT 11   ENDURANCE 12

If Alice is victorious in her battle with the Red Queen, turn to **125**. If not, then her adventure will end here, as the vampire begins to feast…

73

"Falsehood!" booms the guard. Make a note that the guards have the initiative and turn to **163**.

74

Putting the bottle to her lips, Alice takes a gulp of the blue potion before carefully setting the bottle down again upon the table. A moment later, her stomach lurches as the world start to spin about her.

The child feels horribly dizzy, as if she is having to endure a ride on the waltzers at a funfair. (Deduct 1 *Endurance* point.)

And then suddenly the world stops spinning. As the woozy dizziness fades, Alice dares open her eyes again.

She is sitting on the ground beside a gazebo clad in honeysuckle, beneath which, resting upon a glass table, is a glass bottle containing a crimson-coloured liquid. A path leads off east into the maze.

"I'm beginning to get the feeling I've been here before," Alice says to no one in particular, since no one in particular is precisely who is keeping her company at present.

If you think Alice should drink from the bottle, turn to **54**. If not, she must follow the path east – turn to **220**.

75

"Tweedle-dee and Tweedle-dum, I've got an aching in my tum," says the first head as it sniffs the air above the spot where Alice crouches, shaking, hidden beneath the bracken.

"Tweedle-dum and Tweedle-dee, I think I've found it. Time for tea!" the second head roars and the Ogre reaches down with a huge hand, catching Alice up. Dragging her from the undergrowth, the brute throws her onto the bone-strewn ground in front of its cave.

Lose 1 *Endurance* point and turn to **30**.

Keeping the towers of the palace in sight over the tops of the hedges, Alice comes at last to a set of tall gates. Beyond the gates, a drawbridge over a moat leads to the barbican gatehouse of a vast palace.

However, barring her way, standing in front of the gates, are two, burly brutes wearing ill-fitting tabards that make them look like playing cards – the Six and Seven of Clubs in this case.

"Halt! Who goes there?" demands one of the guards. "Friend of foe?"

"Friend?" Alice answers hesitantly, all too aware of how burly and brutish the two guards appear, and how knobbly their clubs look.

"And what is your business at the Palace?" asks the other guard in a high-pitched nasal voice. "Here to see the Queen, I suppose."

"Yes, that's right," replies Alice, playing along with the unwitting guards now.

"Then you'll know what the password is," says the first, an ugly smug grin creasing his lumpen features."

If you want Alice to give the guards a password, turn to **113**. If you want Alice to charge the gates, in an attempt to break through, make a note that Alice has the initiative and turn to **163**. If you want Alice to use the *Curiouser and Curiouser* ability at this juncture instead, turn to **86**.

77

The cake has a strangely familiar taste, like allspice and marzipan. (Regain up to 4 *Endurance* points.)

"Curiouser and curiouser!" cries Alice. "I'm opening out like the largest telescope that ever was!"

Alice looks down at her feet, which seem to be almost out of sight, she is getting so tall.

Take an Insanity test. If Alice passes the test, turn to **121**, but if she fails the test, turn to **107**.

78

As the first of the Spinebacks comes for her, the second holds back, meaning that Alice can fight the horrors one at a time. (Alice has the initiative.)

	COMBAT	ENDURANCE
First SPINEBACK	8	7
Second SPINEBACK	8	7

If Alice defeats both of her opponents, turn to **117**.

79

If the word 'Phantasm' is written on Alice's Adventure Sheet, turn to **128**. If not, turn to **153**.

As Alice approaches the tree a low hum fills the air around her. Bees are buzzing about the flower beds, alighting on the trumpets of foxgloves and crawling inside in search of the plants' sweet nectar, getting their furry legs covered with golden yellow pollen in the process.

As she strolls between the raised beds, Alice takes a moment to watch the insects at their work. Something hums past her ear, taking her attention away from the business-like bees.

Lumbering through the mote-shot sunlight, on stained glass wings three feet across, is a carved wooden rocking horse, with its own leather saddle attached and a mane and tail made of genuine horsehair.

"A Rocking-horse-fly!" Alice says in surprise.

Crawling on the ground at her feet is another curious insect. Its wings are thin slices of Bread-and-butter, its body is a crust, and its head is a lump of sugar.

"And I suppose you're a Bread-and-Butterfly. I hope I don't bump into an actual Dragon-fly!"

Alice has only gone a little further when she hears a curious crackling sound. Flying towards her are two more impossible insects, and the largest she has seen so far. Their bodies are plum-puddings, their wings are huge holly-leaves, but most strange of all, their heads look like large raisins burning in brandy, and it is this which is the source of the crackling sound.

The Snap-dragon-flies dart towards her, their burning raisin heads alive with hot blue flame, and Alice is quite sure that to be burnt by one, or to be grazed by their holly-wings would be more painful than being stung by an angry hornet.

What should Alice do now?

Run away as fast as she can?	Turn to **50**.
Try to dodge past the insects?	Turn to **65**.
Prepare to fend them off?	Turn to **112**.
Try to think of a way out of this tricky situation?	Turn to **35**.

81

Alice enters another clearing, the towering toadstools which surround it the tallest the child has yet seen since entering this weird woodland. Surely, if she were to climb to the top of one of the colossal fungi she would be able to see for miles.

An experienced tree-climber, Alice is confident she can climb to the top of one of the toadstools so that she might survey the countryside beyond. If you want her to do this, turn to **91**. If not, turn to **488**.

Tumbling head over heels, Alice sees that she is fast approaching a rickety bookcase. If you want her to grab a book from a shelf as she falls past, turn to **102**. If you think she should leave her hands free, just in case, turn to **62**.

It is then that the Mouse returns, carrying a tray of tea things.

"Shall I be mother?" asks Alice, glad of the distraction, and proceeds to pour out four cups of tea. After all that's happened to her, she doesn't think it at all strange to be sitting down to tea with a stuffed rabbit pocket watch, a Mouse and a Lizard.

"Mmm… Earl Grey," the Mouse says, closing its eyes and savouring the aroma of the hot steam.

Alice takes a wary sip from her own cup. The tea is indeed delicious and most refreshing. (Add up to 6 *Endurance* points.)

"Now, where was I?" the White Rabbit says. "Oh yes, the Queen of Hearts."

But before he can say any more the Rabbit is interrupted by a sharp cracking sound and a noise like the internal workings of a watch exploding.

All eyes turn to the grandfather clock and watch as the timepiece transforms into an almost humanoid form, with the clock's pendulum swinging from the end of one arm-like appendage, not unlike a flail, while the other ends in the scissoring hands of its face.

"There is a spy in the camp!" shrieks the Rabbit.

Walls might have ears, but a clock has a face and hands. The meeting in the study has been observed and now the Queen of Hearts' spy will eliminate those that threaten her choke-hold on Wonderland.

First to go is the Mouse. One swing of the pendulum sees to that, caving in the poor creature's skull and sending the tea things crashing to the floor.

The return swing sends Bill the Lizard flying into a glass-fronted cabinet of animal skulls, the glass shattering and the woodwork splintering as he lands in a bleeding heap amidst the debris.

"Run, Alice!" screams the White Rabbit. "Save yourself! Stop the Queen!"

The animal is abruptly silenced as the clockwork assassin removes his head with a scything sweep of its other arm.

Alice turns in a panic and throws herself at the door as, with one almighty leap, the transformed Grandfather Clock leaps over the desk, reaching for her with its scissoring clock-hand fingers.

Take an Agility test. If Alice passes the test, turn to **69**. If she fails the test, turn to **56**.

Following the path west, Alice comes to a dead-end. However, strangely, standing before the hedge in front of her is a full-length mirror set within in a polished wood frame. Reflected in the mirror Alice can see the gravel path leading back into the maze… But… But she can't see herself!

"I do declare it's not a mirror at all!" Alice exclaims. She reaches a tentative hand towards the glass and where the glass should be, her hand passes straight through.

If you want Alice to try stepping through the mirror, and see where it takes her, turn to **104**. If not, she will have to retrace her steps through the leafy labyrinth (turn to **70**).

The wind whips waves across the surface of the river, shaking the willows' whip-like fronds. The thunderous rumbling comes again as the face in the clouds starts to laugh.

Alice is helpless in the face of the gale. The wind lifts her off her feet and she is tossed about like just another leaf in the storm.

Sticks and branches whirl about her as the howling gale carries her across the field. She can see the rabbit-hole beneath her now. And then suddenly the wind drops as quickly as it arose and she is falling, plummeting towards the ground, the entrance to the burrow yawning beneath her like a gaping, earthy mouth.

It is then that a spinning branch hits her on the head, knocking her senseless.

Deduct 2 points from Alice's *Endurance* score and turn to **191**.

86

The gates behind the guards suddenly open of their own accord and a trumpeted fanfare announces the arrival of their captain, accompanied by a troop of club-wielding soldiers. The man is seated upon a snorting warhorse. He has angular, aquiline features, and wears a tabard adorned with embroidered hearts, while his steed's barding bears the heraldry of the Queen of Hearts.

"Who have we here?" demands the Captain of the Guard, more knave than knight, as far as Alice is concerned.

"Alice," replies Alice.

"Alice?" the Knave of Hearts bellows. "Seize her at once!"

Alice is an intelligent girl and realises that to resist arrest now, when faced by a whole troop of soldiers, would be to invite certain death, so she allows the playing card guards to take her prisoner. The guards then march her through the gates, over the drawbridge, and into the palace beyond.

Turn to **386**.

The snarls of the Spinebacks are suddenly drowned out by a furious croaking cry and a vast shadow falls across the croquet-ground as a monstrous bird swoops down out of the sky. The colossal avian catches one of the hedgehog-like beasts in its long beak before flying away again, as quickly as it appeared, leaving Alice to fight the last remaining mutant. (Alice has the initiative.)

SPINEBACK   COMBAT 8   ENDURANCE 7

If Alice defeats her opponent, turn to **117**.

88

With powerful strokes, Alice swims towards the shore, the sandy spit of land getting closer with every surge of the sea, until at last she staggers from the water, her arms and legs feeling like they're made of nothing more substantial than blancmange.

The sun beats down on the child from the azure sky overhead as she takes a moment to rest upon a ledge of rock, and empty her shoes of seawater. Before long her dress starts to dry out too.

Behind her the beach rises to a range of grass-topped dunes, and beyond those Alice can see the tops of trees interspersed with carefully-tended topiary. Looking left along the beach, Alice spies the entrance to a rocky cove, while to her right the shoreline curves round to a wide bay.

If you think Alice should investigate the rocky cove first, turn to **138**. If you think she should head instead towards the sandy bay, turn to **258**. Alternatively, if you think she should just head into the dunes towards the well-tended topiary, turn to **312**.

89

As the bizarre vivisect-hybrid bears down on her Alice realises that rather than screaming it is singing, its howls distorted by their passage through the water. "Will you, won't you, will you, won't you, will you join the dance?"

Somehow, the words of the song seem strangely familiar to Alice. And then – she doesn't understand precisely how – the words of another song entirely enter her mind, unbidden.

"Beautiful Soup, so rich and green,
Waiting in a hot tureen!
Who for such dainties would not stoop?
Soup of the evening, beautiful Soup!
Beautiful Soup! Who cares for fish,
Game, or any other dish?
Who would not give all else for two
Pennyworth only of beautiful Soup!
Beautiful Mock Turtle Soup!"

At these final words the monstrous creature turns tail and flees, powerful strokes of its paddle-like flippers transporting it back into the darkness of the ocean depths.

Turn to **118**.

90

Alice remembers visiting mazes before with her Nurse, and has learnt about the Labyrinth of Crete in classical studies with her Governess, so she feels quite at home here.

At the next junction, should Alice go north (turn to **24**), east (turn to **100**), or south (turn to **174**)?

91

Finding plenty of hand- and foot-holds in the stalk of the vertiginous toadstool, Alice clambers up the stem until she finally hauls herself up onto the cap of the fungus.

The wonderful landscape of this strange realm is laid out below her like a map. Far to the south she can see the coast and beyond that, even further out in the wave-washed ocean, a gloomy island. To the west she can see a beautiful garden which appears to belong to a grand house that she spies to the north-west. Directly north of the forest is a quaint thatched cottage with a pair of distinctive chimneys, while to the east Alice can see the imposing battlements and turrets of a once imposing, but now rundown, palace. The way to the palace appears to be blocked by a tortuous maze made of tall yew hedges.

Having learnt all she is going to learn from her vertiginous vantage point, Alice sets off back down the trunk-like stalk of the giant toadstool.

It is then that she spots the monstrous slug making its way up the stem towards her. She finds its rippling, boneless body quite repellent. "I dread to think what might happen if we were actually to come eye to eye-stalk," she says.

There are three different ways for Alice to complete her descent to the forest floor, but which one do you think is the most sensible?

Fight her way past the Slug?   Turn to **181**.

Try to avoid the slug by continuing her descent on the other side of the stalk?   Turn to **101**.

Allow herself to drop to the ground from here?   Turn to **151**.

92

Alice throws the crumbly cake onto the path, close to the tree and almost immediately the Snap-dragon-flies take off after it. Landing on the cake they begin to devour it with rapid scissoring movements of their wasp-like mandibles, leaving Alice able to continue on her way through the garden unhindered.

Cross the Curious Cake off Alice's Adventure Sheet (she cannot use it again) and turn to **146**.

93

"Wrong!" declares the guard. Make a note that the guards have the initiative and turn to **163**.

94

"Well it's your dream, so who else do you expect to do it?" asks the White Rabbit in response to Alice's question.

"A dream? It's more like a nightmare."

"That's what I've been trying to tell you."

"And if you want it to stop, you need to off 'Er Madge," the Lizard chips in. "Surest way is with the Vorpal Sword, one swift chop to the neck. Take the 'ead clean off her shoulders. It's the only way to be sure with 'er kind."

"Now then, Bill, that's enough of that. You'll be giving the poor girl nightmares... Oh, I'm sorry. It's a little late for that, isn't it?"

Turn to **83**.

95

Does Alice have a Coin? If so, and you still want her to throw it into the fountain, turn to **124**. If she doesn't have a Coin, or you don't think she should throw it away so carelessly, turn to **241**.

96

Reaching the rabbit-hole, without a second thought Alice throws herself into the earthy gloom.

Turn to **57**.

As the Spinebacks come for her, two of the playing card croquet arches unfold themselves and stand upright. The playing card guards' bodies are oblong and flat, with hands and feet at the corners, and unkind expressions on their furious faces.

Alice's attention is drawn straight back to the humanoid hedgehogs as they bear down on her. She must fight the horrors (which have the initiative) at the same time.

	COMBAT	ENDURANCE
First SPINEBACK	8	7
Second SPINEBACK	8	7

If Alice defeats the Spinebacks she must then battle the croquet-ground's Playing Card Guards, taking them on together. (In this case Alice has the initiative.)

	COMBAT	ENDURANCE
First PLAYING CARD GUARD	7	6
Second PLAYING CARD GUARD	7	6

If she bests both her opponents, turn to **117**.

98

Bill lies prone amidst the wreckage of the broken cabinet. His body is covered in cuts caused by the broken glass and he is breathing heavily.

"Mr Lizard?" Alice says kneeling down beside him. "Bill? Can you hear me?"

In response, a guttural snarl issues from the Lizard's throat.

"Oh no, it's happening again!" cries the Rabbit. "Get out of here, Alice. Get out of here now! Don't do it, Bill," the Rabbit goes on desperately, "you can control this, you know you can! We've done it before, remember? Alice – get *out*! You won't like Bill when he's angry."

If you want Alice to leave as quickly as she can, turn to **179**. If you want her to stay, turn to **111**.

99

As the monster lumbers towards Alice, the child is distracted momentarily as a broad tooth-filled grin appears in the air beside her. The smile is soon followed by a head, a body, and last of all a tail, and then the Cheshire Cat is there, ready to fight at her side. Spitting its fury, the grinning animal springs at the reptilian beast, claws and teeth bared.

Make a note of the fact that the Alice-Jabberwock has suffered one attack and turn to **119**.

100

Alice is quite enjoying exploring the maze. At the next turn in the path she doesn't hang about but hurries on her way. But which way does she go?

North?   Turn to **110**.

West?   Turn to **90**.

101

Alice slides round to the other side of the toadstool's trunk, but as she does so, she comes into contact with the Slug's trail of slime.

Take an Agility test. If Alice passes the test, turn to **131**. If she fails the test, she slips on the slime – turn to **151**.

102

Alice's fingers close around the cracked leather spine of a slim volume and, as she continues to fall, pulls it from the bookcase.

The wind whistling about her ears, she flicks through the book but can see no pictures and no obvious conversations. "And what is the use of a book without pictures or conversations?" she asks herself out loud.

She stops at a page on which is printed a curious poem that reminds her of a rhyme her Nurse used to sing – but which is, at the same time, quite different – and she starts to read:

"Twinkle, twinkle, little bat!
How I wonder what you're at!
Up above the world you fly,
Like a tea tray in the sky.
Twinkle, twinkle, little bat!
How I wonder what you're at!"

"What a curious poem," Alice says, and then starts as the book in her hands begins to twitch.

As she watches, the book transforms, the cracked leather cover becoming the flapping wings of a large bat, the loosened leaves of its pages fluttering into the air around her. And then she is holding a large, and very angry bat in her hands, which gives a shrill high-pitched shriek, exposing elongated fangs.

Take an Insanity test. If Alice passes the test, turn to **200**. If she fails the test, turn to **214**.

103

Opening the red cloth-bound book, Alice begins to read:

One winter night, at half-past nine,
Cold, tired, and cross, and muddy,
I had come home, too late to dine,
And supper, with cigars and wine,
Was waiting in the study.

There was a strangeness in the room,
And Something white and wavy
Was standing near me in the gloom—
I took it for the carpet-broom
Left by that careless slavey.

"What a curious poem," says Alice. She can almost imagine the strangeness in the room as she reads the verse and evens fancies she can see something white and wavy standing there between the bookcases.

If you think Alice should keep reading, turn to **514**. If you think she has tarried in the library long enough, turn to **504**.

104

Taking a deep breath, Alice steps up to the mirror and then, in another moment she is through the glass.

She is standing at another dead-end in the maze, with another mirror set within a polished wood frame behind her. Checking by the sun overhead, she realises that the gravel path will set her on a course heading west into the labyrinth.

If you want Alice to follow this new path through the maze, turn to **490**. If you would prefer her to step back through the looking-glass, turn to **154**.

"A villain referred to only as the Carpenter," replies the Rabbit in hushed tones, his voice wavering. "I would call him the Queen's executioner, only he doesn't actually kill anyone. Would that he did," the Rabbit adds with a shudder.

"Vivisection is his game," says the Lizard. "'Off with 'is head' is only the beginning; it's what he does with your head afterwards you want to worry about. Taxidermy's just a hobby to him, something he practises on the side."

A vivisectionist who chops up people and animals only to put them back together in grotesque ways? And Alice thought she has seen all the horrors that Wonderland had to offer already. (Add 1 to Alice's *Insanity* score.)

"Now don't go scaring the poor girl, Bill!" the White Rabbit says.

Wringing his cap in his hands whilst looking at the floor, the Lizard makes his apology: "Begging your pardon, miss."

Turn to **83**.

"This must be the tomb of the White King!" Alice declares in both excitement, and shock at the implications of what this means.

Before Alice's eyes, the stone sword held in the marble hands of the carved king at his repose, begins to glow with an inner luminescence. When the light fades again the sword in the White King's hands is stone no more, but a gleaming steel blade, etched with runes of power.

"The Vorpal Sword!" Alice says in a reverent whisper.

Her awed reverie is disturbed by the arrival of another within the mausoleum. Standing within the arch at the top of the stairs is a knight clad in a suit of blood-red armour, his face hidden behind the closed visor of his helm.

The Red Knight says nothing but drawing his black iron blade crosses the chamber, sword raised, and Alice instinctively understands that once again she is expected to fight for her life.

If you are able to and want to use *The Pen is Mightier* ability now, turn to **484**. If you are either not able or not willing, turn to **292**.

107

Alice continues to grow until her head hits the roof of the hall and she is more than nine feet high. Unable to believe her very particular predicament, Alice peers down at the tiled floor – the tiles looking like the tiny tesserae of a mosaic, to the overgrown Alice – and bursts into tears. (Add 1 to Alice's *Insanity* score.)

"You ought to be ashamed of yourself," Alice chides herself, "a great girl like you to go on crying in this way! Stop this moment, I tell you!"

But she can't stop and goes on shedding gallons of tears, until there is a large pool all around her, reaching half down the hall.

A creeping realisation comes over her. "I've been in a situation very like this before. I think I even remember saying those self-same words. Let me see if I can remember what happened next."

It is then that a very peculiar rhyme pops into Alice's mind, and she finds herself inadvertently reciting it out loud:

> "How doth the little crocodile
> Improve his shining tail,
> And pour the waters of the Nile
> On every golden scale!"

Alice is suddenly aware that her shoes and stockings are getting wet.

"That was a narrow escape! I must be shrinking again," she says, the pool of tears seeming to rise as she shrinks toward it (only now it is a veritable Sea of Tears, the walls of the hall having vanished into the distance) until – *splash!* – she finds herself treading water to keep her head above the briny waves.

It is then that she spies two reptilian eyes blinking at her from just above the surface of the water, followed by a line of bronze protrusions covering a ridged back and the slowly lashing tail steering the crocodilian form.

"And now things are worse than ever," the poor child declares, as the crocodile glides towards her.

If you think that now would be a good time to use *The Pen is Mightier* ability, turn to **203**. If you think Alice should prepare to defend herself, turn to **182**.

108

And then the vision changes again and Alice is standing before an ivory tower, overgrown with creepers, within a sinister wood, even as the mists start to thicken about her again. "Whoever lives here?" wonders Alice in a dreamy way.

"Come back," comes the Caterpillar's distant voice again. "Come back…"

If you think Alice should answer the Caterpillar's summons, turn to **185**. If you want Alice to enter the ivory tower instead, turn to **129**.

109

Taking something from the cupboard whilst falling down the well isn't going to be as easy as perhaps it sounds.

Take an Agility test. If Alice passes the test, turn to **133**. If she fails the test, turn to **156**.

110

Mounted on a granite pedestal at the next turning of the trail is a curious statue of an old man balancing an eel on the end of his nose. Which way now?

East?   Turn to **140**.

South?   Turn to **100**.

111

The Lizard gives another snarling hiss, causing Alice to take a wary step away from him, but she cannot tear her eyes away from poor Bill when he too starts to undergo his own terrible transformation.

Bill's body seems to swell with every breath he takes, causing his gardener's shirt to split at the seams. As the tatters of his clothes fall from his ever-expanding body so his snout elongates and his tail grows, becomes longer and thicker.

But it is not only Bill's clothes that are coming apart, his skin is splitting too, the tears following the gashes caused by the broken shards of glass.

Shaking off his shed skin, and now standing on all fours, Bill the Lizard turns his attention to Alice. His eyes burn red and his mouth is full of saurian fangs as long as steak knives. The White Rabbit's gardener is Bill the Lizard no longer; now he has become Bill the Basilisk and he is blocking Alice's way out of the room.

I you want Alice to use *The Pen is Mightier* ability to save herself, turn to **122**. If not, Alice will have to fight for her life once again (turn to **142**).

112

The two Snap-dragon-flies buzz towards Alice with angry intent, and no sign of festive spirit.

If you want to use *The Pen is Mightier* ability to help Alice escape her fate, and you are still able to do so, turn to **393**. If not, turn to **126**.

113

"Go on then. What is the password?" the guard challenges Alice. What should she say in reply?

"Off with their heads!"   Turn to **73**.

"Jam tarts!"   Turn to **93**.

"We're all mad here!"   Turn to **143**.

Before her is another long passage. There is no sign of the White Rabbit but she can hear the tick and rattle of clockwork coming from somewhere up ahead.

There's not a moment to lose. Chasing off down the passage Alice turns a corner and finds herself in a long, low hall, lit by lamps hanging from the roof. There are doors all around the hall but what has really attracted her attention are the two stick-like figures stalking towards her on pin-like legs.

Although they are shaped like men, they most definitely are *not* men, since they are quite clearly made from pieces of metal, and their visible innards look like the workings of a clock.

Tick-tock, tick-tock, go the clock mechanisms as the metal men stalk towards her, a sinister glint in their watch-case eyes. *Tick-tock, tick-tock.*

The horrid vision of these clockwork creations, their brass body parts glinting in the lamplight, fills Alice with dread. (Add 1 to Alice's *Insanity* score.) Quaking in fear, her face as white as a sheet, what should Alice do now?

To try to dodge past the advancing Tick-Tock Men, turn to **5**. To try talking to the clockwork creations, turn to **226**. To attack the Tick-Tock Men, before they can attack Alice, turn to **169**. For Alice to try to think her way out of such a dangerous situation, turn to **246**. To use Alice's *Curiouser and Curiouser* ability, turn to **130**.

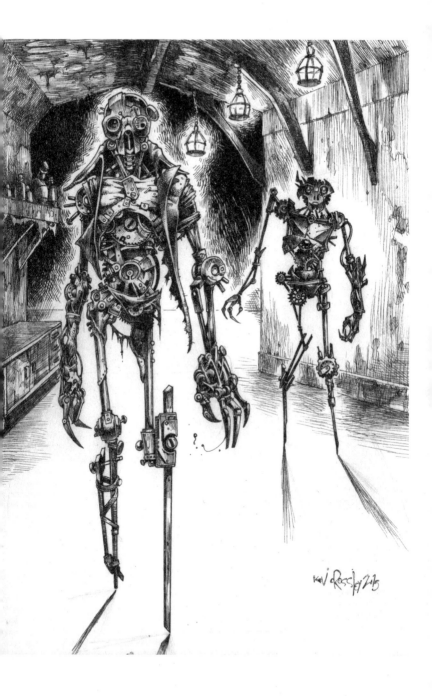

"Jabberwocky!" the child says with a confidence befitting someone much older than her tender eleven years.

"You may pass!" declares the guard.

The two burly brutes heave open the gates, letting Alice out of the maze and into the palace.

Turn to **446**.

"Surely you remember Her Majesty," the Rabbit gasps in disbelief. "Foul-tempered ruler of Wonderland, quick to pass a sentence of death for the slightest offense. 'Off with their heads!' No?"

"What happened to the King of Hearts?" asks Alice, shaking her head.

"Best not to ask."

The Lizard draws a finger across his throat whilst making a strange clicking noise from the side of his mouth.

"Hearsay and rumour, Bill. Hearsay and rumour!" chides the White Rabbit.

"But look what she had done to you!" the Lizard says pointedly.

"Now don't go getting yourself all het up. You know what happens when you get worked up. And you know what they say about walls and ears too. We can't be too careful, not with her Tick-Tock Men about."

Turn to **83**.

Having endured such an unpleasant encounter at the strange croquet-ground, Alice is more than happy to be on her way. But which way is she going?

East?   Turn to **250**.

West?   Turn to **58**.

Exhausted by her encounter with the Mock Turtle, Alice lets the current carry her where it will until finally she is washed up on the sandy shore. The sun beats down on the child as she takes a moment to rest upon a ledge of rock, empty her shoes of water and untangle strands of seaweed from her hair. Before long her dress has started to dry out as well.

Beyond the shore, the beach rises to a range of grass-topped dunes, and beyond those Alice can see the tops of trees interspersed with carefully-tended topiary. Looking left along the beach, Alice spies the entrance to a rocky cove, while to her right the shoreline curves round to a wide bay.

If you think Alice should investigate the rocky cove, turn to **138**. If you think she should head towards the sandy bay, turn to **258**. If you think she should just head into the dunes towards the well-tended topiary, turn to **312**.

If the word 'Metamorphosis' is recorded on Alice's Adventure Sheet, turn to **322**. If not, turn to **231**.

120

"Why, an hourglass has the most moving parts," Alice says, feeling very pleased with herself, "because it is full of so many grains of sand."

One by one, Alice rotates the brass triangle so that it lines up with each letter of the word in turn, giving it one full rotation for the last 'S' just to be sure.

Hearing a click, she looks down to see something drop out of a hole that has appeared in the column of the plinth. Bending down, Alice picks it up between finger and thumb.

It is a shiny gold Coin. She would have said that it was a sovereign, but she doesn't recognise the Queen's face on the reverse. Nonetheless, Alice is delighted with her prize and pops it into her pinafore pocket before continuing on her way.

Add 1 to Alice's *Logic* score for solving the puzzle, and turn to **31**.

"Curiouser and curiouser and curiouser!" Alice exclaims as she continues to grow until her head hits the ceiling and she is more than nine feet tall! (Add one more *Curiouser and Curiouser* box to Alice's Adventure Sheet.)

"What a curious cake," Alice says, looking at the crumbling remains lying in the palm of her huge hand. "I wonder, if I only ate half as much would only grow half as tall?" And with that thought she wraps what is left of the cake in its greaseproof paper case and pops it into her pinafore pocket.

There are two pieces of cake remaining. If Alice eats one she can add 4 *Endurance* points, and if she does so before a battle, she can add 1 to her *Combat* score for the duration of said battle. (Add the Curious Cake to Alice's Adventure Sheet.)

Just as Alice is adjusting to her new size, and imagining all the things she could do now that she's taller – such as pick apples without needing a ladder, or have a conversation with a giraffe – her body starts to shrink again and soon she is back to her normal size. Clearly the effects of curious cake are only temporary.

Turn to **164**.

Suddenly a face appears at the window. It is that of a Weasel, dressed in a similar manner to Bill before his unfortunate transformation.

"'Ere, what's going on?" the Weasel shouts, throwing open the window and climbing into the study. "Is that you, Bill?"

Upon seeing the mustelid, the Basilisk gives a furious hiss, smashing through the study door in its hurry to escape the new arrival.

"Come back 'ere, you!" the Weasel shouts as it sets off in pursuit, leaving Alice alone in the study. She listens as the Basilisk crashes through the house, overturning furniture and breaking windows, until it finds its way out through the front door and an eerie stillness falls over the place once more.

Turn to **168**.

123

Knowing of no way off the island, the child sits down on the floor and starts to weep. Her adventure is over.

THE END

124

Taking the golden Coin from the pocket of her pinafore, Alice casts it into the fountain while making her wish. But what does she wish for?

The agility of an ape?	Turn to **144**.
The wisdom of an owl?	Turn to **161**.
The ferocity of a unicorn?	Turn to **206**.
The strength of a lion?	Turn to **221**.
Peace of mind?	Turn to **187**.

125

Taking the Vorpal Sword in both hands, Alice plunges it into the vampire's shrivelled black heart. The Red Queen gives a gasp and then a soul-wrenching scream as her undead form dies at last. Her body bursts into flame and quickly burns down to nothing but ash, which is then blown away on the powerful wind that suddenly howls through the Palace.

But as the Red Queen's remains are blown to the four winds, so the walls of the palace start to dissolve and melt away like mist…

Blinking the sleep from her eyes, Alice yawns and stretches, finding herself back home in the drawing room, curled up in a corner of the great arm-chair, with a dear little black kitten, sitting in her lap, the cat purring contentedly to herself as she washes her face with a paw.

Alice's nightmare is over and she is home again… Isn't she?

Take an Insanity test. If Alice passes the test, turn to **159**. If she fails the test, turn to **139**.

126

Alice must fight the fire-sparking insects (which have the initiative) at the same time.

	COMBAT	ENDURANCE
First SNAP-DRAGON-FLY	7	5
Second SNAP-DRAGON-FLY	6	5

If Alice kills the insects, like a toddler plucking the wings from a Daddy-Long-Legs, she can continue on her way at last, no longer bothered by the bothersome insects – turn to **146**.

127

The path enters a grotto, yew hedges giving way to rock walls glistening with moisture. The ground underfoot becomes wet and muddy as Alice enters the dank gloom of the artificial cave.

If Alice has been to the Grotto before, turn to **208**. If not, turn to **218**.

Hearing a ghostly wailing, Alice stares in amazement as the Ghost she freed from the book in the library rises from the chessboard in front of the monster. Its discomforting wail becomes a dreadful, soul-chilling howl, and then the phantasm launches itself at the Alice-Jabberwock, tearing the monster's soft underbelly with its spectral talons.

The Jabberwock responds with a sweep of a claw and with a final unearthly moan, the Ghost is snuffed out.

Make a note of the fact that the Alice-Jabberwock has suffered one attack and turn to **153**.

"You must come back, Alice," comes the Caterpillar's distant desperate voice again. "We are losing you…"

"Now I am hearing things," says Alice, dismissing the Caterpillar's voice as being unreal, rather than the vision of the ivory tower she is walking through now. She is struggling to distinguish the difference between what is real and what isn't.

Take a Logic test, and if Alice passes, turn to **149**; but if she fails, turn to **165**.

First she has a conversation with a talking, clockwork rabbit, then she finds herself falling down an impossibly deep well, and now she finds herself being threatened by two skeletal clockwork men. "Curiouser and curiouser," says Alice.

But just when she thinks things cannot possibly get any stranger, before her very eyes one of the Tick-Tock Men starts to transform. As she watches it jerks and twitches and appears to divide itself in two down the middle. More limbs unfold from the bifurcated body parts and Alice finds herself now facing three of the curious clockwork creations rather than just two!

The three horrors scrape their gleaming metal claws together, sending sparks flying from the keenly-honed blades, leaving Alice with no doubt in her mind as to what they intend for her.

If you think Alice should now make use of *The Pen is Mightier* ability, turn to **189**. If not, she will have to prepare to fight them – turn to **150**.

Alice makes her way safely to the ground. Turn to **488**.

Most of the pieces have already been removed from the board. Those that are left are arranged like this:

A note scribbled on a piece of jotting paper and tucked under one corner of the chessboard reads, 'White to move.'

"If white is to play," says Alice, "I wonder how many moves it would take to win."

Do you know how many moves it would take for White to win? If so, turn to the paragraph with the same number as the number of moves required.

If not, Alice has spent enough hiding in the library and should be on her way again – turn to **454**.

133

Alice manages to open the cupboard door with one hand and reach inside with the other, pulling out a large pair of scissors.

Add the Scissors to Alice's Adventure Sheet. If she ever finds herself in combat with one of the strange denizens that inhabit Wonderland she may use the Scissors as a weapon, causing 3 points of damage to her opponent's *Endurance* score with every successful strike, rather than the usual 2.

Now turn to **156**.

134

Following the path east, Alice comes to a dead-end. Before her stands a full-length mirror in a polished wood frame. Alice can see the gravel path behind her reflected in the looking-glass.

"Imagine if there was a way of getting through it," Alice says, putting a hand to the mirror. "Imagine if the glass got all soft like gauze, so that I can get through. Why, it's turning into a sort of mist now, I declare! It'll be easy enough to get through."

And certainly the glass *is* beginning to melt away, just like a bright silvery mist.

If you want Alice to push on through the mirror, turn to **154**. If not, she will have to go back the way she has come (turn to **490**).

"You never were very good at time-keeping," the White Rabbit goes on, regarding Alice through lifeless glass eyes.

"Yes, here I am," says Alice and then, annoyed by the Rabbit's slight, adds, "but where is here, exactly?"

"Why, my home, of course," replies the Rabbit. "What a strange question," he says, addressing this last remark to the Lizard and the Mouse.

"And where is that? *Exactly?*"

The animals stare at Alice in dumbfounded amazement, as if she is a monkey that has just learned to walk and talk, although such a thing is probably commonplace here – wherever here is!

"Why, Wonderland, of course!" the White Rabbit exclaims with growing irritation. "Don't you remember?"

"Remember what?" asks Alice.

"This. Wonderland." – Alice shakes her head – "The Hall of Doors?" – Alice shakes her head again – "The beautiful garden?"

"I am very sorry, Mr Rabbit, but I'm afraid I don't. Some things seem familiar, like you for example, but as if I dreamt it all once upon a time."

"That's because you *did* dream it," the White Rabbit says, regarding her with dead glass eyes. "You'll be wanting some answers then. And tea too, probably. Tea first, I should think."

The White Rabbit picks up a little silver bell from the desk and rings it.

"Then none of this is real," says Alice, taking in the room around her, as well as the animals within it.

"Why does that make it any less real?" the White Rabbit challenges her. "Just because this is your dream, doesn't mean we all fade into nothingness the moment you wake up. Life goes on here, whether you're here to observe it or not."

Alice suddenly feels rather light-headed. "This is all rather a lot to take in," she says, her legs giving way and a padded leather armchair catching her.

"Yes, I can see," the Rabbit says, his tone more sympathetic now. "Where is that tea? Mary Ann! Where is she, useless girl? Would you go and see what she's up to, there's a good chap?" the Rabbit asks the Mouse. With a curt nod, the Mouse exits the study.

Recalling her encounter with the Rabbit beside the river bank, Alice's mind is a-whirl with questions again. Questions such as, who is the Queen of Hearts? Who turned the White Rabbit into a walking timepiece? And how does he expect her to kill anyone?

But which question is the most pressing?

"Who is the Queen of Hearts?"   Turn to **116**.

"Who turned you into a walking
timepiece?"   Turn to **105**.

"How do expect me to kill anyone?   Turn to **94**.

Excitedly, Alice runs down the passageway and into the beautiful, sunlit garden. As she leaves the rat-hole she starts to grow again, until she has returned to her normal size. There will be no going back down the tunnel into the Hall of Doors now. But no matter, the bright, sunlit garden is far more appealing than the gloomy, underground hall.

The garden is boxed in on all sides by tall, dense hedges. Gravel paths lead away to left and right among the flower beds that are fit to bursting with a profusion of brightly-coloured plants. Ahead of Alice, at the centre of the garden, there is a magnificent fountain. It is in the form of a gallant knight on horseback, battling a monstrous winged beast. Water spouts from the monster's mouth as well as the tip of the knight's spear.

To explore the garden further, would you like Alice to head left (turn to **371**), head right (turn to **310**) or make for the fountain at the centre of the garden (turn to **51**)?

137

Its eyes seeming to burn with the fires of Hell itself, the snorting beast tries to gore Alice with its sickle-like tusks. She has no choice but to defend herself against the Black Swine (which has the initiative).

BLACK SWINE　　　　　　COMBAT 7　　　ENDURANCE 7

If Alice bests the beast, turn to **148**.

138

Picking her way carefully over the rocks, Alice finds herself on a stony beach covered with myriad pebbles of every different hue of white, grey, brown and black she could possibly imagine.

"I wonder if there might be some interesting fossils to be found here," she says, but before she can locate a single ammonite the shingle shifts and the entire beach rises up before her.

Alice suddenly finds herself face to face with a monstrous lobster, stones cascading from its rocky carapace. As big as a horse, each of its claws as large as Alice, the Rock Lobster scuttles towards her with all the power of a locomotive. There is no way she can outrun the overgrown crustacean so should Alice prepare to defend herself against the angry shellfish (turn to **158**), or do you want her to use *The Pen is Mightier* ability to alter the story and save herself (turn to **212**)?

kev cRossley 2015

"You really shouldn't purr so loud," Alice says, rubbing her eyes, and addressing the kitten, respectfully, yet with some severity. "You woke me out of – oh! – such a dream! I dreamed I was far from here, and had such adventures, and then I dreamed that I woke up and found myself at home…"

Alice's words falter and she gets up out of the arm-chair, placing the purring kitten carefully back on the cushion, and approaches the large looking-glass that dominates the room.

"Now, Kitty, let's consider who it was that dreamed it all. This is a serious question, my dear, and you should not go on licking your paw like that – as if Dinah hadn't washed you this morning! You see, Kitty, it must have been either me or… Me… Alice… She was part of my dream, of course – but then I was part of her dream, too! Was it Alice? Or was it me? But if it was me, then who am I?"

And so the nightmare goes on, without ending, while in the waking world, at home, Alice wakes, her body home to another entity altogether; one that might look like Alice but who is Alice no more…

Still she haunts me, phantomwise,
Alice moving under skies
Never seen by waking eyes…

THE END

140

A white rose bush has been planted at the next junction in the path. Now which way should Alice go?

North?	Turn to **220**.
South?	Turn to **160**.
West?	Turn to **110**.

141

"Curiouser and curiouser, and curiouser!" declares Alice. "One moment I am shrinking and shrinking, wondering if I might go out altogether, like a candle; the next I'll probably start opening out again, wondering whether I'll stop before my head hits the ceiling."

And then, sure enough, Alice starts to grow again, only stopping when she is her normal size. Turn to **164**.

142

Face to face with the monstrous Basilisk, Alice feels paralysed with fear by the reptile's terrible red-eyed stare.

Take an Insanity test. If Alice passes the test, turn to **190**. If she fails, turn to **202**.

143

"That is not the password. Off with her head!" shouts the guard. Make a note that the guards have the initiative and turn to **163**.

144

The coin lands with a plop in the pool where it proceeds to sink to the bottom, and Alice's wish is granted. Add 1 point to her *Agility* score, and then turn to **241**.

145

Alice is standing at the heart of a tangled forest. The grey-black trunks of the trees are contorted into shapes that speak of torment and pain, their branches clung with moss and snaking creepers. The air is redolent with the aroma of a compost heap and a sour yellow mist hangs in the air. Beads of moisture condense on Alice's skin, sucking the warmth from her body. Strange animal hoots and shrieks echo between the trees and have Alice looking all about her, wondering from where the next threat to her life might come.

"Beware the Jabberwock, my son! The jaws that bite, the claws that catch!" Alice mutters under her breath. "Beware the Jubjub bird, and shun the frumious Bandersnatch!"

And then the strange sounds of the forest are silenced by a blood-curdling howl that cuts through the tulgey wood, threatening to send an already anxious Alice over the edge.

Take an Insanity test and if Alice passes, turn to **367**. If she fails the test, turn to **347**.

146

As Alice makes her way along the path through the garden, she hears a loud rustling sound behind her and can't help but look round. The hedges of the garden are closing in behind her, encroaching on the path and forcing her onwards, in fear of her life once again.

And then she sees a way out – an arch of red brick, smothered with swags of ivy, and beyond it the shadowed depths of a sinister forest. But Alice has no choice, she eithers enters the forest or stays and is swallowed by the hungry hedges. Turn to **397**.

147

Something else that Alice remembers from her Governess's attempts to educate her about the Ancient Greeks was the legend of Perseus and the Gorgon Medusa.

"I might not have snakes for hair," Alice addresses the advancing Stone Satyr, "but I am jolly cross that you would take it upon yourself to threaten a young girl, and my fearsome scowl has got the better of both my Governess and Nurse in the past, not to mention both my sisters!"

With that Alice fixes her furious gaze on the statue as it stalks towards her and, thanks to the dream-like logic of this Wonderland, the Satyr's steps slow and, as they do, cracks start to appear across its marble body. With a sound like a thunderbolt striking the earth, the statue explodes into a thousand stony shards.

Turn to **188**.

148

Alice is trapped in the kitchen with the crazed Cook. The bony old hag strides towards her, the massive cleaver gripped tight in one bloody hand, its keen edge dripping with gore.

If you want Alice to use *The Pen is Mightier* ability at this time, turn to **205**. If not, turn to **222**.

149

"Where am I?" Alice challenges herself. "And how did I get here? I do not recall travelling to this dismal wood or this crumbling ruin. "Why it must just be some curious dream!"

And with that, she opens her eyes…

Turn to **185**.

150

The three Tick-Tock Men converge on Alice, but at least she is ready for them (and so has the initiative in the battle to come).

	COMBAT	ENDURANCE
First TICK-TOCK MAN	7	7
Second TICK-TOCK MAN	6	6
Third TICK-TOCK MAN	6	6

If Alice manages to defeat all of her aggressors, turn to **314**.

151

Falling from such a great height is not without its dangers and although Alice's descent is slowed when she bounces off the cap of another mushroom, when she does hit the ground it is still hard enough to cause her to twist her ankle. (Lose 3 *Endurance* points and deduct 2 from Alice's *Agility* score.)

If Alice is able to continue her journey, she picks herself up, dusts herself down, and sets off again at a hobbling limp – turn to **488**.

Alice surveys the scene before her, splintered wood and broken clockwork lying amidst the carnage that greeted her young eyes upon entering the study.

It is quite clear to Alice that someone wants her dead. But who? And just as importantly, why?

She certainly doesn't feel safe staying in the White Rabbit's House a moment longer. But it is as she is making for the door that the sudden realisation comes over her that the White Rabbit was already dead when they first met beside the river bank, nothing but stuffing and clockwork. Although that could be considered a life of sorts, and, if so, is the Rabbit still alive even now, after having had his head removed from his body?

If you want Alice to find out, turn to **168**. If you would rather get her out of there as quickly as possible, turn to **179**.

153

If the word 'Bonkers' is recorded on Alice's Adventure Sheet, turn to **99**. If not, turn to **119**.

154

In another moment Alice is through the glass, her feet alighting on the gravel path on the other side.

She finds herself at another dead-end in the maze, another mirror in a polished wood frame at her back. Judging by the position of the sun overhead, the path she is on now leads away east into the labyrinth.

If you want Alice to follow this new path through the maze, turn to **70**. If you would prefer her to step back through the misty surface of the looking-glass, turn to **104**.

155

Standing before the glass, her pulse racing, Alice takes a deep breath, closes her eyes, and steps forward…

She feels only the slightest resistance, like a gauzy veil against her face, and the solid stone floor gives way to a squelchy quagmire underfoot. Slowly, she opens her eyes…

Record the word 'Portal' on Alice's Adventure Sheet, write the number '233' next to it, and then turn to **145**.

156

As Alice continues to tumble down the well she sees a dresser racing up to meet her. If you want Alice to grab whatever she can from the dresser, turn to **178**. If not, turn to **12**.

157

The Stone Satyr remains silent as it commences its attack, which only makes the experience all the more terrifying for the poor child. (The Stone Satyr has the initiative.)

STONE SATYR   COMBAT 9   ENDURANCE 10

If Alice somehow manages to defeat the animated statue, turn to **188**.

158

Is Alice armed with a Pair of Scissors? If so, turn to **175**. If not, turn to **195**.

159

"You shouldn't purr so loud," Alice says, rubbing her eyes, and addressing the kitten, respectfully, yet with some severity. "You woke me out of – oh! – such a dream! I dreamed I was far from here, and had such adventures, and then I dreamed that I woke up and found myself at home…"

Alice's words falter and she gets up out of the arm-chair, placing the purring kitten carefully back on the cushion, and approaches the large looking-glass that dominates the room.

Beside the great arm-chair, upon a table standing on the hearth-rug, is a chess set.

"Kitty, can you play chess?" Alice asks the kitten, feeling muddle-headed. "I'm asking it seriously, because I dreamt that I was playing chess. Or at least I think I was playing chess. There was certainly a Red Knight and a White Knight, and the Red Queen and the White King's Castle…"

Alice stumbles over her words again as she peers at the reflection of the room in the great mirror.

"Now, if you'll only attend, Kitty, I'll tell you all my ideas about Looking-glass House. First, there's the room you can see through the glass – that's just the same as our drawing room, only the things go the other way. I can see all of it when I get upon a chair – all but the bit behind the fireplace. Oh! I do so wish I could see that bit! Well then, the books are something like our books, only the words go the wrong way; I know that, because I've held up one of our books to the glass, and then they hold up one in the other room."

Alice breaks off as she tries to read the names on the spines on the books on the bookcase in the Looking-glass house… And finds that she can read them without any problem at all.

"The books in the mirror are the right way round," Alice tells the kitten, "but then… that must mean that we are inside the Looking-glass house."

Alice's mind suddenly feels clear at last. "This isn't real!" she exclaims.

Picking up a poker from beside the fireplace, Alice's takes a step closer to the mirror.

"None of this is real!"

Raising the poker, she swings it at the looking-glass.

The mirror shatters, shards of silvered glass cascading down about her, revealing nothing but the black void of oblivion beyond. And then the fireplace fractures, as does the table and the chess set, the arm-chair, and even the kitten, and Alice's world falls apart around her…

Turn to **49**.

160

The air is thick with the pine-scent of the evergreen boughs all about Alice. Reaching another junction, this time should she head north (turn to **140**), go east (turn to **170**), or make her way south through the maze (turn to **180**)?

161

The coin lands with a plop in the pool where it proceeds to sink to the bottom, and Alice's wish is granted. Add 1 point to her *Logic* score, and then turn to **241**.

Alice endures the agony of her body being torn apart by the monstrous beast, her head rolling away across the swampy ground until it comes to rest beside the root bole of a gnarled tree...

Alice opens her eyes. She is back in the library and there is no sign of the battle she has just been involved in having taken place here. (Restore half the *Endurance* points Alice lost in her battle with the Jabberwock.)

Deciding that it is best if she doesn't read any more books, just in case she finds herself trapped in one of them for good, Alice puts the slim volume back on a shelf and leaves the library.

Alice may now also use *The Pen is Mightier* ability a total of four times, rather than three. Make a note of this on Alice's Adventure Sheet, and then turn to **454**.

163

The two thugs on the gate lower their weapons as the burlier and uglier of the two gives the command, "Attack!"

Can Alice use the *The Pen is Mightier* ability to save herself now? If so, and you want her to do so, turn to **183**. If not, turn to **193**.

164

Alice is still stuck in the Hall of Doors. If she hasn't done so already, she could try drinking the contents of the bottle on the table (turn to **387**), or alternatively she can keeping trying the doors to see if one of them will actually open (turn to **339**).

165

The courtyard of the ivory tower is full of stone statues of knights on horseback and infantry soldiers. Alice makes her way between theses silent sentinels to the castle keep, climbing a spiral stone staircase to the top.

Within the uppermost chamber of the tower she finds a white marble sarcophagus. Carved into the lid is an armoured king at his repose, a stone sword gripped in his hands. As Alice watches, the statue blinks and the marble figure starts to gnash his teeth, a hideous transformation overcoming the carving as the mists return.

The dead king's features flatten and bright orange fur bursts from his face. His eyes turn yellow and his teeth becomes large fangs as he opens his mouth wider and wider as he gives voice to a savage roar.

Turn to **452**.

Alice has found her way into a tidy little room with a table in the window. Lying on the table are a fan and a pair of white kid gloves. Covering one wall is what can only be described as a very extensive rabbit family tree – or should that be family warren? – but of more interest to Alice is the bottle standing next to a looking-glass. There is no label with the words 'Drink Me' on it but Alice has a feeling that, "*Something* interesting is sure to happen whenever I eat or drink anything."

If you think Alice should drink from this bottle, turn to **177**. If not, she will have to leave the room through another door to her left (turn to **516**).

Alice backs away from the advancing statue and is unable to stifle the terrified cry that escapes her mouth. The shrill scream echoes around the chamber, the acoustics of the grotto amplifying it, until Alice's eardrums are throbbing from the noise. (Add 1 to Alice's *Insanity* score.)

But it is not only Alice who is adversely effected by the resonating scream. The stalactites that hang from the roof of the cave start to vibrate in sympathy until – just as the Satyr is about to grab Alice – with a sharp crack, the largest breaks away from the ceiling and plummets to the ground. As luck would have it, the stone spear lands directly on top of the animated statue, smashing it into a thousand pieces that scatter across the floor at Alice's feet, where they can do her no harm.

Turn to **188**.

168

The Rabbit's eyelids flicker open one last time and Alice can hear the grinding of gears as he articulates his message.

"Seek out the Seer, only he can help you remember what has been forgotten. Enter the Fungus Forest and find the Caterpillar. The mists will lead you to him."

And then the White Rabbit speaks no more, and with one final whirring click, his internal clockwork falls silent too.

Turn to **179**.

169

Her heart pounding in her chest, Alice runs at the sinister Tick-Tock Men as the mechanical horrors scrape their gleaming metal claws together, sending sparks flying from the keenly-honed blades.

If you think Alice should now make use of her *The Pen is Mightier* ability, turn to **189**. If not, turn to **209**.

170

Alice comes to another turn in the trail. Should she go north (turn to **257**) or west (turn to **160**)?

As the Grandfather Clock climbs over the desk, in order to be able to reach her, Alice steels herself for battle. (The Grandfather Clock has the initiative.)

GRANDFATHER CLOCK   COMBAT 8   ENDURANCE 9

If the Grandfather Clock makes a successful hit against Alice, roll one die (or pick a playing card). If the number rolled is odd (or the card picked is red) the elder Tick-Tock Man cuts her with its scissor-like clock-hand fingers, causing Alice 2 *Endurance* points of damage. However, if the number rolled is even (or the card picked is black) then the mechanical horror hits her with its swinging pendulum, causing her 3 *Endurance* points of damage.

If Alice survives her epic battle with the Grandfather Clock, turn to **152**.

The monstrous creature lies dead at Alice's feet, its head no longer attached to its sinuous neck.

> One, two! One, two! And through and through
> The vorpal blade went snicker-snack!
> He left it dead, and with its head
> He went galumphing back.
>
> "And hast thou slain the Jabberwock?
> Come to my arms, my beamish boy!
> O frabjous day! Callooh! Callay!"
> He chortled in his joy.
>
> 'Twas brillig, and the slithy toves
> Did gyre and gimble in the wabe;
> All mimsy were the borogoves,
> And the mome raths outgrabe.

Alice closes the book. She is back in the library. There is no sign of the hard fought battle she has just won having taken place here. (Restore Alice's *Endurance* score to the level it was before she fought the fictional Jabberwock.)

Deciding that it is best if she doesn't read any more books, just in case she finds herself trapped in one of them forever, Alice puts the book back on the shelf and leaves the library.

Alice may now also use *The Pen is Mightier* ability a total of four times, rather than three. Make a note of this on Alice's Adventure Sheet, add 1 to her *Combat* score, and then turn to **454**.

173

At the south-east corner of the garden Alice finds herself at a turn in the gravel path surrounded by a number of marvellously trimmed topiary. She stares in wonder at the artistry and horticultural skill that has been demonstrated here. One of the hedges has been cut to resemble a charging Unicorn, another looks like a rearing Lion, and there is one shaped like a Wyvern, with its wings outstretched and great thorns for claws. And all of them are life-sized.

As the child is marvelling at the mythological monsters, the Wyvern turns its head towards her, hissing, the Lion gives a guttural growl, and the Unicorn gives a shrill whinny. Alice's first instinct is to run but the foliage creatures quickly surround her, blocking off any obvious means of escape.

Her heart pounding in her chest, Alice senses that she doesn't have long before the thorn-clawed creatures rip her to shreds and turn her into just so much compost to feed the roots of the hedges. What is she to do?

Try talking to the topiary?	Turn to **198**.
Try to vault over the living bushes?	Turn to **266**.
Prepare to fight?	Turn to **299**.
Try to think her way out of danger?	Turn to **217**.
Use the *Curiouser and Curiouser* ability?	Turn to **417**.

174

"Well here's an annoyance beyond all annoyances," says Alice, stopping before a large pit that has been dug across the path before her. There is no way round it and the only way Alice will be able to cross it is if she jumps across.

If you want Alice to attempt to jump across the pit, *take an Agility test*; if she passes she clears the pit and continues on her way (turn to **510**), but if she fails she misses the edge and plunges into darkness (turn to **204**).

If you would rather Alice not attempt to jump across the pit, she will have to go back the way she came (turn to **90**).

175

Unfortunately, the Scissors are ineffective against the stony shell of the Rock Lobster and so Alice will not gain the damage bonus she would normally receive from using the Scissors in battle. Better to save them than end up blunting them against the rock-hard carapace. Now turn to **195**.

176

"You'll chew 'er bones, one by one?" challenges the right-hand head. "But what about me?"

"You can suck the marrow out of 'em after I'm done," replies the left-hand head.

"Contrariwise, I could chew 'er bones and you could such the marrow out," counters the first head to speak.

"I know what you're thinking," says the head on the left; "you're going to chew 'er bones *and* suck out all the meaty juices!"

"But it isn't so, nohow!" argues its brother.

With the two heads lost in their argument now, Alice creeps away from the cave and upon reaching the safety of the treeline, when she is sure she is out of sight of the Ogre, she sets off at a run.

As she hears the sounds of blows being exchanged, as the battle of words becomes a battle of pugiling fists, Alice sees the battlements of a ruined fortress appear over the tops of the twisted trees away ahead of her.

Turn to **512**.

The effects of the contents of the bottle take affect much sooner than Alice had expected: before she has drunk half the bottle, she finds her head pressing against the ceiling, and she has to stoop to save her neck from being broken. "That's quite enough," she says. "I hope I shan't grow any more – as it is, I can no longer fit through the door."

But Alice keeps on growing and growing, and very soon has to kneel down on the floor: in another minute there is not even room for this, and she is forced to lie down with one elbow against the door and the other arm curled round her head. Still she goes on growing, until, as a last resort, she puts one arm out of the window, and one foot up the chimney. "Now I can do no more, whatever happens."

Luckily for Alice, the little magic bottle has now had its full effect, and she grows no larger. (Add 4 to Alice's *Endurance* score.) Still it is very uncomfortable, and there seems to be no way of her getting out of the room again as things stand, so what should Alice do?

Drink the rest of the contents of
the bottle in the hope that it might
make her shrink again?   Turn to **197**.

Eat a piece of Curious Cake
(if she has such a thing)?   Turn to **215**.

Drink a tot of Shrinking Potion
(if she has some left)?   Turn to **225**.

Wait and see if the effects of the
potion wear off?   Turn to **235**.

If you would rather Alice use her` *Curiouser and Curiouser*
ability, turn to **186**.

178

Flinging out a hand, Alice snatches a jar from the dresser
shelf. Written on a label stuck to the glass in a spidery
hand are the words 'Orange Marmalade', and the jar is
full.

Add the Jar of Marmalade to Alice's Adventure Sheet
and make a note that it contains enough for four portions.
Alice may choose to eat a portion of the Marmalade at
any time, apart from when she is in the middle of combat,
and will replenish up to 4 *Endurance* points by doing so.

Now turn to **12**.

Alice runs from the house, tears streaming down her cheeks, so overwhelmed is she by what she has just witnessed. Behind her lies death and destruction, while before her lies a gloomy forest. And yet even its dark depths seem preferable to remaining at the White Rabbit's House a moment longer.

Turn to **397**.

Every turning seems to bring Alice to yet another branching of the ways. Which way should she go now?

North?	Turn to **160**.
South?	Turn to **210**.
West?	Turn to **4**.

181

The Slug recoils at Alice's advance at first, but then acidic slime begins to bubble from its mouth and the child knows that this battle is not one that is going to be easily won.

If you want Alice to use *The Pen is Mightier* ability in her moment of need, turn to **232**. If she has a jar of Slug Pellets, now would seem like a good time to use them (turn to **211**), otherwise she is going to have to fight the gigantic garden mollusc (turn to **201**).

182

The Crocodile's jaws crank open exposing teeth like iron spikes. Steeling herself accordingly, Alice prepares for the fight of her life. (Alice has the initiative.)

CROCODILE   COMBAT 7   ENDURANCE 8

If Alice is victorious, turn to **240**. If it is the Crocodile that is victorious, Alice's adventure ends here.

183

The brutes both charge Alice at the same time, but this is their fatal mistake. The Six of Clubs trips, accidentally bringing his heavy cudgel down on the head of his companion. Knocked unconscious, the Seven of Clubs falls to the floor, dropping his own weapon hard on the head of the other.

With both guards knocked out, Alice is free to come and go from the maze as she pleases. Turn to **213**.

184

"Well whose idea was it to dig a pit across the path?" asks Alice, her brow crumpled in irritation. The only way across the obstacle is to jump across.

If you want Alice to attempt to jump over the pit, *take an Agility test*; if she passes she clears the pit and continues on her way (turn to **90**), but if she fails she misses the edge and plunges into darkness (turn to **204**).

If you would rather Alice not attempt to jump the pit, she will have to go back the way she has just come (turn to **510**).

185

"Thank goodness!" exclaims the Caterpillar, the spiracles along its body opening and closing in breathless agitation. "I was starting to think I had lost you to a higher state of being, never to return."

"Return to where?" Alice asks, still feeling as if body and mind are not quite one.

"Why *here* of course," says the Caterpillar. "Wonderland! I only wish we were meeting again under better circumstances."

"So what circumstances are we meeting under?" says the child.

"It's the Queen of Hearts. She's even madder than she was before."

"We're all mad here," Alice mutters under her breath.

"Her lunacy has infected this reality, turning the dreamscape of Wonderland into a nightmarish realm of imagined horrors and manifest phobias. Do you see?" says the Caterpillar. "That is why the Queen must die."

Alice doesn't understand half the words the Caterpillar has been using, but she understands that everyone she meets in Wonderland seems dead set on her doing away with the monarch of mayhem and madness.

"Do you have any questions before you set off on your way again?"

"Yes, I do," says the child, after pondering the question for a moment. "If we've met before, and you were a caterpillar then, why aren't you a butterfly now?"

"Old Father William says I have a bad case of neoteny. Now, if you want one last piece of advice, steer clear of the Duchess's madhouse. The Nightmare has already well and truly taken hold there. Make for the Palace instead and remember, keep moving forwards, never turn back. Now, be on your way."

Record the word 'Metamorphosis' on Alice's Adventure Sheet and then turn to **316**.

Stuck in the room as she is, all squashed up in such a small space, Alice starts to feel very hot. Picking up the fan from the table (which has been pushed into the corner of the room thanks to her unnatural growth) Alice starts to fan herself.

"It was much pleasanter at home," thinks poor Alice, "when one wasn't always growing larger and smaller. I almost wish I hadn't gone down that rabbit-hole! I do wonder what *can* have happened to me! When I used to read fairy-tales, I fancied this kind of thing never happened, and now here I am in the middle of one! There ought to be a book written about me, that there ought! And when I grow up, I'll write one – but I'm grown up now," she adds in a sorrowful tone. "At least there's no room to grow up any more here. But then shall I never get any older than I am now? That'll be a comfort, one way – never to be an old woman – but then – always to have lessons to learn! Oh, I shouldn't like that!"

"Oh, you foolish Alice!" she answers herself. "How can you learn lessons in here? Why, there's hardly room for you, and no room at all for any lesson-books!"

Except there *is* room for lesson-books now, and a writing desk, and a governess, since Alice has started to shrink again.

"How *can* I have done that?" she wonders, and then realises it must be the fan she is holding. She drops it hastily, just as she returns to her normal size, and in time to avoid shrinking away altogether.

"What is going on in there?" comes a voice from behind the other door in the room.

Curious as to the identity of the owner of the voice Alice turns the handle… Turn to **516**.

187

The coin lands with a plop in the pool where it proceeds to sink to the bottom, and Alice's wish is granted. Subtract 2 points from Alice *Insanity* score, and then turn to **241**.

188

The Stone Satyr now just so much garden rubble, suitable only for using to build a rockery, Alice leaves the grotto – but which way is she going? South (turn to **420**) or west (turn to **410**)?

189

"If you're run by clockwork," Alice says, observing the Tick-Tock Men through narrowed eyes, "you must need someone to wind you up, to make sure that you keep time, but I don't see a key anywhere."

The mechanical men hesitate at this, and look at each other, before resuming their advance. But as they do so their movements begin to slow, as does the ticking of their mechanical hearts. Beat by beat, step by step, the Tick-Tock Men finally come to a shuddering halt, leaning forward at the waist, their talon-hands hanging uselessly at their sides.

Turn to **314**.

190

The Basilisk is a monster of legend that put the fear of God into the hearts of those that heard tell of how this King of Serpents could make plants wither and animals die with its baleful gaze alone. And now this eleven year-old child has to fight one. (The Basilisk has the initiative.)

BASILISK   COMBAT 9   ENDURANCE 9

If Alice is victorious in her battle against the Basilisk, turn to **168**.

191

Alice is brought to her senses again as she lands with a soft thud atop a pile of dry leaves. Lying on her back among the leaves, she finds herself staring up at what appears to be a circular well shaft.

She feels like she barely has her wits about her; the blow to the head she received was clearly much worse than she first thought and has left her feeling quite dizzy.

Deduct 1 point from Alice's *Logic* score and 1 point from her *Combat* score as well, and then turn to **114**.

192

Done with their childish rhymes, the Ogre's two heads give a terrifying roar and the Ogre lumbers towards Alice, its huge club raised above its head. (The Ogre has the initiative.)

OGRE   COMBAT 10   ENDURANCE 11

Every time the Ogre wounds Alice the gigantic tree-trunk club causes her 3 *Endurance* points damage rather than the usual 2.

If Alice somehow manages to defeat the two-headed monster, turn to **295**.

193

Alice has to fight the club-wielding gate guards at the same time.

	COMBAT	ENDURANCE
SIX OF CLUBS	8	9
SEVEN OF CLUBS	9	8

If Alice overcome her opponents, turn to **213**.

194

Back in the entrance hall of the house, Alice makes her way towards the front door, passing a small teak writing desk with brass trimmings as she does so.

With a raucous creaking of wood, the writing desk unexpectedly unfolds itself before reforming itself into an entirely different shape.

Alice is taken aback to find a large wooden bird, with a brass beak and gleaming metal talons, blocking her way out of the March Hare's house.

The flapping of its wings sounding like a squeaky desk lid being opened and closed repeatedly, the bird goes for Alice.

If Alice is still able to use *The Pen is Mightier* ability, and you want her to do that now, turn to **227**. If not, or you don't want her to use it now, turn to **207**.

The Rock Lobster's granite-like shell is so tough that successful hits against it will only cause 1 *Endurance* point damage. No matter what the outcome, this will definitely be a battle to remember. (The Rock Lobster has the initiative.)

ROCK LOBSTER   COMBAT 9   ENDURANCE 9

If Alice somehow manages to defeat the lobster, turn to **238**.

"Stop right there!" shouts the Knave of Hearts. Moving as fast as a striking cobra, he seizes Alice in a grip as strong as steel. And then, there at his shoulder, is the Red Queen.

"I see you've already met my knight in shining armour," she purrs. "Knave no more, he has been reborn as my champion, my Red Knight."

In her exhausted state, Alice finds herself unable to resist the Red Queen this time as the vampiress turns her penetrating gaze on the child once more. The Queen's lips part, exposing elongated snake-like fangs, and as

Alice stands there, not moving to protect herself despite the danger she is in, the leech closes them again about the child's neck and begins her blood-feast.

The part of Alice that is still Alice, thinks she hears the rumour of a voice carry to her on the wind, a voice that says, "Wake up, Alice dear!"

But Alice can't wake up. She is under the control of the Red Queen now. She will never wake up again.

THE END

197

Hoping against hope that downing the rest of the potion will have the opposite effect of downing the first half, Alice gulps it down.

She immediately starts to grow again. The room is no longer able to contain her continually expanding body. Frist the ceiling plaster cracks and the window shatters, and then the very walls give way as the house collapses around her gigantic form.

Below her, a trio of curious animals scamper away from the house as the remaining walls, and half the roof, collapse in chaos about them. Free of the restrictions of the building, the once neat little house now just so much broken masonry and other building materials lying amidst its tidy lawns, Alice steps free of the demolished structure.

"Oh, you foolish Alice!" she scolds herself. "Whatever made you think that drinking the rest of the potion would make you smaller?"

(Reduce Alice's *Logic* score by 1 point.)

Angry at herself for doing something so foolish, Alice strides off towards a dark forest, and, with each step, she starts to shrink, until she is her old size again.

Turn to **291**.

198

"Good afternoon," Alice begins, "or should that be 'Good Morning'? I'm afraid I have no idea what time of day it is, although by the rumbling of my stomach it could be past luncheon. So instead I shall say 'Good Day'."

The living topiary respond with snarls and growls and unearthly shrieks, and lash out at Alice with their thorny talons. Lose 3 *Endurance* points, and if Alice is still able to, turn to **299** and prepare for battle!

As Alice reads on she imagines the bookcases of the library becoming the tangled trees of a wood, haunted by the hoots and whistles of its bizarre denizens.

> He took his vorpal sword in hand:
> Long time the manxome foe he sought —
> So rested he by the Tumtum tree,
> And stood awhile in thought.
>
> And as in uffish thought he stood,
> The Jabberwock, with eyes of flame,
> Came whiffling through the tulgey wood,
> And burbled as it came!

"What was that?" Alice starts and looks about her. The library is gone, to be replaced by the encroaching branches and creepers of a dank forest. But what was it she heard?

The noise comes again. It sounds like someone trying to talk through a mouthful of treacle.

There is a tremendous snapping of branches and Alice turns to see a hideous monster bearing down on her from out of the trees. It looks not unlike a dragon, or a wyvern, with a beak-like snout, a serpentine neck, and

a pairs of wings extending from its shoulder blades. Its hands and feet end in curling black claws. (Make a note of Alice's current *Endurance* score.)

The Jabberwock opens its malformed maw and gives another gargling scream before launching itself at Alice on the stubs of its ragged wings. The wretched child has no choice but to defend herself against its slashing claws and snapping beak. (The Jabberwock has the initiative.)

JABBERWOCK   COMBAT 10   ENDURANCE 12

If Alice wins the battle, turn to **172**. If she loses the battle, turn to **162**.

200

Keeping her wits about her, despite holding an angry bat in her hands, Alice declares, "I'm sure the poem actually goes 'Twinkle, twinkle, little star!'"

As soon as she says the word 'star' the lanterns lining the well shaft flare into life, bathing the tunnel in light. The bat gives a pained shriek and immediately flies off to find some dark crevice among the bookshelves where it can hide.

Turn to **62**.

201

While Alice is battling the Slug she also needs to keep one hand holding on tight to the trunk of the toadstool, which means that for the duration of this fight she must temporarily reduce her *Combat* score by 2 points. The Slug, on the other hand, has no trouble maintaining its position as it spits acidic slime in her direction, hoping that some of it might hit. (Alice has the initiative.)

SLUG   COMBAT 5   ENDURANCE 6

If Alice wins the fight, the Slug curls into a ball and falls from the stalk of the mushroom, allowing the child to complete her descent unmolested (turn to **131**).

202

Alice is rooted to the spot with fear before the mythological monster. The Basilisk lashes out with a clawed foot, striking her leg and sending her tumbling backwards. (Lose 2 *Endurance* points and 1 *Agility* point.)

Shaken from her reverie by the attack, Alice prepares to defend herself against the monster's next attack.

Turn to **190**.

As the Crocodile glides towards her through the water, the second verse of the strange poem enters Alice's mind unbidden:

"How cheerfully he seems to grin,
How neatly spread his claws,
And welcomes little fishes in
With gently smiling *jaws*!"

With that, a distinctive triangular fin breaks the waves, followed by a bullet-nosed brass-body gouting clouds of steam from its scorched-metal gills. The oceanic predator's jaws open, and in that moment the hunter becomes the hunted. The steam-shark's jaws close upon the Crocodile and then both are gone, back into the briny depths below.

Remember to tick off one *The Pen is Mightier* box on Alice's Adventure Sheet, and then turn to **240**.

Alice plunges in the dark depths of the pit, the entrance becoming a dwindling rectangle of light above her. But now, as she looks down, she can see a circle of light widening beneath her as she hurtles towards it.

Wincing as she emerges into bright sunlight again, Alice lands with a bump on another gravel path. (Lose 1 *Endurance* point.)

"Well!" Alice thinks to herself. "After such a fall as that, I shall think nothing of tumbling down-stairs! How brave they'll all think me at home! Why, I wouldn't say anything about it, even if I fell off the top of the house!"

Picking herself up she looks about her, taking in her new surroundings. Turn to **330**.

205

As the harridan lunges at her, Alice dodges out of the way. The cannibal Cook comes for her once again, and once again Alice manages to escape the sweeping arc described by the cleaver.

Alice can feel the heat issuing from the hearth at her back now. Shrieking like a lunatic, the hag comes at her one last time, trips over the large cat that has suddenly appeared in front of the fire and falls headfirst into the flames.

The Cook pulls herself free almost immediately but her hair and mob cap are already on fire. Wailing like a banshee, the Cook runs from the kitchen, lighting up the passageway beyond as she goes until Alice can hear nothing but the crackling of the coal in the hearth and the bubbling of the human stew in the cauldron.

Looking for the cat, Alice sees nothing but a lingering grin that must have stretched from ear to ear floating above the hearth, and then that too is gone.

Turn to **242**.

206

The coin lands with a plop in the pool where it proceeds to sink to the bottom, and Alice's wish is granted. Add 1 point to her *Combat* score, and then turn to **241**.

207

"Well now we know why a raven is like a writing-desk!" Alice says as she prepares to fight for her life once again. (The Raven Writing-Desk has the initiative.)

RAVEN WRITING-DESK   COMBAT 7   ENDURANCE 8

If Alice wins her battle with the unnatural bird, turn to **267**.

208

On this occasion Alice is thankfully saved the unwanted attentions of animated effigies. Nonetheless she has no desire to linger within the gloomy grotto and so hurries through it; but in which direction is she headed?

South?   Turn to **420**.

West?   Turn to **410**.

The Tick-Tock Men prepare to meet Alice's assault with weirdly lurching movements that are strangely out of time with the ceaseless ticking of their internal mechanisms. (As Alice has brought the fight to the Tick-Tock Men, she has the initiative in this battle).

	COMBAT	ENDURANCE
First TICK-TOCK MAN	7	7
Second TICK-TOCK MAN	7	7

If Alice manages to defeat both her aggressors, turn to **314**.

210

At yet another turn in the path, Alice comes upon the statue of two parrot-like birds. One has been painted red, the other yellow.

"Red lory, yellow lory," considers Alice as she walks past. "Red lory, yellow lory. Red lory, yellow lory."

Which way now?

North?   Turn to **180**.

West?   Turn to **304**.

211

Wrapping her legs around the trunk of the toadstool, Alice takes the jar from her pocket, unscrews the lid, and tips the startlingly blue pellets onto the Slug.

The garden pest immediately begins to throw its body into all sort of twisted contortions and Alice could easily believe that it is in agonising pain. Ultimately the Slug curls into a ball and falls from the stem, allowing her to complete her descent unmolested by molluscs.

Cross the Slug Pellets off Alice's Adventure Sheet and turn to **131**.

212

"Do you know what a delightful thing a Lobster Quadrille is?" Alice suddenly pipes up. "First you form a line along the seashore, you advance twice" – saying this she strides forward to meet the Lobster's pincer attack – "each with a lobster as a partner" – she grabs hold of the Lobster, one hand one each claw, the crustacean having apparently started to shrink – "and then you throw your partner as far out to sea as you can!"

With that, Alice pirouettes on the spot and hurls the Rock Lobster out to sea. Half a mile from the shore it disappears with a plop beneath the waves.

The Lobster dealt with, Alice makes her way back to the beach, where she can now either make her way towards the sandy bay (turn to **258**), or head into the dunes, in the direction of the well-tended topiary (turn to **312**).

213

Alice looks down at the defeated guards, in their playing card tabards, and considers the heavy cudgels they were using as weapons.

If you think Alice could put one of these to good use, turn to **223**. If you would rather she ignore the spoils of war, turn to **243**.

214

The bat has large pointy ears, large leathery wings, a pair of over-large fangs, and a very bad attitude.

If Alice wants to use her *The Pen is Mightier* ability to get her out of trouble, tick off one of the boxes on Alice's Adventure Sheet and turn to **200**. If not, turn to **234**.

215

Quickly Alice pops the cake into her mouth and swallows it down. But rather than shrinking, she starts to grow again. The room is soon no longer able to contain her ever-expanding body. Frist the ceiling goes, then the window, until finally the very walls of the house give way around her gigantic form.

Below her, a trio of curious animals scamper away from the house as the remaining walls, and half the roof, collapse in chaos about them. Free of the restrictions of the building, the once neat little house now just so much broken masonry and other building materials lying amidst its tidy lawns, Alice steps free of the demolished structure.

"Oh, you foolish Alice!" she scolds herself. "Whatever made you think that eating that cake would make you smaller?"

(Reduce Alice's *Logic* score by 1 point.)

Angry at herself for doing something so foolish, Alice strides off towards a dark forest, and, with each step, she starts to shrink, until she is her old size again.

Turn to **291**.

216

With its ear-chimneys and fur-thatch, whoever built the house Alice is now approaching was quite clearly following the lepus style of architecture. There is a long table set out under a tree in front of the house, with a large arm-chair placed at one end.

If you have the word 'Revelation' recorded on Alice's Adventure Sheet, you will also have a number associated with it; turn to the paragraph with the same number now.

If you do not have the word 'Revelation' recorded on Alice's Adventure Sheet, turn to **318**.

As the Unicorn, Lion and Wyvern close on her, Alice wracks her brain for a way out of this particularly thorny predicament.

Take a Logic test. If Alice passes the test, turn to **237**. If she fails to come up with a solution, turn to **299**.

In the centre of the grotto stands a marble statue of a forest spirit, the kind Alice has read about in books of classical mythology. As she walks past the sculpture a sound not unlike a pestle being ground slowly in a mortar echoes from the craggy walls of the cave. Alice turns to see the statue coming to life.

She takes in its goat-like legs, its protruding horns, its curly stone beard, and the devilish leer on its face and knows that whatever the animated statue intends for her, it can be nothing good.

If you want Alice to employ *The Pen is Mightier* ability, turn to **147**. If you would rather she employ the *Curiouser and Curiouser* ability, turn to **167**. If not, Alice will have to protect herself as best she can – turn to **157**.

219

Opening the slim leather-bound volume, Alice begins to read:

> 'Twas brillig, and the slithy toves
> Did gyre and gimble in the wabe;
> All mimsy were the borogoves,
> And the mome raths outgrabe.

> "Beware the Jabberwock, my son!
> The jaws that bite, the claws that catch!
> Beware the Jubjub bird, and shun
> The frumious Bandersnatch!"

"What a curious poem," says Alice, "and yet it seems strangely familiar too."

If you think Alice should keep reading, turn to **199**. If you think she has dallied in the library long enough, turn to **454**.

220

The path Alice is following turns a sharp ninety degrees at the point where there stands a statue of a lobster performing a quadrille with a salmon.

If you want Alice to head south, turn to **140**. If you want her to go west, turn **230**.

221

The coin lands with a plop in the pool where it proceeds to sink to the bottom, and Alice's wish is granted. Add 2 points to her *Endurance* score, and then turn to **241**.

222

"You know what they call me?" the hag shrieks as she capers across the smoky kitchen, ready to slice Alice into rasher-thin slices. "Bloody-Bones, on account of how I don't like to waste a thing from a carcass, and I don't just mean the offal, but right down to the blood and the bones."

With that the Cook swings her cleaver at Alice and the terrified child is forced to retaliate. (Bloody-Bones has the initiative, and for the duration of this battle Alice must reduce her Combat score by 1 point, due to sneezing so much from all the pepper that is in the air.)

BLOODY-BONES   COMBAT 9   ENDURANCE 8

If Alice wins her battle with Bloody-Bones, turn to **242**.

223

Prising a club from the fingers of the Six of Clubs, Alice tests its weight in her hands.

If Alice chooses to use the Club in battle, every time she lands a successful blow, roll two dice (or pick a card). If you roll 2-10 (or you pick an Ace up to a Jack), Alice's strike causes 3 *Endurance* points of damage to her opponent. However, if you roll 11 or 12 (or pick a Queen or King), Alice's blow knocks her opponent out, removing them from the fight.

Turn to **243**.

224

Blocking Alice's way onwards through the maze is a stone archway, within which is set a heavy iron portcullis. Approaching the gate, Alice grabs hold of the portcullis and tries to lift it. She feels the heavy gate move slightly, but it will take all her strength to lift it.

Take an Endurance test. If Alice passes, she manages to raise the portcullis with her bare hands (turn to **244**). If she fails, it will not budge, and she is forced to retrace her steps (turn to **320**).

225

Pulling out the 'Drink Me' bottle, Alice downs the last of the cherry-tart, custard, pineapple, roast turkey, toffee and hot buttered toast-flavoured infusion, and immediately starts to shrink. In no time at all she is back to her original size and feeling very pleased with herself for her quick thinking.

(Strike the Shrinking Potion from Alice's Adventure Sheet, but add 1 to her *Logic* score.)

"What is going on in there?" comes a voice from behind the other door in the room.

Curious as to the identity of the owner of the voice Alice turns the handle… Turn to **516**.

226

"Good day to you," says Alice, having been brought up to always be polite, no matter what the occasion. The Tick-Tock Men say nothing, but continue their relentless advance. With time running out, the disappearing seconds marked by the ticking of the mechanical men's inner workings, Alice is going to have to try something else – and quickly!

If you think Alice should try to dodge past the advancing Tick-Tock Men, turn to **5**. If you think she should attack the Tick-Tock Men, before they can attack her, turn to **169**.

"Well now we know why a writing-desk is like a raven," Alice says, before adding, "which means that surely a raven is also just as much like a writing-desk."

At those words, with a strangled creaking croak, the raven folds its wings, tucks its head beneath its breast, and becomes a writing-desk once more.

Without waiting for the writing-desk to turn back into a raven, Alice hurries out of the house.

Turn to **267**.

228

Hurrying away from the house, beneath a glowering sky, Alice is a little startled when she sees a large moggy sitting on the bough of a tree a few yards off.

"There you are," says the Cat, grinning from ear-to-ear, "I was starting to worry that we would never get the chance to speak."

If you have the word 'Revelation' recorded on Alice's Adventure Sheet, you will also have a number linked to it; add 47 to that number and turn to the paragraph with the same number. If not, turn to **253**.

Alice peruses the shelves for some time, passing over many books as being far too dull and dry for her liking. "After all," thinks Alice, "what is the use of a book without pictures or conversations?"

She finally settles on two tomes with interesting titles but which one should she read? *Jabberwocky* (turn to **219**) or *Phantasmagoria* (turn to **103**)?

The path Alice is following ends at a white gazebo, draped with honeysuckle. Beneath the gazebo is a glass table, upon which is a glass bottle containing a crimson-coloured liquid.

"Hello!" says Alice. "This is all starting to look very familiar."

If you think Alice should drink from the bottle, turn to **54**. If not, the only other option open to her is to turn back the way she has just come (turn to **220**).

231

How many attacks have already been made against the Alice-Jabberwock?

None?	Turn to **418**.
One?	Turn to **287**.
Two?	Turn to **328**.
Three?	Turn to **363**.
Four?	Turn to **513**.

232

The air is suddenly rent by a keening cry that has Alice looking to the sky in abject dread of what might be descending to attack her now.

She hears the ruffling of feathers and a sinister shadow falls across the forest as some avian monster swoops down and snatches the grotesque Slug from the stalk beneath you.

It only takes a moment and then the bird is gone again, and the Slug along with it. Not wanting to remain in such an exposed position any longer herself, Alice wastes no time in descending the toadstool herself.

Turn to **131**.

233

Alice agrees that there's not a moment to lose, but how will she return to the palace to finish the job she started there?

If Alice has a Golden Feather, turn to **276**. If not, but Alice is wearing a Wig, turn to **326**. If Alice has neither of these things, turn to **305**.

234

Shrieking shrilly the Bat attacks. (In this battle the Bat has the advantage.)

BAT   COMBAT 6   ENDURANCE 5

If Alice manages to defeat the furious Bat, turn to **62**.

235

It seems that usually, if Alice is prepared to wait long enough, the effects of anything she has eaten or drunk will wear off relatively quickly, so that is what she resolves to do now.

Suddenly she feels someone trying to open the door she didn't enter by, but, as the door opens inwards, and Alice's elbow is pressed hard against it, that attempt proves a failure. "What is going on in there?" comes a voice from behind the door.

Alice is about to answer when she hears a shrill scream and the crash of breaking glass. This is followed by sounds of a disturbance. Her heart racing she cries out "What's going on?" herself, and "Who's there?"

There are more screams and then an eerie silence falls over the house, one that is absolute other than for the pounding of Alice's pulse in her ears.

It is only then that she realises she has started to shrink, and very soon she is back to her normal size. Her heart still racing, she tries the door, which had previously been jammed by her elbow.

It opens onto a snug study. At least it must have been snug until the massacre occurred. Blood covers the walls and even drips from the ceiling. Lying on the floor, their viscera spilling out across a once fine Persian rug are the bodies of a Mouse, dressed like a bank clerk, and a Lizard wearing clothes for gardening in.

Flopped in a chair behind a leather-topped writing desk is the body of the White Rabbit, stuffing and mangled clockwork spilling from rents in his skin. His head is lying on the desk, glass eyes blinking mechanically.

The eerie stillness is disturbed only by the dull ticking of a grandfather clock, and the clicking eyelids of the White Rabbit. Such sights are not for the likes of eleven year-old girls. (Add 1 to Alice's *Insanity* score.)

"Who could have done such a thing?" she gasps, her voice barely more than a whisper.

And then the question is answered for her as, with a creaking of mahogany and oak, the grandfather clock transforms before her eyes, unfolding itself until it looks not unlike one of the Tick-Tock Men Alice encountered in the Hall of Doors.

The clock's heavy pendulum weight hangs from the end of one arm-like appendage, looking rather like a flail, while the other arm ends in the scissoring hands of the clock face. And the hands are still wet with the blood of the slaughtered animals.

There is barely time for Alice to take all this in, never mind come up with some cunning ploy to get out of danger, so she will either have to use *The Pen is Mightier* ability to save herself, if that option is still open to her (turn to **247**), or she will have to prepare to defend herself (turn to **171**).

236

"I remember this place," says Alice as she passes through a gate in the rickety fence. "Why, it's the March Hare's House! The last time I was here the March Hare was having tea with the Hatter and the Dormouse, but there's no sign of them. I wonder where they could be."

If you want Alice to approach the table, turn to **256**. If you want her to look inside the March Hare's House, turn to **381**.

"What do you use to get rid of nuisance plants?" Alice ponders, and then her face brightens as she comes up with the answer. "Why, weed-killer of course!" But where is Alice going to get weed-killer from? Even if there was a potting shed somewhere in the garden containing the necessary supplies, she would still have to get past the monstrous topiary to find it.

And then the answer comes to her – the Shrinking Potion that enabled her to enter the garden in the first place!

If you want Alice to use the Shrinking Potion on the plants, turn to **255**. If not, turn to **299**.

The crustacean dead, and looking not unlike the remains of an epicure's Lobster Thermidor, Alice starts to pick at the scraps. The Lobster's flesh is very sweet, and if Alice eats some it will add 4 *Endurance* points.

She briefly considers using one of its claws as a weapon but they are large and cumbersome. Instead, she picks up a piece of the Lobster's carapace. It is big enough and hard enough to act as an effective shield, should Alice wish to take it.

If she does, record the Shell Shield on Alice's Adventure Sheet and make a note that it will reduce the damage caused by enemy attacks by 1 *Endurance* point. However, carrying it will also impede Alice's movements and so you must reduce her *Agility* score by 2 points for as long as she has it in her possession. Alice may discard the Shield at any time (losing both the benefit and the burden it brings), but she will not be able to recover it again during the course of her adventure.

When she is done with the rocky cove, Alice may either make her way towards the sandy bay (turn to **258**), or head into the dunes instead, in the direction of the well-tended topiary (turn to **312**).

239

Opening the door Alice enters an extensive library. Bookcases twice as tall as she is line the walls and are filled with dusty leather-bound tomes on all subjects, from Shoes, and Ships, and Sealing-Wax, to Cabbages and Kings.

In the centre of the room, on a little table, a game of chess appears to be in progress, but there is no sign of anyone around who might be playing it.

What should Alice do now?

Peruse the books in the library? Turn to **229**.

Take a closer a look at the game of chess? Turn to **132**.

Leave the library and be on her way? Turn to **454**.

240

The Crocodile having been sent to the bottom of the Sea of Tears, treading water, Alice looks about her. She can no longer see the walls of the hall, and above her, rather than a cracked plaster ceiling, all she can see is sky dotted with smudges of white cloud. She is all at sea in the middle of an ocean of tears.

Turning her attention back to the distant horizon, Alice suddenly spots land between the rise and fall of the waves. She could try swimming for the shore (turn to **290**), or call for help, in the hope that someone might hear her and come to her aid (turn to **440**). Alternatively she could use the *Curiouser and Curiouser* ability to try to get herself out of her latest predicament (turn to **434**).

241

The cascading water does look particularly refreshing. If you think Alice should drink from the fountain, turn to **71**. If not, it's time to look somewhere else – turn to **380**.

The cannibal Cook will never threaten, or indeed eat, anyone ever again. Despite a grumbling ache in her belly, at the thought of eating anything she might find in the macabre slaughterhouse-kitchen, Alice suddenly loses her appetite.

However, on the table is the Cook's over-sized Pepper Grinder that she was so fond of employing in her cookery. If Alice wants to take the Pepper Grinder with her record it on Alice's Adventure Sheet; before a battle one twist of the Pepper Grinder will set her opponent sneezing, reducing their *Combat* score by 1 point for the duration of the battle. (There is enough pepper left in the grinder for Alice to use this trick five times but it will only work against living creatures, and not animated inanimate objects such as Tick-Tock Men.)

Keen to leave this house of horrors as quickly as she can, Alice lets herself out through the back door of the kitchen.

Turn to **228**.

243

Stepping over the bodies of the Six and Seven of Clubs, Alice pushes open the gates and escapes the maze at last.

Turn to **446**.

244

Heaving the portcullis up over her head, Alice shuffles underneath before letting it fall again, only with her now on the other side. Shaking the lactic acid burn from her arms, she sets off again through the maze. Turn to **360**.

245

In her flight from the Red Queen, Alice suddenly turns a corner and finds herself standing in chill chamber, empty except for the large, heart-shaped mirror hanging from the wall opposite her.

But as Alice enters the room, her reflection in the mirror shifts and changes, becoming a vista of a darkened forest lurking on the other side of the looking-glass. It is hardly the most inviting place but surely going anywhere would be better than staying here, still hunted through the palace by the blood-thirsty Red Queen, as long as Alice can actually pass through the mirror, of course.

If you want Alice to try to reach the sinister wilderness beyond the looking-glass, turn to **155**. If not, turn to **196**.

246

As Alice tries to think of a way out of her dire situation, the Tick-Tock Men continue to advance with lurching movements that are strangely out of time with the ceaseless ticking of their internal clockwork mechanisms.

Take a Logic test. If Alice passes the test, turn to **263**. If she fails the test, turn to **278**.

247

As the Grandfather Clock climbs over the desk to reach the child, its movements slow and its wooden body stiffens, until finally it comes to a dead stop.

"Someone must have forgotten to wind the clock this morning," Alice says, "much to my good fortune."

Turn to **152**.

248

Remembering the prickly encounter she had to endure last time she was here, Alice hurries across the rutted lawn and continues on her way. In which direction is she heading?

East?   Turn to **250**.

West?   Turn to **58**.

249

The instant Alice turns around she finds herself looking at a blank wall. The front door, and indeed the entire entrance hall, have gone, the blank wall making it look like there was never a door there at all!

(Add 1 to Alice's *Insanity* score.)

Having no choice but to go onwards, deeper into the house, should Alice go through the door at the end of the passageway (turn to **454**), or investigate the room to the left on the way (turn to **239**)?

250

The path Alice is following turns sharply by ninety degrees. Should she head north (turn to **270**) or go west (turn to **465**).

251

Alice watches in appalled amazement as all the crockery and cutlery that has been carefully laid out on the table rises into the air and comes together to form a distinctly humanoid shape. The strange creature – if it can even be called a creature – has knives and forks for fingers, and a large teapot for a head.

The Tea Service stalks across the tablecloth, with rattling clattering steps, reaching for Alice with its cutlery claws.

If Alice is able to use *The Pen is Mightier* ability, and you want her to take this course of action, turn to **281**. If not, turn to **55**.

252

The garden is planted with all manner of rose bushes, but at its centre there stands a larger rose-tree. The roses growing on it are white, but three gardeners are busy painting them red. Each of the gardeners is wearing a tabard with the image of a playing card embroidered upon it. They are numbered Two, Five and Seven, and all of them are Spades, as befits a group of gardeners. Or should that be a sprinkling?

As Alice approaches the rose-tree she hears the gardeners arguing with one another.

"Look out now, Five! Don't go splashing paint over me like that!" says Two.

"I couldn't help it," says Five, in a sulky tone, "Seven jogged my elbow."

At which Seven looks up and says, "That's right, Five! Always lay the blame on others!"

If you want Alice to talk to the gardeners, turn to **453**. If you would rather she sneak past before they're aware she's even there, turn to **433**.

253

"I'm very sorry, Puss," Alice begins, "but who are you?"

"Who am I?" asks the Cat in disbelief, its smile never once faltering. "Why, I am the Cheshire Cat, but then you should know that already. The real question should be, who are you?"

"But I'm Alice," replies the child indignantly.

"You might *say* that, but how can I be sure?" replies the Cat. "If you don't know who I am, even though we've met before, how can you be sure that you know who you are?"

"Well how do you suggest we resolve this problem?" Alice challenges the Cheshire Cat in return.

"By asking and answering a series of questions. I will ask them and you must answer them correctly to prove that you are who you say you are."

Unless you want Alice to ignore the feline and continue on her way (turn to **216**), it looks like she has little choice but to play the Cheshire Cat's game (turn to **303**).

254

Blocking Alice's way onwards through the maze is a stone archway set within which is a heavy iron portcullis. Approaching the gate, Alice grabs hold of the portcullis and tries to lift it. She feels the heavy gate move slightly, but it will take all her strength to lift it.

Take an Endurance test. If Alice passes the test, she manages to raise the portcullis with her bare hands (turn to **264**). If she fails the test, she cannot shift it, and will have to retrace her steps (turn to **360**).

255

Taking the bottle from her pocket and unstoppering it, Alice proceeds to pour what is left of the Shrinking Potion onto the root-like feet of the advancing topiary. The effect is almost instantaneous.

Before Alice's very eyes, the hedge-born creatures begin to shrink. Soon they are no taller than she is. Not long after that they are no bigger than dogs. They finally stop shrinking when they are the size of garden ornaments.

Alice looks at them, her brow furrowed in annoyance. "Now be off with you!" she tells the topiary, stamping her foot to emphasise her point. "And next time, think twice about picking on someone smaller than you," she adds, entirely failing to see the irony in what she is saying.

The curious foliage creatures scamper away with a rustle of leaves, leaving Alice free to continue on her way through the mysterious garden.

Turn to **146**.

256

"Perhaps the Hatter and the Hare succeeded in stuffing the poor Dormouse inside the teapot," Alice says to herself as she approaches the table, which has been laid out for tea. Leaning across the table she lifts the lid of the huge teapot to look inside.

At once, the teapot launches itself into the air and smashes Alice in the face. Blood immediately starts to pour from her nose and she reels back from the blow, her head in a spin.

Lose 1 *Endurance* point and for the duration of the battle to come, reduce Alice's *Combat* score by 1 point as well.

Now turn to **251**.

257

Alice turns a corner and, much to her relief, finds herself at the heart of the labyrinth. (If this is the first time you have been here, gain 2 *Endurance* points.)

Unlike the lethal labyrinth of King Minos that she learnt about in classical studies, there is no bull-headed Minotaur lurking at the centre of this maze. Instead, what Alice finds is a beautifully-kept square of grass and at its centre a heart-shaped pool.

Alice can see no obstacles to her continued progress through the maze, so what should she do now?

Leave through the trimmed hedge arch to the north?	Turn to **340**.
Leave through the trimmed hedge arch to the south?	Turn to **170**.
Linger for a moment and take a closer look at the pool?	Turn to **353**.

258

As Alice makes her way along the beach towards the bay, she sees a number of oyster shells lying discarded on the sand. It soon becomes clear to her that the shells form a line, leading her further around the headland into the bay.

If you want Alice to keep following the trail of shells, turn to **273**. If not, she can either explore the rocky cove, back the other way (turn to **138**), or head into the dunes (turn to **312**).

Entering the house, Alice finds herself creeping through a darkened entrance hall, her cautious footsteps echoing from the high ceiling, with its plaster stucco work, and its looming marble columns.

Off to the right Alice can see a small, unassuming door, while on the opposite side of the hall an open doorway leads deeper into the house.

If you want Alice to open the door to see what lies beyond, turn to **482**. If you think Alice should leave the hall through the open doorway ahead of her, turn to **502**?

Turning her attention to the box under the table, which now seems to be the size of a packing trunk, Alice heaves off the lid. Inside is a large cake in a large paper case, upon which the words 'EAT ME' have been painstakingly marked out in currants. It looks delicious.

"Well, I'll eat it," says Alice, considering what had happened when she followed the instructions on the bottle, "and see what happens" – and takes a big bite.

Turn to **77**.

261

Passing between trim box hedges, Alice reaches a crossroads where four gravel paths meet. Ahead of her is an ornate wrought-iron gate, which stands ajar, beyond which is a very grand house indeed. To her right she can see a tree growing at the north-east corner of the garden.

Wanting only to keep moving forwards, and not retrace her steps or head back in the direction from which she has come, ignoring the path to her left, should Alice go through the gate in front of her (turn to **319**) or make her way towards the tree away to her right (turn to **80**)?

262

"Yes, it is his business!" says Five, "and I'll tell him – it was for bringing the cook tulip-roots instead of onions."

Seven flings down his brush. "Well, of all the unjust things–" he starts to protest, when his eye chances to fall upon Alice.

"Hey! It's her!" he shouts and the others looked round too. "It's the one the Queen wanted taken dead or alive!"

"Well that doesn't sound at all friendly," says Alice unhappily.

Whatever you think she should do now, she is going to have to do it quickly. Should Alice:

Run for it?	Turn to **46**.
Prepare to fight?	Turn to **503**.
Use something suitable she has found in the maze?	Turn to **463**.

263

An idea suddenly comes to her. Rather than running away from the menacing mechanical men, Alice runs towards them. Metal claws unsheathed, they swing at her, just as she throws herself onto the tiled floor and slides past between them.

There is a metallic shearing sound followed by a crash as something hits the floor. Alice is on her feet in seconds and looks back over her shoulder to see the head of one of the clanking horrors lying in pieces on the floor.

Alice has no choice but to defend herself as the remaining automaton bears down on her with long, scissoring strides. (As Alice is still struggling to get up, the Tick-Tock Man has the initiative in this battle.)

TICK-TOCK MAN   COMBAT 7   ENDURANCE 7

If Alice manages to overcome the automaton assassin, turn to **314**.

264

Raising the portcullis above her head, Alice passes beneath it before it can drop again. Safely on the other side, the child sets off once more through the maze. Turn to **320**.

265

Alice must fight the strutting, squawking Borogoves at the same time.

	COMBAT	ENDURANCE
First BOROGOVE	7	7
Second BOROGOVE	7	6

If Alice kills the birds, she hurries off again through the swamp before anything else unpleasant can make an appearance. Turn to **286**.

266

Being an active outdoorsy sort, Alice has climbed plenty of trees in her time – much to her Governess's chagrin – and aren't bushes just small trees?

Running at the nearest shrub monster – the Unicorn – Alice takes the creature entirely by surprise when she grabs hold of one of its hidden branches and hauls herself up onto its back.

Take an Agility test. If Alice passes, turn to **288**. If she fails, turn to **277**.

Outside again, Alice takes a deep breath to calm herself, before deciding what to do next.

If you want her to approach the table under the tree, turn to **327**. If you think she should be on her way before anything else untoward can happen to her, turn to **15**.

At long last Alice finally finds her way back to the spot where she first entered the tulgey wood, pursued by the Red Knight, unbeknownst to her at the time. Standing before the looking-glass, she watches as the reflection of the forest behind her melts away to become a view of the mirror room back in the Queen of Hearts' Palace.

Without a moment's hesitation, Alice closes her eyes and steps through, the glass becoming a silvery mist before her. And then she is back in the palace and the Red Queen is waiting for her.

Turn to **41**.

269

Alice starts as an even darker shadow falls across the footstep of the grand house and the air is rent by a terrible croaking cry. The Frog Footman breaks off its attack and looks up, just as a huge bird – with a wingspan as wide as a croquet-ground is long – swoops down from the sky, and snatches the amphibian up in its beak before flying away again, leaving Alice alone at the entrance to the dark house.

Turn to **259**.

270

A little further on the path forks again. Should Alice go east (turn to **300**), south (turn to **250**) or west (turn to **280**)?

271

Unable to think her way out of danger, Alice readies herself as best she can, and prepares to enter into a duel with the Tea Service. (Alice has the initiative, unless she has been smashed in the face by the teapot.)

TEA SERVICE   COMBAT 8   ENDURANCE 7

If Alice weathers this tempest in a teapot, turn to **298**.

272

Beyond the maze to the south, Alice can make out the buttresses and the turrets of the palace, seemingly closer than ever before.

Which way should she go now?

North?   Turn to **480**.

East?   Turn to **413**.

South?   Turn to **76**.

273

Alice follows the trail round into the peaceful bay where gentle waves lap the shore. There is something lying there on the sand, at the end of the line of discarded shells. Something large and blubbery, with a hide like cracked leather. As Alice watches, the creature's sides rise and fall with each snoring breath.

If you want Alice to approach the sleeping creature, turn to **293**. If you think it best to let sleeping sea mammals lie, turn to **312**.

274

At another junction in the path Alice is following through the maze, tucked away in the corner, is a quaint potting shed. If you think Alice should take a look inside, turn to **294**; if not, turn to **284**.

"Well, they do say that the best form of defence is attack," Alice tries to convince herself, although she's not sure who 'they' are to give such warmongering advice. 'They' also say only to seek battle after the victory has already been won.

If Alice is able to use *The Pen is Mightier* ability to resolve this battle in her favour, turn to **519**. If not, or you do not want her to use that ability now, turn to **499**.

Hearing the sound of strong wingbeats coming from beyond the walls of the ivory tower, Alice races back down the stairs into the courtyard at the foot of the keep.

"Oh, Gryphon! Dear Gryphon! You're alive!" Alice cries, tears streaming down her cheeks.

"Do you have the sword?" the Gryphon asks as the child buries her face in its feathers.

"I do," Alice replies with a sniff.

"Then climb on my back once more and let us return to Wonderland."

Alice does as the Gryphon says and with one bound, the magnificent creature takes to the sky again. They fly over

the foetid forest, eventually coming to land in a clearing before the mirror portal by which Alice arrived on the island of the Jabberwock.

It is then that a blood-curdling howl breaks the eerie silence of the wood. It is the same howl Alice heard when she first arrived here, only it is so close now that she can almost feel the breath of the beast at her back.

"Do what needs to be done," the Gryphon tells Alice as she jumps down from his back. "I will guard the portal to make sure that nothing follows you through."

Alice opens her mouth as if about to speak but then stops herself. The Gryphon is right. She has to finish this.

The glass becoming a silvery mist at her touch, she steps through… And then she is back in the palace, where the Red Queen is waiting for her.

Turn to **41**.

277

The Unicorn bucks, throwing Alice off before she can vault over its back. She lands hard on the gravel path, jarring her shoulder and grazing her arm.

Lose 2 *Endurance* points. If Alice is still able to, turn to **299** and prepare for battle!

278

Trying to come up with an escape plan while two mechanical monsters are bearing down on her is very off-putting for Alice. Unable to think of something in time, she panics and screams as she looks up into the watch-case eyes of the automaton assassins. (In this fight, the Tick-Tock Men have the initiative.)

	COMBAT	ENDURANCE
First TICK-TOCK MAN	7	7
Second TICK-TOCK MAN	7	7

If Alice manages to defeat her aggressors, turn to **314**.

279

The Frog Footman towers over Alice now, its body muscular and glistening with slime. Opening its mouth again, it tries to ensnare Alice once more with its lash-like tongue. (The Frog Footman has the initiative.)

FROG FOOTMAN   COMBAT 8   ENDURANCE 8

If the Footman scores two consecutive hits against Alice it manages to catch her with its tongue and pulls her into its mouth where it bites her causing double the usual amount of damage. (Being in possession of a shield will not protect Alice from the Frog's bite.)

If Alice slays the Frog Footman, turn to **259**.

280

The gavel path ends at a white-painted arbour, smothered with wisteria. Sat upon a table, inside the arbour, is a glass bottle containing a bright blue liquid.

"I wonder what will happen if I drink from the bottle?" Alice says to herself, suspecting that she knows exactly what will happen if she drinks the potion contained within.

If you want Alice to drink from the bottle, turn to **74**. If not, the only other option open to her is to go back the way she has just come – turn to **270**.

281

"Well, this really isn't my cup of tea at all!" declares Alice, crossly. "If it was up to me, I'd see you sent packing to a village fete and have the local children smash you to pieces with wooden balls." And saying that, she takes hold of the end of the table cloth and, giving it a sharp tug, whips it out from under the Tea Service.

Cups, plates, sugar bowl and teapot all come crashing off the end of the table, the knives, forks and spoons landing amongst the broken pieces of crockery.

Turn to **298**.

282

Walking beneath a trellis walk bedecked with vivid purple wisteria, Alice reaches a crossroads in the garden's gravel paths. Ahead of her is an open white wooden gate that leads, via a gravel path, to a neat little house, while to her left the hedges of the garden have been trained and trimmed to resemble all manner of exotic animals.

Wanting only to keep moving forwards, and not retrace her steps or head back in the direction from which she has come, ignoring the path to her right, should Alice go through the gate in front of her (turn to **2**) or make her way towards the topiary at the south-east corner of the garden, turn to **173**.

"Cheshire Puss!" she exclaims in delight. "How wonderful to see a friendly face in Wonderland."

The Cat says nothing, but merely fixes Alice with its emerald eyes, with a grin on its face that stretches from ear to ear.

"Would you tell me, please, which way I ought to go from here?"

"That depends a good deal on where you want to get to," says the Cat.

"I need to reach the Queen of Hearts' Palace, or so I have been led to believe," says Alice.

"Ah, then you will need to make your way through the Maze to get there," the Cat tells her.

"And do you know the way through?"

"I may do," comes the Cat's cryptic reply, "but before I can divulge such information and give away my secrets, first I must determine who you are."

"And how do you suggest we do that?" Alice asks the Cheshire Cat.

"By asking and answering a series of questions. I will ask them and you must answer them correctly to prove that you are who you say you are."

Unless you want Alice to ignore the feline and continue on her way (turn to **216**), it looks like she has little choice but to play the Cheshire Cat's game (turn to **303**).

284

Leaving the potting shed behind, which path should Alice take to continue on her way through the labyrinth? Should she go:

East?   Turn to **330**.

South?   Turn to **350**.

As Alice proceeds along the path, the tendrils of mellow mist that snake around the trunks of the towering toadstools thicken to become a miasmic haze, thick with the sweet smell of mould and decay.

She finds herself entering a hollow, at the centre of which is a large mushroom. It is about the same height as herself; and when she has looked under it, and on both sides of it, and behind it, it occurs to her that she might as well look and see what is on the top of it.

Stretching herself up on tiptoe, Alice peers over the edge of the mushroom, and she finds herself nose to nose with a monstrous larva at least twice as long as she is tall. Its head is a bulbous mass of soft rippling flesh, while a series of pseudopods and jointed legs run the length of both sides of its undulating body. And the thing appears to be smoking a hookah pipe.

Take an Insanity test. If Alice passes the test, turn to **323**. If she fails the test, turn to **306**.

The ground beneath her feet becomes firmer, mud giving way to hard ground, as Alice eventually reaches the far side of the swamp.

The path Alice is following through the tulgey wood forks in front of a gnarled leafless tree, which has a particularly pronounced, bulging root bole. Standing before the tree, Alice considers which way to proceed.

To the right, the path becomes a rocky trail as it climbs between tumbled boulders into a range of scarred crags beyond. To the left, the path winds and wends its way between looming oaks into a denser region of the forest.

Alice feels weary after trudging through the swamp, and everything that came before that. If you would like Alice to rest awhile here, at the foot of the tree, turn to **297**. If you think it best she doesn't delay and should be on her way again, should she follow the path to the left (turn to **364**) or the path to the right (turn to **22**)?

287

"And now you die!" roars the monster, the child's voice transformed to become a rumbling dragon-roar. Preparing to wield the Vorpal Sword one more time, Alice readies herself for her final battle.

(Alice has the initiative in this battle, but the Vorpal Sword will only cause 3 *Endurance* points of damage to the monster's iron-hard scales, rather than the usual 4.)

JABBERWOCK   COMBAT 11   ENDURANCE 18

If Alice somehow manages to slay the Jabberwock, turn to **520**.

288

The Unicorn bucks, trying to throw Alice off, but she is too quick for the strange, shrub-like creature, launching herself into the air and over its rump, landing in a crouch on the path beyond.

Without daring to look behind her to assess the creatures' reaction to her escape, Alice sprints away, the gravel crunching noisily with her every running footfall. Turn to **146**.

289

The door handle turns and Alice steps over the threshold.

"Here!" the Footman suddenly shouts. "You can't go in there! You're not invited!"

Alice turns to see the Frog Footman running towards her and as it does so it begins to swell, its uniform ripping along the seams, no longer able to contain the alarmingly metamorphosing amphibian.

The Frog opens its wide mouth and a long tongue shoots out like a whip, missing Alice by a hair's breadth.

If she is still able to use *The Pen is Mightier* ability, now might be a good time for Alice to do so (turn to **269**). If not, she must prepare to meet the angry Footman's attack (turn to **279**).

Her water-logged clothes threatening to drag her to the bottom of the briny deep, with confident strokes, Alice starts to swim for the shore, dearly hoping that there aren't any more crocodiles at large!

Take an Endurance test. If Alice's passes the test, turn to **88**. If she fails, turn to **23**.

As Alice enters the forest she passes from broad daylight into a sinister, unwelcoming twilight. Following the path deeper into the preternatural gloom, the trees give way to towering fungal forms, toadstools that appear to be taller than the trees themselves, so that Alice starts to wonder if she has shrunk with every step she has taken into the forest.

And then the path she is following comes to an abrupt end before a tree trunk that has fallen across the path, blocking the way onward. Climbing onto the top of the log Alice sees that the path continues on the other side of a boggy hollow, but she will have to somehow navigate the dank depression to reach it.

Between Alice and the continuance of the path are several massive toadstools of the fly agaric genus, with broad red caps speckled with white blemishes. Perhaps Alice could jump from one to the other and so cross the hollow that way. Alternatively she could just slide down into the ditch and cross the muddy ground beneath the fungi and make her way across that way.

Which is it to be? To climb down into the leaf mould and mud at the bottom of the hollow, turn to **301**. To try jumping from one toadstool to the next and cross that way, turn to **311**.

292

Alice goes to take the Vorpal Sword from the king's stone cold grasp but it is trapped and there isn't time to free it before the Red Knight is on her, and Alice is forced to defend herself as best she can. (The Red Knight has the initiative in this battle.)

RED KNIGHT   COMBAT 11   ENDURANCE 12

If Alice bests the Knight in single combat, turn to **484**.

293

Creeping up to the beached beast, wondering if it needs to be rolled back into the sea, Alice is taken by surprise when the creature rears up on its thick tail and lashes out at her with a huge flipper-like appendage.

Take an Agility test. If Alice passes the test, turn to **348**, but if she fails the test, turn to **332**.

Opening the creaky wooden door, Alice steps into the musty gloom of the shed. The air is thick with the smell of compost and spider-webs curtain the small cracked window.

On a bench Alice finds several items of interest. One is a stoppered bottle containing a dark brown liquid. A label, written on card, is tied to the neck of the bottle. On it, in a spidery hand, have been written the words 'Bloom's Patent Plant Provender'. There is also a jar containing bright blue pellets labelled 'Slug Knacker'. Hanging from a nail on the wall is a Spade, its blade shaped like a spade on a playing card.

If Alice doesn't already have one, the Spade might prove an effective weapon, causing 3 *Endurance* points damage every time she makes a successful strike against an opponent. If you want Alice to take the Slug Pellets or Bloom's Patent Plant Provender with her, record whatever she takes on Alice's Adventure Sheet.

Now turn to **284**.

The Ogre dead, Alice decides against exploring its cave, not knowing what else might be lurking within, and instead sets off again through the wood. It is not long before she sees the battlements of an ancient fortress appear above the tops of the sickly trees ahead of her.

Turn to **512**.

The next door is locked, and so is the one after that. Alice keeps trying one door after another, the sound of the Tick-Tock Men's clockwork getting louder, as they come closer, all the time.

And then, just when she thinks she can almost feel their outstretched metal talons at her back, the handle she is trying turns, the door opens, and she throws herself through, slamming it shut again behind her.

Alice is surprised to find herself suddenly bathed in bright sunshine. She is standing at the end of a winding gravel path that leads to a neatly kept house. She can make out a polished brass plate on the front door of the house but she cannot make out the name engraved upon it.

Turn to **2**.

Alice is quite happy to rest awhile beneath the leafless tree, and consider what might await her at the end of either path. (Regain 2 *Endurance* points.)

However, as in uffish thought she sits, the sounds of the tulgey wood encroach on her position again, a whiffling, and a burbling, and the clip-clop of a horse's hooves somewhere far off through the mist and murk.

Alice looks up at the tree with its overhanging branches and the cracks in its pitted bark that she could almost believe form eyes and a mouth. "Would you tell me, please, which way I ought to go from here?" Alice asks, addressing the tree.

At that, the bark of the trunk splits and opens like a mouth, lined with teeth made of huge wooden splinters.

"Oh no!" exclaims Alice. "This won't do at all!" And tries to take a step back from the snarling tree. But she can't move.

While she has been resting in the shadow of the Tumtum Tree, the pernicious plant's roots have snared her feet. Tentacle-like tendrils shoots out of the trunk, wrap around Alice's arms and start pulling her towards the gaping, splinter-lined maw. Straining with all her might, Alice starts to fight back.

Take an Endurance test. If Alice passes, turn to **307**; if she fails, turn to **317**.

298

Alice decides that she has had enough of this place, but as she is wondering which way to go, she catches sight of a broad grin, floating two feet above the path that leads east away from the fur-thatched cottage. Unable to contain her curiosity she sets off along the path, even as the smile fades back into thin air.

Turn to **6**.

299

The topiary terrors bear down on the terrified child, their thorny talons bared. To use *The Pen is Mightier* ability, turn to **439**. If you do not want Alice to use this ability, or she is no longer able to, turn to **428**.

300

Some call the yew tree the Tree of Death, since it grows abundantly in graveyards. Some people even believe that its shadow is particularly dark and potent. Perhaps that is why the paths of the maze are so shaded, and the way ahead so obscured.

Coming to another junction, which way do you want Alice to go now?

East?   Turn to **320**.

South?   Turn to **330**.

West?   Turn to **270**.

301

Sliding down the muddy bank into the hollow, Alice begins to pick her way through the mulch, mud and mould. It is only then that she notices wriggling movement in the deeper shadows underneath the toadstools.

The rotting detritus of the forest is alive with massive fly larvae. Their pulsating white bodies writhe and twist towards Alice as, thanks to some unknowable preternatural sense, they detect her presence and wriggle towards her.

Alice sets off at a run, but before she can escape the maggot pit she is bitten by their scissoring mandibles several times. Roll one die, divide the number rolled by two, rounding fractions up, and deduct this final total from Alice's *Endurance* score. (Alternatively, pick a card – counting picture cards as being worth ten – divide the card's value by four, round any fractions up, and deduct this total from Alice's *Endurance* score.)

If Alice survives her brush with the maggots, turn to **361**.

302

The Red Knight dead, Alice turns back to recovering the Vorpal Sword. Carefully easing it from between the effigy's fingers, Alice weighs it in her hands. The blade is perfectly balanced and unbelievably feels as light as a feather. The treasured Vorpal Sword hers at last, Alice prepares to leave the ivory tower.

Hearing the clatter of armour and steel behind her, Alice turns in time to see the Red Knight rise from the floor and throw himself at her in one sudden, fluid movement, batting the blade from her hand.

The vampiric knight pulls off his helm, revealing a hideous, near-skeletal face beneath. Unable to defend herself, Alice's adventure end here, as the monster sinks his fangs into her neck and starts to drink her blood. Her adventure might be over, but her nightmare is only just beginning...

THE END

303

"Very well," says the Cat. "Your first question: Are you mad?"

How should Alice reply?

"Yes, we're all mad here." Turn to **335**.

"No, I don't want to go among mad people." Turn to **313**.

304

The path Alice is following widens to form a ring around a pond, the surface of which is thick with lily-pads.

If Alice has visited the Pond before, turn to **324**. If this is the first time she has been here, turn to **334**.

The only way Alice knows of escaping the island and returning to the Queen of Hearts' Palace is back through the mirror portal in the tulgey wood.

Running back down the stairs and out of the ivory tower, Alice races between the rows of silent statues, out of the castle courtyard and back into the foetid forest.

It is dark between the trees, as dark as if night has already fallen. A blood-curdling howl breaks the eerie stillness of the wood. It is the same howl Alice heard when she first arrived here, only it is so close now that she can almost feel the breath of the beast upon her neck.

Alice turns, Vorpal Sword at the ready, and comes face to face with the beast that has been hunting her ever since she set foot on the island of the Jabberwock.

"Beware the Jabberwock, my son! The jaws that bite, the claws that catch! Beware the Jubjub bird, and shun the frumious Bandersnatch!" Alice whimpers to herself.

The beast is more than twice as tall as she is. It stands on two legs like a man but has the head and shaggy pelt of a wolf. Saliva drools from its lupine fangs while its claws are fingernails grown to cruel barbed talons. (Add 1 to Alice's *Insanity* score.)

If you want Alice to use *The Pen is Mightier* ability now, turn to **315**. If she is unable to, or you would prefer that she didn't, turn to **325**.

306

Alice screams in terror, turns tail and flees. Add 1 to Alice's *Insanity* score and turn to **316**.

307

Breaking free of the carnivorous tree's thorny grasp and without delaying a moment longer, choose a path – any path – so that Alice might escape the lair of the Tumtum Tree. But which way should she go?

Left?   Turn to **364**.

Right?   Turn to **22**.

The rose-tree starts growing at an astonishing rate, claw-like woody limbs emerging from its trunk while the flowers themselves mutate and change, their petals becoming one great, thorn-lined mouth.

Two screams as the transformed rose-tree grabs him with one woody appendage and promptly lowers him into its monstrous mouths. The remaining gardeners soon meet their ends as well, as the plant crushes Five beneath one splayed-root foot, whilst trapping Seven in the thorn-lined constricting coils of another tentacle-like growth.

The gardeners all dead, Alice has no intention of sharing their fate and prepares for battle. (Alice has the initiative.)

'ROSE'   COMBAT 10   ENDURANCE 10

If Alice is armed with a Pair of Scissors, any successful strikes she makes against the carnivorous plant will cause 3 *Endurance* points damage, rather than the usual 2.

If Alice defeats the rampaging rose-tree, turn to **36**.

Alice goes timidly up to the door, and knocks.

"There's no sort of use in knocking," comes a voice from behind her.

She turns and, looking down, sees a large Frog dressed in the style of a Footman, curled wig and all.

"No there's no use in knocking," the Frog Footman goes on, "and that's for two reasons. First, because I'm on the same side of the door as you are; secondly, because they're making such a noise inside, no one could possibly hear you."

And certainly there is a most extraordinary noise going on within – a constant howling and sneezing, and every now and then a great crash, as if a dish or kettle has been broken to pieces.

"Please, then," says Alice, "how am I to get in?"

"There might be some sense in your knocking," the Footman replies, "if we had the door between us. For instance, if you were inside, you might knock, and I could let you out, you know."

Clearly the Frog Footman isn't going to be any help so what should Alice do now? Open the door herself and enter the house (turn to **289**), or give up on trying to get in at all and be on her way (turn to **228**).

The garden is a horticulturist's paradise. Beds of tiger-lilies, bordered by daisies, fill the air with their heady perfume, making Alice feel almost relaxed after all her bizarre experiences since falling down the rabbit-hole.

But there is something peculiar about these flowers. At first she takes it for a trick of the light or a change of pattern on the petals, but the closer she looks she soon realises that many of the flowers have faces.

"Why, I do believe that I have seen something like these curious flowers before," Alice says, "and if I recall rightly, they can talk as well. You can talk, can't you?" she asks, turning to a particularly tall Tiger-Lily.

The Tiger-Lily turns its head to look at her and then its flowery features crumple into an expression of pain and it emits a terrible, ear-piercing scream from between its petal lips. The Tiger-Lily is soon joined by the rest of the flowers, until their blood-chilling cries become deafening.

Alice throws her hands over her ears and starts to run. Everywhere she looks she sees the scream-twisted faces of the flowers, as the sky overhead darkens, and the piercing shrieks threaten to overwhelm her senses.

Take an Insanity test. If Alice passes the test, turn to **333**, but if she fails, turn to **321**.

311

Flinging herself forward, Alice lands on the first of the massive toadstools on her knees. Picking herself up she prepares to make another leap. However, the subsequent landing platforms are further apart.

Take four separate Agility tests. As soon as Alice fails an Agility test, turn to **341**. But if she passes all of them, turn to **331**.

312

Leaving the beach Alice heads into the dunes. Struggling up one of the low sandy hills, fighting the cascading sand as it shifts ever downwards, threatening to take her back to the beach, she finally reaches the top and there before her sees a beautiful landscape of woods, walled gardens bursting with exotic plant life, and carefully-manicured lawns. She can make out buildings too, from a quaint thatched cottage with a pair of chimneys that look just like rabbit's ears, to a grand house built in the Palladian style, and, away to her right, a fine palace of spiralling turrets and heart-carved crenulations.

Descending the dunes again, Alice finds herself at the end of a winding gravel path that leads to a neatly kept house. She catches sight of a polished brass plate on the front door of the house, shining in the light of the sun, but she cannot make out the name engraved upon it.

Pausing only to empty the sand from her shoes, Alice sets out along the path…

Turn to **2**.

"Wrong!" declares the Cat, and with that, it vanishes, beginning with the end of the tail, and ending with the grin, which remains some time after the rest of it has gone.

"Well! I've often seen a cat without a grin," thinks Alice; "but a grin without a cat! It's the most curious thing I ever saw in my life!"

Add 1 *Curiouser and Curiouser* box to Alice's Adventure Sheet and then turn to **216**.

The mechanical killers dealt with, Alice starts to explore the Hall of Doors. There are tall doors and small doors, some with golden handles, others half-hidden behind drapes, but they all have one thing in common; they are all locked.

The child can't help feeling that she has found herself in a situation very similar to this once before, but she can't quite remember when. It is as she is struggling to recover the memory, lost in her ruminations, that she notices the three-legged table standing in the middle of the hall. It is made of solid glass which must be why she didn't see it before now.

On top of the table are two objects, a tiny golden key and a bottle. The key appears far too small to open any of the doors around the hall. The bottle, on the other hand, is much more interesting. It is full of a strangely fluorescing liquid that changes colour before Alice's very eyes; one moment it's cherry-red, then next a custard yellow. A label tied round the bottle's neck reads 'DRINK ME'.

It is as Alice is studying the objects on top of the table that she spies something through the glass, sitting on the floor beneath it. It is a little glass box.

What should Alice do now?

Take the tiny golden key?	Turn to **329**.
Drink the contents of the bottle?	Turn to **387**.
Open the glass box?	Turn to **3**.
Keep trying the doors around the hall?	Turn to **339**.

315

Alice begins to back away from the Bandersnatch, but then she feels the curious warmth of the Vorpal Sword in her hand and her courage returns.

"You're not a Jabberwock!" Alice says indignantly, now advancing on the beast. "In fact you're not in the least bit frightening. In fact you remind me of a dear, sweet puppy. You're nothing but a puppy dog!"

With every step the child takes towards the beast, the Bandersnatch takes a pawing step backwards. And with every step backwards the beast takes, so it becomes less like a beast and more like a man, until Alice is facing a hunched wretch of a fellow, with untidy black hair. "I didn't mean any harm," the man says. "I never meant any harm to any of my child-friends." And then he turns, gives a pathetic whimpering howl – but a human howl this time – and flees into the forest.

Turn to **268**.

316

The strange mist obscures the way through the warped wood and Alice can't be sure that it isn't playing with her perceptions so that she can't trust her own senses, but eventually she emerges from between the towering toadstools, leaving the mind-altering mists behind her. Taking a number of deep breaths of fresh air to clear her head, Alice looks about her.

She is standing at the top of a steep slope. Below her, at the bottom of the incline, to the north, on the other side of a rickety fence, she can see a curious house, with chimneys shaped like ears and its roof apparently thatched with fur. To the north-west there stands a grand house built in the Palladian style. Beyond the cottage Alice can see the towering yew hedge walls of a maze that appears to cover acres of ground.

In which direction should Alice go now? To head towards the grand house, turn to **319**. To make for the fur-thatched cottage, turn to **216**.

317

The Tumtum Tree has Alice in its clutches now, and will not easily give her up; and Alice considers a future in which she becomes fertilizer for the pernicious plant.

If Alice is still able to use *The Pen is Mightier* ability, and you want her to employ that power now, turn to **337**. If not, turn to **358**.

318

There is no one sitting at the table, even though it has been laid for tea.

If you want Alice to take a seat at the table, turn to **327**. If you would rather she look inside the house instead, turn to **381**.

319

As Alice approaches the grand house, the wind sends scrags of cloud scudding across the face of the sun and the sky darkens.

Keen to get out of the wind and sudden cold, Alice considers how best to proceed. Should she knock on the door (turn to **309**) or enter the house without knocking (turn to **259**)?

320

The deeper Alice ventures into the maze the more overgrown its paths become until she is having to push past brambly tangles just to keep moving forward. It is one of these protruding thorny creepers that snags her leg, tearing her stockings and drawing blood. (Lose 1 *Endurance* point.)

At another right-angled turn in the labyrinth, do you want Alice to go south (turn to **224**) or west (turn to **300**)?

321

Rose and larkspur, violet and dahlia, it seems as if every flower in the garden is screaming at Alice now and she can bear it no longer. (Add 1 to her *Insanity* score.)

Alice runs on, tears of terror streaming down her face, not knowing where she is going. Roll one die (or pick a playing card). If the number rolled is odd (or the card picked is red), turn to **173**. If it is even (or the card is black), turn to **344**.

322

Alice is startled to hear a fluttering of wings, as a huge blue butterfly emerges from one of the spinning mirror shards orbiting the chessboard plateau – its wingspan as wide as the dining room table at home – and bombards the monster with puffball fungi that it is holding tight to its body with its spindly legs. The Alice-head is obscured by a clouds of spores and Alice hears a child-like wheezing and coughing.

Make a note of the fact that the Alice-Jabberwock has suffered one attack and turn to **231**.

323

The colossal Caterpillar rears back, the hookah falling from its mouthparts, its body rippling hideously as it does so. Manipulating its mandibles in an unnatural way, the Caterpillar says, "Alice! Is that you?"

Not sure whether she should be more surprised by the fact that the Caterpillar can speak or that the gigantic butterfly larva seems to know who she is, confused and bemused, Alice says in a dreamy voice, "I hardly know, sir, just at present – at least I know who I *was* when I got up this morning, but I think I must have been changed several times since then."

The Caterpillar sucks on the hookah pipe and then says, "So you think you've changed, do you?"

"I'm afraid I am, sir," says Alice; "I can't remember things as I used – and I don't keep the same size for ten minutes together!"

"Can't remember what things?" says the Caterpillar.

"Well…" Alice hesitates. "This place for a start. Everything seems strangely familiar even though I haven't been here before."

"What you mean is, you don't remember being here before, and that's hardly the same thing, is it?" replies the Caterpillar sagely.

The Caterpillar takes another puff on the hookah, closing its eyes as it savours the smoke, and then goes on. "The question is, what is it more important for you to remember? Things that have already happened or things that have yet to happen?"

"I can't remember things before they happen," Alice says indignantly, starting to feel like she has had enough of this nonsense.

"It's a poor sort of memory that only works backwards," the Caterpillar remarks.

"What sort of things do you remember best?" Alice ventures to ask.

"Oh, things that happened the week after next," the Caterpillar replies in a careless tone. "Things that happened later today. For instance, I remember you standing at the gates to the Royal Palace and uttering the password 'Jabberwocky'."

(If anyone ever asks Alice the direct question "What is the password?" deduct 50 from the number of the paragraph you are reading at the time and turn to this new paragraph immediately.)

"It's dreadfully confusing!" declares Alice.

"Which is precisely why you need to remember," says the Caterpillar. "So what's it to be? The future" – the immense larva points to the edge of its mushroom – "or the past?" it asks, offering her the hookah pipe.

Alice is not in the habit of accepting strange substances from even stranger strangers but then neither does she normally have conversations with giant caterpillars. So what should Alice do now?

Nibble at the edge of the mushroom?	Turn to **21**.
Take a puff on the hookah pipe?	Turn to **346**.
Politely decline both and leave this strange place?	Turn to **336**.

324

Leaving the pond, which way should Alice go? East (turn to **210**) or west (turn to **510**)?

325

As the beast prowls towards her, Alice prepares to use the Vorpal Sword to defend herself once again. (The Bandersnatch has the initiative.)

BANDERSNATCH   COMBAT 11   ENDURANCE 10

If Alice manages to kill the creature, turn to **268**.

326

Alice hears a buzzing, almost right in her ear, and a large wasp flies out of the wig Alice is wearing – and suddenly Alice has a mad idea!

If Alice has a tot of Shrinking Potion, turn to **491**. If not, there's no use Alice getting a bee in her bonnet about it, she will just have to abandon her mad idea; turn to **305**.

327

Sitting herself down in the large arm-chair, Alice surveys the delights spread out before her. There are plates of cucumber sandwiches, jam tarts and slices of pink and yellow sponge cake wrapped up in a layer of marzipan, and a large teapot, of course. There is also all manner of cutlery, including a large bread-knife, and the silver tea tray used to bring everything to the table.

What should Alice do now?

Pour herself a cup of tea?	Turn to **338**.
Prepare herself a picnic?	Turn to **349**.
Pick up the bread-knife?	Turn to **359**.
Take a closer look at the tea tray?	Turn to **369**.
Leave the table and be on her way?	Turn to **15**.

328

Rallying, the Alice-Jabberwock gives a roar of fury and launches itself at Alice across the chessboard plain. "And now you die!" the monster roars.

Preparing to fight for her life one last time, Alice readies herself for her final battle.

(Alice has the initiative in this battle, but the Vorpal Sword will only cause 3 *Endurance* points of damage to the monster's iron-hard scales, rather than the usual 4.)

JABBERWOCK   COMBAT 10   ENDURANCE 15

If Alice manages to slay the Jabberwock, turn to **520**.

329

The key is very finely wrought, but it is far too small to open any of the locked doors Alice has come across so far. Nonetheless, she drops it into the pocket in the front of her pinafore for safe keeping, just in case. (Record the Golden Key on Alice's Adventure Sheet.)

What would you like Alice to do now?

Drink the contents of the bottle?   Turn to **387**.

Open the little glass box?   Turn to **3**.

Keep trying the doors around the hall?   Turn to **339**.

330

The statue of a tortoise, its shell covered with patches of moss, has been positioned at another of the maze's interminable turnings. Its head seems to be pointing westwards.

Which way should Alice go now?

North?   Turn to **300**.

West?   Turn to **274**.

331

Alice makes it to the other side, landing back on the path, unscathed and still in one piece. Add 1 to her *Agility* score and turn to **361**.

332

The flipper catches Alice across the face, drawing blood and sending her flying. She lands on the sand, amidst the discarded oyster shells, banging her head on a half-buried rock. Alice sits up woozily, her head spinning.

(Deduct 1 point from Alice's *Agility*, *Logic* and *Combat* scores, and lose 2 *Endurance* points as well.)

Emitting a bullish bellow, the huge Walrus shuffles its way across the sand towards the addle-witted child, its savage intentions plain.

If Alice is still able to use *The Pen is Mightier* ability, now might be a good time to do so (turn to **394**) otherwise she is somehow going to have to fight the beast (turn to **377**).

333

Alice keeps running, whilst repeating over and over out loud, "I've been in many gardens before, but none of the flowers could talk. I've been in many gardens before, but none of the flowers could talk!"

And then, at long last, she is past the screaming flower beds, the storm clouds dissipate once more, and she finds herself at a parting of the ways. Turn to **344**.

334

As Alice approaches the pond, a pair of bulbous eyes breaks the surface and with one almighty leap a huge frog hops out of the water and lands on the path in front of her. Opening a mouth as wide as Alice is tall, a whip-like tongue shoots out towards the child.

"Goodness me!" she gasps. "I do believe this frog considers me a fly and wishes to eat me!"

What should Alice do to protect herself? If you want her to use the *Curiouser and Curiouser* ability, turn to **385**. If you want her to use *The Pen is Mightier* ability, turn to **345**. If not, Alice will need to defend herself – turn to **375**.

335

"Correct," purrs the Cheshire Cat. "You're mad, bonkers, completely off your head. But I'll tell you a secret. All the best people are. And now for my second question: Why is a raven like a writing desk?"

What should Alice say this time?

"Poe wrote on both!"   Turn to **313**.

"Because it can produce a few notes,
tho they are very flat; and it is nevar put
with the wrong end in front!"   Turn to **354**.

336

"Thank you but no thank you," says Alice, who has been brought up to be polite to strangers, even if the strangers in question are gargantuan butterfly larvae.

Turning away from the mushroom she considers which way it is best to go now.

"Are you content now?" the Caterpillar calls after her. "Would you rather not know who you really are or why you have been drawn back to Wonderland?"

The Caterpillar is being very persistent; perhaps it would be wisest to take its advice.

If you think Alice is best off not eating or smoking anything out of the ordinary – she is, after all, only eleven years-old – turn to **316**. If you think Alice should relent, do you think she should eat some of the mushroom (turn to **21**) or take a puff on the pipe (turn to **346**)?

337

Thunder rumbles across the glowering sky overhead and lightning flashes between the burgeoning storm clouds. With a crack loud enough to rend the sky in twain, a bolt of incandescent energy sears down from the heavens and strikes the Tumtum Tree.

Alice is momentarily blinded by the burst of actinic light. As the echoes of the thunderclap recede into the distance, so Alice's vision returns. Before her stands the lifeless Tumtum Tree, its blackened trunk rent in two by the lightning strike that saved Alice's life.

Turn to **307**.

338

"Why, I'm quite parched," Alice declares reaching for the teapot. As she does so the teapot hops out of the way.

Alice reaches for the teapot once again, and once again it skips away from her clutches. Only it is not the only thing on the table that is moving now; the cutlery has started to rattle loudly as it dances on the tablecloth.

Turn to **251**.

339

Alice returns to testing the handles of the doors around the hall. She can think of no other way of getting out of this place now, after falling down the interminable rabbit-hole.

Suddenly a handle turns and the door she is trying opens a crack. However, it is at this exact moment that she spots a low curtain that she had not noticed before, covering the wall beside the unlocked door. Pulling back the drape reveals another door, only fifteen inches high, with a golden lock. This tiny door is locked.

If Alice has a Golden Key, and if you want her to try it in the golden lock, turn to **351**. If not, she opens the other door instead (turn to **366**).

340

The ground at Alice's feet is now a well-tended green sward rather than gravel. As the pathway turns at a right-angle, Alice must once again decide which way she wants to go.

For Alice to go east, turn to **350**. For Alice to head south, turn to **257**.

341

Alice misjudges her leap and misses her landing point, bouncing off the side of the next toadstool and tumbling down into the bottom of the stinking hollow. The mulch and mud break Alice's fall, even if she does end up filthy from head to toe, but she is not out of danger yet.

The seething muck is alive with gigantic maggots. Their pulsating white bodies writhe and twist towards Alice as, thanks to some inexplicable preternatural sense, they detect her presence and wriggle towards her.

Alice sets off at a run, but before she can escape the pit of maggots she is bitten by their scissoring mandibles several times. Roll one die, divide the number rolled by two, rounding fractions up, and deduct this final total from Alice's *Endurance* score. (Alternatively, pick a card – counting picture cards as being worth ten – divide the card's value by four, round any fractions up, and deduct this total from Alice's *Endurance* score.)

If Alice survives her brush with the gigantic fly larvae, turn to **361**.

342

As Alice proceeds along yet another passageway, certain that she is heading towards the heart of the Palace, she hears voices coming from up ahead, and they are arguing with one another.

"I told you butter wouldn't suit the works!" a nasal voice snaps.

"It was the best butter," comes a second, meek voice in reply.

"Yes, but some crumbs must have got in as well," grumbles the first voice.

"You shouldn't have put it in with the bread-knife," yawns a third.

"But it was the best butter, you know," comes the second again.

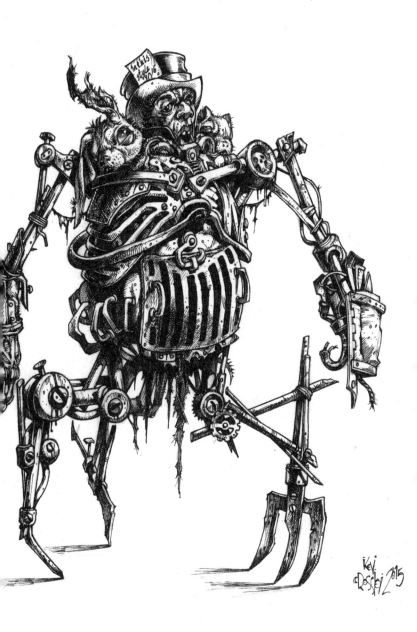

From out of the gloom at the other end of the passageway, emerges the most bizarre and horrifying amalgam of metal and living flesh Alice has ever seen.

The abomination standing before her now was quite clearly once three separate creatures – a man, a hare, and a dormouse – but now they have been made into one by some mad genius. All that is left of the three individuals are their heads, which have been mounted on top of a skeletal metal armature. The brass and steel components of its body have been constructed around a large kettle-like boiler, and steam gouts from its spout with every step the hideous automaton takes. There appears to be some form of grease dripping from the cogs and gears that make up the inner workings of the abomination.

The head of the Dormouse is clearly fighting the urge to doze off, while the hare's eyes and ears twitch and jerk erratically. The man's head, positioned between the other two, wears a top hat that is one size too big, and has a card bearing the words 'In this Style 10/6' tucked into the hatband.

It is the Hatter who is the first to catch sight of Alice.

"She's here!" he shrieks, breaking off from his constant bickering. "Alice is here!"

"Off with her head!" screeches the Hare.

"Time for tea," mutters the drowsy Dormouse.

It would appear that Alice must fight for her life once again. If you want her to use *The Pen is Mightier* ability, and she still can, turn to **392**. If not, Alice must prepare for battle – turn to **372**.

Turning to the thick undergrowth growing beside the path, Alice throws herself into cover among the nettles and ferns, and can't help but be both scratched and stung by the pernicious plants. (Lose 1 *Endurance* point.)

Alice is forced to stifle a gasp as something huge and hideous emerges from the cave. It is vaguely humanoid in form but is clad only in animal skins. One strong arm it is dragging a massive club, made from a whole tree branch, and its muscular, malformed body is covered with a host of healed scars.

But what has attracted Alice's attention, and has her shaking in an apoplexy of fear, is the fact that the lumbering brute has not one, but two heads, growing from lumpen necks upon its shoulders.

The two-headed Ogre sniffs the air sharply as if it has caught the scent of something – or should that be someone?

"Tweedle-dee and Tweedle-dum, I smell the blood of human scum," growls the head on the left.

"Tweedle-dum and Tweedle-dee, I'm gonna eat 'im for my tea," rumbles the head on the right, the Ogre coming closer to Alice's hiding place with every thudding footfall.

Is Alice carrying some Cheese about her person? If so, turn to **75**. If not, the Ogre stops, turns around, and then stomps off into the forest, following something else's scent – turn to **501**.

Alice looks about her in a daze after her traumatic encounter with the fearsome flowers. To her left, past a trellis walk bedecked with vivid purple wisteria, she can see the fountain. Ahead of her the hedges of the garden have been sculpted with shears and guiding bamboo canes to resemble all manner of exotic animals, while to her right is an open white wooden gate that leads, via a gravel path, to a neat little house.

To approach the fountain, turn to **51**. To go through the gate to the right, turn to **2**. To head for the topiary at the south-east corner of the garden, turn to **173**.

The air is suddenly rent by a dreadful screeching cry that shocks Alice to her core and sends her scampering for the cover of a yew hedge. The huge Frog, equally startled, looks to the sky as a sinister shadow falls across the maze. Before it can hop out of the way, a huge bird – something like the Roc from the Voyages of Sinbad – swoops down, snatches the overgrown amphibian up in its mouth, and flies away again, its cry echoing from the distant hills as it flies away.

Alone again, and not wanting to linger here a moment longer, Alice hurries on her way, but which way does she go? East (turn to **210**) or west (turn to **510**)?

Tentatively putting the mouthpiece of the pipe between her lips, Alice breathes in and almost chokes on the sweet-tasting smoke that fills her mouth and throat. Once the coughing fit has subsided, she tries again.

Inhaling deeply, she closes her eyes as the smoke fills her lungs and curious, cloudy visions fill her mind...

She opens her eyes again – or is it her mind's eye? – but sees nothing but shifting mist and coiling blue smoke. Then the fog banks part and Alice finds herself standing at the entrance to the rabbit-hole under the hedge again, peering down into darkness. She takes a step forwards, over the edge of the void, unable to stop herself, as if in a trance...

And then she is at the bottom of the hole. Before her is a long passage, and the White Rabbit is in sight, hurrying down it. Alice knows, somehow, that there is not a moment to be lost, and away she goes like the wind, and is just in time to hear the Rabbit say, as it turns a corner, "Oh my ears and whiskers, how late it's getting!" She is close behind it when she turns the corner...

And finds her way into a tidy little room with a table in the window, and on it a fan and two or three pairs of tiny white kid gloves. She is just going to leave the room, when her eye falls upon a little bottle standing near the looking- glass. There is no label upon it but nevertheless she uncorks it and put it to her lips, and before she has drunk half the bottle, she finds her head pressed against the ceiling...

And Alice is looking up at a large mushroom, about the same height as herself; and when she has looked under it, and on both sides of it, and behind it, it occurs to her that she might as well look and see what is on the top of it.

Stretching herself up on tiptoe, Alice peeps over the edge of the mushroom, and her eyes immediately meet those of a large caterpillar that is sitting on the top with its arms folded, quietly smoking a long hookah.

And the Caterpillar turns to her and says, "Alice you must come back now. Come back…" And its voice seems to be coming from both far away and all around her at the same time…

And then she is standing before a grand house set within acres of parkland, even as the mists start to thicken about her. "Whoever lives here?" wonders Alice in a dreamy way.

"Come back," comes the Caterpillar's distant voice again. "Come back…"

If you think Alice should answer the Caterpillar's summons, turn to **357**. If you would rather Alice open the door and enter the palatial house instead, turn to **379**.

347

The howl has Alice imagining all sorts of horrible things are out to get her, and she starts at every rustle in the undergrowth and every half-glimpsed shadow between the trees.

Add 1 to Alice's *Insanity* score and turn to **367**.

348

Alice deftly dodges the flailing flipper and takes a step back as the Walrus flops down onto the sand. Giving a gruff bark, the beast lollops towards her.

Strange scars criss-cross the animal's body, some still displaying the pin-holes of stitch marks, and there is something unsettlingly human about the Walrus's eyes, as if it was not always a Walrus. (Add 1 to Alice's *Insanity* score.) But there is also a furious intent reflected in the creature's human gaze, leaving Alice in no doubt as to what the Walrus intends.

If Alice is still able to use *The Pen is Mightier* ability, now might be a good time to do so (turn to **394**), otherwise Alice is either going to have to fight the brute (turn to **377**), or run for it (turn to **67**).

Considering it wise to prepare a picnic to take with her on the journey that still lies ahead of her, Alice takes several of the triangular sandwiches, tarts and pieces of cake, wraps them in a napkin and pops them into her pocket.

Alice has enough provisions with her for four meals. Every time she eats a meal she can gain 4 *Endurance* points.

Now what would you like Alice to do?

Pour herself a cup of tea?	Turn to **338**.
Pick up the bread-knife?	Turn to **359**.
Take a closer look at the tea tray?	Turn to **369**.
Leave the table and be on her way?	Turn to **15**.

A red rose bush has been planted at the next junction in the path. Now which way should Alice go?

North?	Turn to **274**.
South?	Turn to **370**.
West?	Turn to **340**.

351

The key fits the lock perfectly; the tumblers turn and the door opens. Beyond it lies a small passage, not much larger than a rat-hole. Kneeling down, Alice looks along the passage into the loveliest garden she has ever seen.

It pains her heart to gaze upon the well-tended lawns and beds of bright flowers. She longs to leave the dark hall and wander about among the cool fountains she can see beyond the end of the passageway, but she cannot even get her head through the doorway.

If you think Alice should try the normal-sized unlocked door instead, turn to **366**. If you'd rather that she drank the contents of the bottle, turn to **355**. However, if you want her to open the little glass box, turn to **368**.

352

Alice throws herself out of the way and the charging boar-like beast hurtles past her and through the kitchen door. Thinking quickly and fast on her feet, Alice runs to the door and pulls it shut before the pig-baby can correct its mistake and charge her again.

Now turn to **148**.

As Alice gazes into the still waters of the pool, a slight breeze sends ripples undulating across the pool and the reflection of the sky above changes to become an image of a grim-looking palace that holds about its battlements a sinister atmosphere, despite the ostentatious heart-shaped ornamentations.

Another moment and the scene changes again, this time to that of a dingy, steam-filled kitchen. Seconds pass and the scene changes yet again, this time revealing an intersection in the maze.

"I wonder if, as well as looking upon these other places, I could transport myself to one of them by entering the pool," ponders Alice.

What do you think Alice should do?

Enter the heart-shaped pool?   Turn to **403**.

Keep watching the waters?   Turn to **373**.

Leave the heart of the maze by
passing beneath the topiary arch
to the north?   Turn to **340**.

Continue on her way by passing
beneath the topiary arch to the south?   Turn to **170**.

"Right again," says the Cat, "or at least I think that's the right answer. Although, to be honest, I'm not sure if that particular riddle really has an answer at all."

Alice sighs wearily. "I think you might do something better with the time," she says, "than waste it in asking riddles that have no answers."

"Very well. Question Three!" declares the Cat. "'Do you play croquet with the Queen today?'

How should Alice reply this time?

"Yes!"	Turn to **313**.
"I should like it very much, but I haven't been invited yet."	Turn to **376**.

Alice puts the bottle to her lips and takes a sip. The liquid, which is now coloured pinkish-red again, tastes like cherry-tart.

"Delicious!" says Alice and takes another swig. The taste tantalises the taste-buds, the flavour changing on her tongue from one moment to the next – a mixture of cherry-tart, custard, pineapple, roast turkey, toffee and hot buttered toast.

"What a curious feeling!" the child declares as a curious feeling overcomes her. It feels as if her organs are contracting inside her, her skeleton shrinking in response, followed by the rest of her. "I must be shutting up like a telescope."

And indeed she is, as the table soars above her, its glass legs growing to the size of tree trunks. When she is only ten inches high, Alice stops shrinking.

Curiously, the bottle has shrunk along with her (as have her clothes) and it still has one measure of the potion left inside. (Add the Shrinking Potion to Alice's Adventure Sheet.)

Alice's face brightens up at the thought that she is now the right size to go through the little door into the lovely garden, and without a moment's delay that is precisely what she does. Turn to **136**.

356

"I wish you were here, dear Gryphon, to return the favour you owe me now," Alice says, finding herself stroking the golden feather in her pocket.

Suddenly there is a great squawking cry, a furious flapping of wings, and the Gryphon flies into the throne room.

"Come on! Climb onto my back!" says the Gryphon and Alice is not inclined to argue, given her current situation.

"Don't let them get away!" shrieks the Red Queen as the Gryphon takes off again with the child on his back.

"I couldn't kill her!" Alice cries as her emotions overcome her. "I tried, but I couldn't do it!"

"There is a way," the Gryphon says. "There is a weapon, so legend says, that has the power to slay anyone and anything."

"What weapon?" Alice asks, a glimmer of hope entering her heart.

"Its name has gone down in legend as the Vorpal Sword," the Gryphon replies, "but it lies many leagues from here, on the island of the Jabberwock."

"How do we get there?" Alice asks, her question a desperate plea.

"There might be a way," the Gryphon says swooping through a door into a bare stone chamber and setting Alice down in front of the large, heart-shaped mirror hanging on the far wall.

"I'll hold off the Queen as best I can," the brave creature says. "You find the sword!" And with that it flies out through the door again, ready to do all it can to stop the vampire catching up with Alice.

As Alice looks at the mirror, the reflection of the room dissolves, revealing a dismal wood beyond the looking-glass. It hardly appears to be the most inviting place but surely anywhere would be better than where she is now, hunted by the blood-thirsty Red Queen, just so long as she can actually pass through the mirror.

If you want Alice to try to reach the sinister forest beyond the looking-glass, turn to **155**. If not, turn to **196**.

"Thank goodness!" exclaims the Caterpillar, the spiracles along the sides of its body opening and closing in breathless agitation. "I was starting to think I had lost you to a higher state of being, never to return."

Alice feels a little woozy and a little dizzy, as if her mind is not wholly connected to her body. But then, the strange melange of memories stirred up from the depths of her unconscious, Alice remembers…

"I remember it all!" she exclaims excitedly. "The rabbit-hole, the Hall of Doors, the White Rabbit's House, meeting you for the first time, the Duchess and her baby, the Cheshire Cat, the mad tea party, playing croquet with the Queen…"

Alice breaks off, temporarily out of breath and overwhelmed by her recollections.

"Welcome back to Wonderland," says the Caterpillar. "I only wish we were meeting again under better circumstances."

"So what circumstances are we meeting under?" says the child.

"It's the Queen of Hearts. She's even madder than she was before."

"We're all mad here," Alice mutters under her breath.

"Her lunacy has infected this reality, turning the dreamscape of Wonderland into a nightmarish realm of imagined horrors and manifest phobias. Do you see?" says the Caterpillar. "That is why the Queen must die."

Alice doesn't understand half the words the Caterpillar

has been using, but she understands that everyone she meets in Wonderland seems dead set on her doing away with the monarch of mayhem and madness.

"Do you have any questions before you set off on your way again?"

"Yes, I do," says the child, after pondering the question for a moment. "You were a caterpillar when we met previously, so why aren't you a butterfly by now?"

"Old Father William says I have a bad case of neoteny. Now, if you want one last piece of advice, steer clear of the Duchess's madhouse. The Nightmare has already well and truly taken hold there. Make for the Palace instead and remember, keep moving forwards, never turn back. Now, be on your way."

Record the words 'Revelation' and the number '236' on Alice's Adventure Sheet, along with the word 'Metamorphosis', and then turn to **316**.

358

As its vine-like limbs drag Alice closer and closer to the tree's champing maw, she manages to free first one arm and then the next, and starts to fight back against the pernicious plant (which has the initiative in this battle).

TUMTUM TREE   COMBAT 8   ENDURANCE 10

If Alice defeats the tree she has not killed the plant, but only cut herself free of its clutches – turn to **307**.

The bread-knife could be used by Alice as a weapon, if she doesn't already have one.

If you decide to take the Bread-Knife, add it to Alice's Adventure Sheet. If she ever finds herself in combat using the Bread-Knife, any successful strikes she makes against an opponent will cause 3 points of damage, rather than the usual 2.

Now what do you want Alice to do?

Pour herself a cup of tea?   Turn to **338**.

Make herself a picnic to take with her?   Turn to **349**.

Take a closer look at the tea tray?   Turn to **369**.

Leave the table and be on her way?   Turn to **15**.

360

No matter which path Alice takes, there is always another branching of the ways, and another decision to be made. Which way should she go now?

North?   Turn to **254**.

South?   Turn to **400**.

West?   Turn to **44**.

361

Not much further on Alice comes to a fork in the path. If you want Alice to follow the left-hand branch, turn to **407**. If you want her to follow the right-hand path, which disappears into the mist among the fungi-trees, turn to **285**.

362

As she meets the Spider's many-eyed stare, a rhyme she last heard years ago, back in the Nursery, pops into Alice's head:

"Will you walk into my parlour?"
said the Spider to the Fly,
'Tis the prettiest little parlour that ever you did spy."

Alice suddenly becomes aware of a droning susurrus and looks up to see a fly – which looks about as big as a cat – come buzzing down towards her. The Spider sees it too and springs.

Snatching the startled fly from the air, the Spider rapidly binds its victim in silk that it exudes from spinnerets at the end of its abdomen, before scuttling back under the door with its ensnared prey held between two legs.

"Up jumped the cunning Spider, and fiercely held her fast.
He dragged her up his winding stair, into his dismal den,
Within his little parlour — but she ne'er came out again!"

Finishes Alice, with a heartfelt sigh of relief. Turn to **260**.

363

Blood running from the wounds it has already received, the Alice-Jabberwock falters. But then, shaking off those injuries, the monster rallies and comes for Alice, while the child prepares to fight for her life one last time.

(Alice has the initiative in this battle, but the Vorpal Sword will only cause 3 *Endurance* points of damage to the monster's iron-hard scales, rather than the usual 4.)

JABBERWOCK   COMBAT 9   ENDURANCE 12

If Alice manages to slay the Jabberwock, turn to **520**.

Alice finds the path she is following skirts the base of a craggy peak, the steep face of which looks to have been savaged by the claws of some gargantuan beast. Not much further on Alice comes to a cleft in the side of the rock.

Approaching the mouth of the cave Alice is startled to hear a snorting grunt and the sound of footsteps approaching from the gloom of the cave. It is then that she notices the bones strewn across the entrance, some of which appear to be human in origin.

What should Alice do?

Run for it?	Turn to **501**.
Stand her ground?	Turn to **399**.
Try to find somewhere to hide?	Turn to **343**.

"I should quite enjoy a game of croquet," says Alice, but where are the balls and mallets?

Just then she spies a pink mallet resting against a bench at the edge of the lawn, and a moment later she sees what she supposes pass for balls in this warped Wonderland.

Hunched in the middle of the lawn are two large spiky balls. "Why," says Alice, "they look just like hedgehogs."

As if having just heard the child, the balls twitch and start to roll towards her. They are only a few feet away when they unfurl and get to their feet.

Alice has never seen hedgehogs like these before. As tall as men, with a thick cloak of quills covering their backs, their fingers end in sharp claws and their eyes burn with a bestial fury. Giving a blood-curdling cry, the mutated humanoid hedgehogs bound towards her.

Take an Insanity test and if Alice passes, turn to **515**; if she fails, turn to **485**.

Alice is surprised to find herself bathed in bright sunshine, which spills in through the open door. She is standing at the end of a winding gravel path, which leads to a neatly kept house. Alice can make out a polished brass plate on the front door of the house that shines in the impossible sunlight – she is deep underground after all – but she cannot make out the name engraved upon it.

If you want Alice to step through the doorway and follow the path to the house, turn to **2**. If you would rather that she closed the door again she will either have to drink the contents of the curious bottle (turn to **355**) or examine the glass box under the table (turn to **368**).

Wondering what could have created such a chilling sound, Alice decides that the longer she stays where she is, the more likely it is that the monster will find her.

She can make out a vague path through the wood ahead of her and so, with nowhere else to go, sets off along it. However, the ground underfoot steadily becomes softer and softer until Alice is picking her way through a stinking bog. Fat-bodied flies hum overhead, only to be plucked from the moist air by warty, amphibian creatures squatting, half-submerged in their brackish pools.

Suddenly a pair of creatures pull themselves from the slime and onto the narrow path Alice is precariously following through the marsh. They look like a cross between a lizard and a salamander, but their sinuous bodies are marked with distinctive black and white stripes, and their claws are curled like corkscrews. The creatures hiss as they stalk towards the wretched child, opening their mouths to expose myriad sharp pointed teeth.

How do you think Alice should resolve her current predicament?

Try to leap over the creatures and
hurry on along the path beyond? Turn to **459**.

Attack the newt-like creatures? Turn to **275**.

Try to think her way out of this
situation? Turn to **383**.

Alternatively, Alice could use the *Curiouser and Curiouser* ability, if that option it still available to her (turn to **509**).

368

Inside the box is a dainty cake in a paper case, on which the words 'EAT ME' have been painstakingly marked out in currants. It looks delicious.

So what's it to be – 'Eat Me' (turn to **77**) or 'Drink Me' (turn to **387**)?

The tea tray is large and heavy and could be used as a shield, should Alice wish to use it as such.

If she does, record the Tea Tray on Alice's Adventure Sheet and make a note that it will reduce the damage caused by enemy attacks by 1 point. However, carrying it will also impede Alice's movements and so you must reduce her *Agility* score by 1 point for as long as she still has it in her possession. Alice may discard the Tea Tray at any time, losing both the benefit and the burden it brings, but she will not be able to recover it again during the course of her adventure.

What should Alice do now?

Pour herself a cup of tea?	Turn to **338**.
Prepare herself a picnic to take with her?	Turn to **349**.
Pick up the bread-knife?	Turn to **359**.
Leave the table and be on her way?	Turn to **15**.

The air is thick with the distinctive aroma of the evergreen boughs all about Alice. Reaching another junction, Alice comes to a bubbling fountain and is glad to take a drink of the refreshing water. (Add 2 *Endurance* points.)

Choosing a way onward, do you want Alice to head north (turn to **350**), go east (turn to **390**), or make her way south through the maze (turn to **405**)?

371

Walking between the flower beds bursting with colour, the air filled with their aromatic scent, Alice begins to feel wonderfully relaxed. (Subtract 1 point from Alice's *Insanity* score). Reaching the north-west corner of the garden she comes upon a brass sundial mounted on a weathered stone plinth. The gravel path turns right, leading eastwards further into the garden.

If you want Alice to take a closer look at the sundial, turn to **391**. If you would rather she continue on her way through the garden, turn to **31**.

372

"How dreadfully savage!" exclaims Alice as the Automaton sends a piston-driven fist hurtling towards her, missing and fracturing the flagstones at her feet. (The Abominable Automaton has the initiative.)

ABOMINABLE AUTOMATON   COMBAT 10   ENDURANCE 10

If the Automaton injures Alice, roll two dice (or pick a card); if the number rolled is 10, 11 or 12 (or the card picked is a picture card), the poor child is also scalded by a rush of super-heated steam from the kettle which causes an additional 2 *Endurance* points of damage.

If Alice survives her encounter with the Carpenter's creation, turn to **402**.

Alice does not have to wait long before the image in the pool changes again.

She sees a resplendent throne room, a hideous woman, short and plump, squatting like a toad upon her royal seat. She is speaking to a tall man, with angular, aquiline features, who wears a tabard emblazoned with embroidered hearts.

Somehow, instinctively, Alice knows who these two villains are; the Queen of Hearts and her loyal lieutenant the Knave of Hearts. And neither of them seem as scary as she first supposed them to be.

(Reduce Alice's *Insanity* score by 1 point.)

And then the scene shifts once more, and now Alice is looking at the looming trunk-like stems of a fungal forest.

What should Alice do now?

Enter the heart-shaped pool? Turn to **403**.

Leave the heart of the maze by passing
beneath the topiary arch to the north? Turn to **340**.

Continue on her way by passing
beneath the topiary arch to the south? Turn to **170**.

"Shut up!" the Cook barks at the yowling baby again, as its sobs start to sound like a piggy grunting.

"Here! You nurse it!" the cannibal crone screeches at Alice, plucking the baby from its cradle and flinging it at her.

Alice deftly catches the infant, even though it is a queer-shaped creature and holds out its arms and legs in all directions. The poor little thing is snorting like a steam-engine, and keeps doubling itself up and straightening itself out again, so that it is as much as Alice can do to keep hold of it.

"Don't grunt," Alice scolds the child. "That's not at all a proper way of expressing yourself."

The baby grunts again, and Alice looks anxiously into its face to see what's the matter with it. There can be no doubt that its turned-up nose is more like a snout than a real nose; also its eyes are getting extremely small for a baby. Alice does not like the look of the thing at all.

"If you're going to turn into a pig, my dear," says Alice seriously, "I'll have nothing more to do with you. Mind now!"

The wretched creature grunts again and kicks Alice, so violently that she cannot help but drop it on the floor. As Alice watches the baby's blanket appears to swell, as the infant inside undergoes a hideous metamorphosis. First a great twitching snout emerges from beneath the knitted shawl, followed by a set of curving yellow tusks. Cloven feet that were once an infant's hands and feet kick free of the woollen mantle as the creature shakes itself free of the blanket.

Standing before Alice is a large, porcine beast, covered in stiff black hair and with a murderous fire in its eyes. With a triumphant guttural grunt it charges at her.

If Alice is still able to use *The Pen is Mightier* ability, and you want her to use it now, turn to **352**. If not, turn to **137**.

375

Arming herself, as best she can, Alice prepares to fight the feisty Frog. (Alice has the initiative.)

FROG   COMBAT 7   ENDURANCE 6

If Alice bests the ferocious Frog in battle, turn to **395**.

376

"It *is* you!" utters the Cheshire Cat in delight. "You really are the right Alice."

"What do you mean, the right Alice?" the child asks, suddenly suspicious.

"The Alice who will save us from the Nightmare."

"The Nightmare?"

"The one you are living through right now. The mad

monarch must be deposed or psychosis will consume the realm leaving behind nothing but a wilderness of phobias made flesh and crippling anxieties."

Alice feels the cold hand of fear grip her heart. "But how am I supposed to save Wonderland?"

"You must make your way to the heart of madness, within the Palace, and dethrone the Queen of Hearts. But to reach the Queen's Palace you must first navigate the Maze. Upon reaching the centre, to find your way out go north, then east, then south, then south again, west, south and south again."

(Add 1 point to Alice's *Logic* score for gaining this useful piece of information.)

"Now be on your way," says the Cat, as it starts to vanish, beginning with the end of the tail – "Time is wasting." – and ending with the grin, which remains some time after the rest of it has gone.

And so Alice sets off on her way once more.

Record the word 'Bonkers' on Alice's Adventure Sheet and then turn to **216**.

Snorting in rage, the Walrus tries to gouge Alice with its spear-like ivory tusks. Let battle commence! (The Walrus has the initiative.)

WALRUS   COMBAT 8   ENDURANCE 8

If Alice is victorious, despite the seemly impossible odds, turn to **414**.

Alice loses herself in the winding passageways of the Queen of Hearts' Palace, hoping to do the same with the Red Queen. And her plan appears to be working, as very soon the vampire's banshee screams of frustration fade into the distance, becoming nothing but distant echoes.

Turning a corner, a panting Alice suddenly runs slap bang into a tall man, wearing the heraldry of the Queen of Hearts, a cold steely look in his unblinking black gaze. Alice's first reaction is one of shock until she realises that a servant of the Queen of Hearts might prove an effective ally now.

That is until a cruel smile spreads across the Knave of Hearts' face, revealing elongated canines and Alice spies the two puncture marks at the villain's throat.

Turn to **196**.

The Caterpillar's call fading into the distance, Alice opens the door and goes in.

The door leads straight into a large kitchen, which is full of smoke from one end to the other: the Duchess is sitting on a three-legged stool in the middle, nursing a baby; the cook is leaning over the fire, stirring a large cauldron which seemed to be full of soup.

"There's certainly too much pepper in that soup!" Alice says to herself, as well as she can for sneezing.

There is certainly too much of it in the air. Even the Duchess sneezes occasionally; and as for the baby, it is sneezing and howling alternately without a moment's pause. The only things in the kitchen that do not sneeze, are the cook, and a large cat which is sitting on the hearth and grinning from ear to ear.

"Please would you tell me," says Alice, a little timidly, for she is not quite sure whether it is good manners for her to speak first, "why your cat grins like that?"

To which the cat replies, "We're all mad here. I'm mad. You're mad."

"How do you know I'm mad?" says Alice.

"You must be," says the Cat and starts to vanish, beginning with the end of the tail, and ending with the grin, which remains some time after the rest of it has gone, "or you wouldn't have come here."

"Well! I've often seen a cat without a grin," thinks Alice; "but a grin without a cat! It's the most curious thing I ever saw in my life!"

And then she is standing in front of a large house, with chimneys shaped like ears and its roof thatched with fur.

There is a table set out under a tree in front of the house, and the March Hare and the Hatter are having tea at it: a Dormouse is sitting between them, fast asleep, and the other two are using it as a cushion, resting their elbows on it, and talking over its head. "Very uncomfortable for the Dormouse," thinks Alice; "only, as it's asleep, I suppose it doesn't mind."

The table is a large one, but the three are all crowded together at one corner of it: "No room! No room!" they cry out when they see Alice coming.

"There's plenty of room!" says Alice indignantly, and she sits down in a large arm-chair at one end of the table.

"Have some wine," the March Hare says in an encouraging tone.

The Dormouse slowly opens his eyes. "I wasn't asleep," he says in a hoarse, feeble voice: "Did you ever see such a thing as a drawing of a muchness?"

"Really, now you ask me," says Alice, very much confused, "I don't think –"

"Then you shouldn't talk," says the Hatter.

This piece of rudeness is more than Alice can bear: she gets up in great disgust, and walks off.

"I'll never go there again!" she says. "It's the stupidest tea-party I ever was at in all my life!"

Just as she says this, she notices a tree in front of her with a door leading right into it. "That's very curious!" she thinks. "But everything's curious today. I think I may as well go in at once." And in she goes.

Turn to **389**.

380

To go north, turn to **261**. To go east, turn to **146**. To go south, turn to **282**.

381

Entering the house Alice finds herself in a gloomy entrance hall. In the half-dark she can make out a portrait in an oval frame, hung on the wall in front of her, of a proud looking hare and underneath it, on the frame itself, has been painted the name, 'March Hare'.

Making her way further into the house, Alice finds furniture overturned, plates broken, and pictures hanging askew from their hooks. These are clear signs of a struggle, but what has happened to the inhabitants of the house?

If you think Alice should keep searching the house, in the hope of either finding its inhabitants, or at least more conclusive proof as to their fate, turn to **401**. If you think she should get out of there as quickly as she can, turn to **194**.

382

Taking a deep breath, in an attempt to avert total arachnophobia, deciding that the best form of defence is attack, Alice braces herself, just as the Spider springs at her. (Alice has the initiative in this battle.)

SPIDER   COMBAT 7   ENDURANCE 6

If Alice overcomes the Spider, turn to **260**.

"Think!" Alice bullies herself. "There must be a way out of this pickle I've got myself into."

Take a Logic test. If Alice passes, turn to **411**. If she fails, turn to **275**.

384

The Cook tugs a large cleaver from a chopping block on the kitchen table, and it is then that Alice catches sight of the hunks of bloody meat that are in the process of being butchered upon it. There is something distinctly unsettling about the shape of those pieces of meat.

The child finds her eyes drawn to the bubbling copper over the fire as something bobs to the surface. It is a human head, its hideous features locked in a permanent state of shock. The look of shock on the dead woman's face is mirrored by that of Alice's appalled expression. (Add 1 to Alice's *Insanity* score.)

Alice has seen little since tumbling down the rabbit-hole to match this house of horrors. If you want her to use the *Curiouser and Curiouser* ability in the hope of saving her sanity, turn to **374**. If not, turn to **148**.

385

"Curiouser and curiouser," says Alice, meeting the Frog's bug-eyed gaze. "I have never seen so large an amphibian."

The surface of the pond heaves again and a second huge Frog leaps from the pond to land on the path beside the first.

Alice is hopping mad at this change in circumstances. Arming herself, as best she can, she prepares to fight both the belligerent bullfrogs. (Alice has the initiative.)

	COMBAT	ENDURANCE
First FROG	7	6
Second FROG	6	7

If Alice defeats both of the greedy Frogs, turn to **395**.

386

The Guards drag Alice down to the deepest, bat-haunted dungeon of the palace and there throw her into a cold dank cell, with moss creeping up the wet walls, slamming the door behind her. There is the sharp click of a key turning in the lock, followed by the sound of retreating footsteps, and Alice is left alone in the near-dark of the prison cell.

But Alice is a resourceful child and does not intend remaining a prisoner any longer than she can help it, and, fortunately for her, the simple-minded Guards did not think to search her before locking her up in the cell.

If Alice is in possession of a Skeleton Key, turn to **396**. If not, but Alice still has a tot of Shrinking Potion left, and you want her to drink it now, turn to **457**. If Alice has neither of these things, turn to **416**.

387

Since the bottle is not marked 'POISON', Alice puts it to her lips and takes a sip. The liquid, which is now a pinkish-red colour again, tastes like cherry-tart.

"Delicious!" says Alice and takes another swig. It has the most wonderful flavour, like a mixture of cherry-tart, custard, pineapple, roast turkey, toffee and hot buttered toast.

"What a curious feeling!" the child declares as a curious feeling overcomes her. It feels as if her organs are contracting inside her, her skeleton shrinking in response, followed by the rest of her. "I must be shutting up like a telescope."

And indeed she is, as the table soars above her, its glass legs growing to the size of tree trunks. When she is only ten inches high, Alice finally stops shrinking.

Curiously, the bottle has shrunk along with her, as have her clothes, and it still has one measure of the potion left inside. (Add the Shrinking Potion to Alice's Adventure Sheet.)

What should she do now? If you want Alice to continue trying the doors around the hall, turn to **406**. If you want her to open the glass box (if she hasn't already), turn to **260**. If you want her to use the *Curiouser and Curiouser* ability to resolve this reversal of fortunes, turn to **141**.

388

Knowing that not only her life but her very soul depend on her getting away, Alice runs from the throne room, hoping to lose the Red Queen within the labyrinthine passages of the Palace.

Take a Logic test and an Endurance test. If Alice passes both of these tests, turn to **245**. If she fails either test, turn to **378**.

389

Alice finds herself standing in a most unremarkable drawing room. It least it would be unremarkable but for the white-haired, uncommonly fat, old man performing acrobatic stunts. One minute he is standing on his head, the next he is turning back-somersaults, and before Alice knows it, he is polishing off a platter of roast goose, bones, beak and all!

Alice is so amazed by his antics that she cannot let what she is seeing pass without remarking upon it, but what should Alice focus on asking about?

The old man's ability to stand on his head?	Turn to **412**.
The way he can turn back-somersaults?	Turn to **432**.
His ability to devour the goose, including the bones and the beak?	Turn to **442**.

390

A little further on the path forks again. Should Alice go east (turn to **400**), south (turn to **410**) or west (turn to **370**)?

391

"How strange," says Alice, as she regards the sundial, for rather than the hours of the day, around the rim of the circular brass dial plate are marked the letters of the alphabet. Standing on tiptoe so that she might see better, Alice rests a hand on the triangular gnomon and feels it move at her touch. "Curiouser and curiouser."

Around the rim of the plinth on which the sundial stands Alice can make out the words of an inscription, half-hidden by patches of orange and white lichen. It reads:

A sundial is the timepiece with the fewest moving parts,
So what, pray, is the timepiece with the most moving parts?

Take a Logic test and if Alice passes, turn to **409**. If she fails, turn to **429**.

392

"Did I hear you say you used butter to grease your gears?" Alice suddenly asks the three-headed Automaton.

"Yes, but some crumbs got in as well," replies the Hatter.

"And treacle," mumbles the Dormouse.

"Treacle?" exclaim the Hatter and Hare together.

"Well I think they're clogging up your steam regulator," says Alice knowingly.

And sure enough, the workings of the Automaton do appear to be jamming shut the pressure release value. The whole contraption starts to vibrate and rattle about furiously, so much so that Alice fears the boiler might explode at any moment.

"I want a clean cup!" shrieks the Hatter, as the Automaton appears to lose control of its actions, its arms flailing in all directions while it struggles to remain on its feet.

Darting past the rattling Automaton, Alice dashes away along the corridor.

"Oh my ears and whiskers!" she hears the Hare say, and the Palace is rocked by a splintering explosion that sends pieces of twisted metal and shards of hot pottery skimming over Alice's head, causing her to duck, lest she lose her head altogether.

Turn to **402**.

393

"I wonder if that's the reason insects are so fond of flying into candles," Alice says after she has taken a good look at the insect with its head on fire, "because they want to turn into Snap-dragon-flies!"

Suddenly a shadow falls across the garden as a cloud passes in front of the face of the sun, and the rain starts to fall. The shower does not last long but leaves Alice's clothes and hair soaking wet. The Snap-dragon-flies do not get off so lightly, however. The sudden downpour has doused their flames and now they lie on the gravel path struggling to take to the air again as their plum pudding bodies dissolve around them.

Wringing the worst of the wet from her hair and shaking out her dress, so that it might dry more quickly in the sun, Alice is able to continue on her way at last, no longer troubled by the troublesome insects.

Turn to **146**.

Suddenly the Walrus gives a gruff bark and falls flat on its face in the sand. Alice watches for any sign of movement but there is nothing, not even a twitch of the big brute's moustache.

Alice decides to try calling out to the Walrus to see if that garners any response. "But what to say?" she muses. And then it comes to her.

"The time has come," the damsel says,
"To talk of many things:
Of shoes – and ships – and sealing-wax –
Of cabbages – and kings –
And why the sea is boiling hot –
And whether pigs have wings."

After several moments Alice dares to take a step towards the Walrus and prods it with her foot, but there is no sign of a response.

"I suppose the greedy creature must have eaten something that didn't agree with him," she remarks, taking in the numerous oyster shells strewn about the beach.

Turn to **414**.

395

Alice covers up any sign of her latest struggle by making sure that all the incriminating evidence ends up in the pond.

Not wanting to linger here a moment longer, she hurries on her way, but does she go east (turn to **210**) or west (turn to **510**)?

396

Her heart pounding with the rush of adrenaline, Alice puts the key in the lock of the cell door and turns it. There is a click and the door swings open. Having checked that the way is clear, Alice heads off into the Palace.

Turn to **342**.

397

As Alice enters the forest she passes from daylight into a sinister, twilit gloom. As she moves deeper into the preternatural darkness, she realises that the trees are giving way to towering fungal forms that appear to be taller than the trees themselves. Alice starts to wonder if she has changed size as she has followed the path through the forest.

Finally, the path she is following between the looming fungi forks. If you want Alice to follow the path the left-hand branch, turn to **407**. If you want her to follow the right-hand path, as it disappears into the mist, turn to **285**.

398

The Red Queen lies dead on the floor of the throne room. Perhaps now Alice's nightmare will come to an end.

But as she stands over the vampire's body – her hands on her knees, gasping for breath – the Red Queen rises once more, apparently able to shrug off injuries that would have proved fatal to any mere mortal, her brutalised flesh knitting back together.

"And now, Alice dear, it's my turn," says the vampire, offering her a cruel smile.

If Alice hadn't already seen what horrors the harridan was capable of, witnessing the life-leech's resurrection might just have sent her mind plummeting over the edge into the abyss of insanity. As it is, all she knows for certain is that she doesn't have the means of defeating the Red Queen and must simply try to escape. But how can she outrun an opponent who is faster and stronger than she is, not to mention capable of healing from what should have been lethal wounds?

How should Alice try to escape the Red Queen?

Run away, as fast as she can? Turn to **388**.

Use a Gryphon's Feather (if she has one)? Turn to **356**.

Alternatively, if the word 'Phantasm' is recorded on Alice's Adventure Sheet, you will also have a number associated with the word; turn to the paragraph with the same number now.

Alice remains exactly where she is as something huge and hideous emerges from the cave. It is vaguely humanoid in form but is clad only in animal skins. One strong arm is dragging a massive club, made from a whole tree branch, and its muscular, malformed body is covered with a host of healed scars.

But what has attracted Alice's attention, and has her shaking in an apoplexy of fear, is the fact that the lumbering brute has not one, but two heads, growing from lumpen necks upon its shoulders. Four eyes fix on Alice and a pair of malevolent smiles spread across the Ogre's two faces.

"Tweedle-dee and Tweedle-dum, I smell the blood of human scum," growls the head on the left.

"Tweedle-dum and Tweedle-dee, what d'you want with him and me?" rumbles the head on the right.

Thinking fast on her feet Alice suddenly says, "I have come to challenge you!"

"What sort of a challenge?" asks the second head, suspicion creasing its ugly brow.

How should Alice respond?

"A test of wits!"   Turn to **511**.

"A test of strength!"   Turn to **30**.

400

At yet another turn in the path, Alice comes upon the statue of a duck of all things! Which way now?

North?   Turn to **360**.

West?   Turn to **390**.

401

On a shelf in a larder Alice finds a jar labelled 'Treacle Mine Treacle', another labelled 'Yesterday's Jam', and next to that 'Tomorrow's Jam'. However on the shelf below she also finds bread and cheese and a large walnut cake.

Finding a clean muslin cloth, she helps herself to enough food to make four meals. Every time she eats a meal she can add 4 *Endurance* points. (Add the Bread, Cheese and Cake to Alice's Adventure Sheet.)

Her combing of the house doesn't furnish her with any further clues as to the whereabouts of the missing inhabitants, and so she decides it is best she went on her way again.

Turn to **194**.

402

The Hatter-Hare-Dormouse-Automaton destroyed, Alice continues on her way deeper into the depths of the Palace.

It is as she is passing a sturdy iron-bound oak door that she hears a plaintive sobbing. Being a caring child, she calls out, "Who's there? Are you alright?" and "What's the matter?"

But whoever is on the other side of the door appears too distressed to answer. Alice cautiously tries the door but it is locked. However, hanging from a hook nearby is a large iron key.

If you want Alice to use the key to unlock the door, turn to **421**. If you think it best that she not tarry for any reason and hurry on her way, turn to **431**.

403

Boldly, Alice steps into the pool, but rather than feeling wet she feels as if she is entering a silvery cloud. Then her head goes into a dizzying spin as the world whirls about her.

Roll two dice, or pick a card from the deck. If you roll 2-4, or the card is a Spade, turn to **454**. If you roll 5-7, or the card is a Diamond, turn to **6**. If you roll 8-10, or the card is a Club, turn to **427**. If you roll 11-12, or the card is a Heart, turn to **446**.

Alice must fight the fire-sparking insects at the same time. However, every time one of them successfully injures her it will cause 3 points of damage rather than the usual 2, due to the increased strength of the insects' flames.

	COMBAT	ENDURANCE
First SNAP-DRAGON-FLY	7	6
Second SNAP-DRAGON-FLY	7	6

If Alice defeats the Snap-dragon-flies, she can continue on her way at last, no longer troubled by the bothersome insects – turn to **146**.

The path ends before an ornate gate, decorated with wrought iron flowers and ivy leaves. The gate is locked, by not one but six separate locks. However, as Alice looks closer she sees that each lock actually has the appearance of a clock.

There is one on the top left, one on the top right, one on each side, and one at the bottom right of the gate, and another at the bottom left. Each clock has two hands, but the minute hands are locked in place as follows:

Top Left – half past the hour

Top Right – quarter to the hour

Middle Right – on the hour

Bottom Right – on the hour

Bottom Left – quarter past the hour

Middle Left – half past the hour

Alice soon discovers that the hour hands of the clocks are able to move, apart from the one on the top left which is stuck on 3.

"I suppose I shall have to set the clocks to the right times in order to open the gate," Alice says, her brow knitting as she concentrates on the puzzle.

Take a Logic test. If Alice passes, turn to **415**. If not, turn to **435**.

406

The trouble is Alice is far too short to reach any of the door handles, let alone able to try and turn them to find out if any of the doors are actually unlocked.

However, it is then that she spots a low curtain that she hasn't noticed before. The curtain is still taller than she is but pulling it back reveals another door, only fifteen inches high, with a golden lock.

The tiny door is locked, but if Alice has a Golden Key, she could try it in the golden lock (turn to **425**). If not, she will have to try something else (turn to **445**).

The path is almost like a tunnel through the fungal forest, so far do the caps of the gigantic mushrooms spread over the path, their spore-filled gills creating a vaulted roof above Alice's head. And then the proliferation of fungi parts and the child enters a clearing.

Four different paths lead off from the clearing. The first is lined by puffballs, the second passes beside a mass of over-sized yellow-orange fungi, the entrance to the third is marked by a tree-sized toadstool, and the fourth vanishes into mist among the mushrooms.

Which path should Alice follow now?

The puffball pathway?	Turn to **427**.
The fungal footpath?	Turn to **478**.
The toadstool trail?	Turn to **81**.
The route leading into the mist?	Turn to **285**.

Alice is just about to leave the Jubjub Bird's crag-top eyrie, when she spots something lying in the bottom of the nest. Moving aside some of the moss and feathers, whilst being careful not to touch any of the manky bones, Alice finds a rucksack. Inside are some dry biscuits and a wedge of strong-smelling hard cheese. (There is enough food for two snacks, each of which will add 4 *Endurance* points.)

Deciding that she has risked spending enough time here already, Alice begins her descent of the cliff-face. Reaching the bottom without further mishap, the child begins to make her way back down through the crags, towards the treeline, watching out for any loose stones that might send her tumbling down the side of the peak, or uneven rocks that might have her going over on her ankle.

Eventually, her descent is done and Alice finds herself re-entering the tulgey wood, although now she can see the battlements of the ruined fortress over the tops of the unhealthy-looking trees.

Turn to **512**.

409

"How many different ways of measuring the time are there?" Alice wonders. "The Egyptians had their water clocks, for many years people had nothing more than the humble hourglass, and now there are great Grandfather clocks, with their swinging pendulum weights, and pocket watches with the most intricate escapements."

She looks at the sundial again. "I suppose if I could work out the answer to the riddle I should spell it out by turning the gnomon to line up with each letter in turn, until I have spelt out the whole word."

Can you help Alice solve the riddle of the sundial? If so, turn each of the letters in the answer into a number using the code A=1, B=2... Z=26, add the numbers together and then turn to the paragraph with the same number. (If the paragraph makes no sense, you have failed to answer the riddle correctly and will have to return here.)

If you are unable to answer the riddle, Alice has no choice but to continue on her way (turn to **31**).

410

The path Alice is following turns sharply by ninety degrees once again. Should she head north (turn to **390**) or go east (turn to **127**).

411

Alice considers that she might have something that she could use to defend herself against the strange creatures in the pocket of her dress, but what exactly?

Some Slug Pellets?   Turn to **438**.

Mr Bloom's Patent Plant Provender?   Turn to **449**.

If Alice possesses neither of these items, she will have to try a different approach (turn to **275**).

"You are old, Father William," Alice begins,
"And your hair has become very white;
And yet you incessantly stand on your head –
Do you think, at your age, it is right?"

"In my youth," Father William replies to the child,
"I feared it might injure the brain;
But, now that I'm perfectly sure I have none,
Why, I do it again and again."

Alice considers the old man's words of wisdom but cannot fault such logic. (Add 1 to Alice's *Logic* score.)

And now the curious old man is standing there balancing a writhing eel on the end of his nose.

"You are old," says the child, "one would hardly suppose
That your eye was as steady as ever;
Yet you balanced an eel on the end of your nose —
What made you so awfully clever?"

"I have answered your question, and that is enough,"
Says the old man; "don't give yourself airs!
Do you think I can listen all day to such stuff?
Be off, or I'll kick you down stairs!"

With that, the mists return until Alice can barely see her hand in front of her face. And then she opens her eyes…

Turn to **357**.

413

The path Alice is following gives way to lush grass and she enters a Rose Garden, within the confines of the maze. If Alice has been here before, turn to **423**; if not, turn to **252**.

414

Looking at the Walrus, lying there dead upon the beach, nothing more than food for the crabs now, Alice considers that one of the animal's tusks would make a handy weapon indeed.

If you want Alice to arm herself in this way, record the Walrus Tusk on Alice's Adventure Sheet, and whenever she is involved in combat any hit she delivers using the elongated ivory tooth will cause 3 *Endurance* points of damage, rather than 2.

Leaving the sandy bay, Alice considers which way to go now.

If she hasn't already done so could make her way across the beach to explore the rocky cove (turn to **138**), otherwise it's time for her to head inland (turn to **312**).

"I'm going to have to be clock-wise about this," Alice says.

If you can solve the puzzle, turn to the number that is the same as the total you reach when you add up all of the numbers that the hour hands should be pointing to. If not (or if the paragraph you turn to doesn't make any sense, meaning you have got the answer wrong), turn to **455**.

There are always a couple of hairpins and a nail file lying forgotten in the pocket of Alice's dress and she puts these to good use now, unfolding the pins to create a useable set of lock-picks.

Poking them into the lock, Alice starts to manipulate her improvised tools in an attempt to manoeuvre the moving parts of the lock to let herself out.

Take a Logic test and an Agility test. If Alice passes both these tests, turn to **436**, but if she fails either of them, turn to **426**.

"My, how realistic you are," says Alice, addressing the Wyvern. "I'm only glad you can't actually breathe fire, considering you're really nothing more than a trimmed tree."

Barely are the words out of her mouth than the Wyvern opens its gaping jaws and a torrent of flame issues forth. Throwing up her hands to protect her face, the startled child dives for the relative safety of the ground, although she does suffer some burns to her arms. (Lose 4 *Endurance* points.)

However, the Lion and the Unicorn do not get off so lightly. Their foliage and wooden stems catch light and the flames quickly consume them. The Wyvern shares their fate, as it manages to set itself ablaze with its fiery breath.

The topiary now nothing more than burnt sticks of charcoal lying on the ground, if she is able to, Alice picks herself up and continues on her way.

Turn to **146**.

"Beware the Jabberwock, my girl! The jaws that bite, the claws that catch!" the Alice-Jabberwock laughs. "Tea time!"

The monster's child-like voice becomes a rumbling, deep-throated roar. Raising the Vorpal Sword one last time, Alice readies herself for her ultimate battle. (The Jabberwock has the initiative. Also, the Vorpal Sword will only cause 3 *Endurance* points of damage to the monster's iron-hard scales, rather than the usual 4.)

JABBERWOCK   COMBAT 12   ENDURANCE 21

If Alice somehow manages to slay the Jabberwock, turn to **520**.

419

"Beware the Jabberwock, my son! The jaws that bite, the claws that catch!" Alice chants. "Beware the Jubjub bird, and shun the frumious Bandersnatch!"

The blood-curdling howl Alice first heard within the tulgey wood comes again, only it sounds much closer now. Alice can't help but give a cry of fear, whilst the Jubjub bird takes off in a panic, considering it safer to be in the air than remain on the ground and face whatever it is that is coming this way.

Turn to **408**.

420

The path turns again and Alice comes upon the statue of a kitten. "She looks just like my dear Dinah," Alice remarks, sniffing back her tears. Do you want Alice to go north (turn to **127**) or west (turn to **430**).

421

Unlocking the door, Alice eases open the iron-banded oak door, and peers into the darkened cell that lies on the other side.

Lying upon a bed of rotten straw, its head resting on one outstretched leg, is a curious beast that is half-eagle and half-lion. Startled by the sudden shaft of light that is cast through the open door, the Gryphon lifts its head from its leg and blinks myopically at the child.

"Alice?" it says in astonishment. "Is that really you?"

"Yes, I'm Alice," says Alice.

"But what brings you back to Wonderland?" asks the mythical beast.

"I'm not really sure, other than everyone keeps telling me I have to kill the Queen. Was it her who imprisoned you here?"

"It was," replies the Gryphon, hanging its head in shame. "I think she intended to send me to see the Carpenter."

"The Carpenter?"

"It's best you don't ask."

And then an idea strikes Alice like a thunderbolt. "You could help me, a big strong beast like you."

"I can't thank you enough, young lady, for freeing me from my incarceration," states the Gryphon, "but I can't stay here a moment longer. I couldn't bear to be captured again!"

And with that the Gryphon takes off, back the way Alice has just come, half-flying and half-leaping down the corridor.

But the Gryphon has left something behind on the floor at Alice's feet. It is a shimmering golden feather. Picking it up, marvelling at the way it shines in the light of the torches that line the passageway, Alice puts it in her pocket for safekeeping.

Add the Gryphon's Golden Feather to Alice's Adventure Sheet, and turn to **431**.

422

The climb is harder, and takes Alice longer, than she had anticipated, but finally she reaches the ledge upon which rests the ramshackle nest. It is even bigger up close than it appeared when she was standing at the bottom of the cliff-face.

It is much easier for Alice to climb into the nest, using the branches from which it has been randomly constructed to aid her. The interior is lined with feathery down, which looks like is comes from a very large bird indeed, and swags of moss. However, there are no eggs in the nest, only the bones of whatever its inhabitant last ate.

Alice starts, as a discordant cry echoes over the island's peak and she turns in time to see the nest's owner returning.

The bird is massive beyond all measure – "Like something out of the Arabian Nights!" exclaims Alice. As the bird swoops down to land, its terrible tearing talons raised ready to strike, Alice finds herself in fear of her life once again.

If you want Alice to use *The Pen is Mightier* ability, and she still can, turn to **419**. If not, turn to **451**.

423

The gardeners are gone, their rose bushes left untended. Perhaps choosing a way Alice hasn't been before, will you send her off east into the maze (turn to **490**) or west (turn to **272**)?

424

Alice does her best to dodge the flying frying-pan but isn't quite quick enough; the handle delivers her a glancing blow to the temple.

Lose 2 *Endurance* points and decrease both Alice's *Combat* and *Logic* scores by 1 point.

Now turn to **384**.

425

The key fits the lock perfectly; the tumblers turn and the door opens. Beyond it lies a passage, and beyond that the loveliest garden Alice has ever seen, with well-tended lawns, beds of bright flowers, and cool, sparkling fountains.

If you think Alice should make her way down the passage into the garden, turn to **136**. If you think she should look inside the little glass box first, turn to **260**.

426

Unable to pick the lock, Alice is forced to give up when one of the bent hair clips snaps and the nail file becomes wedged in the lock.

Unable to escape, Alice makes herself comfortable, as best she can, in the corner of the cell and waits. And waits. And waits. But no one comes, no matter how much she howls, or screams, or begs. She is simply left there, forgotten, a prisoner of her own mind, while, back in the waking world, her physical form is usurped by another, who brings mayhem and madness wherever she goes...

Alice's adventure in Wonderland is over, but the true Nightmare is only just beginning.

THE END

As Alice makes her way along the pathway the puffballs begin to encroach upon the trail until Alice is afraid that she might accidentally cause one of them to release its spores as she eases her way past.

Take an Agility test. If Alice passes, turn to **437**. If she fails, turn to **448**.

Fenced in on all sides by the advancing topiary, Alice must fight the hedge-born horrors (which have the initiative) at the same time.

	COMBAT	ENDURANCE
UNICORN	8	6
LION	9	7
WYVERN	7	6

If Alice defeats the garden's guardians, she is able to continue on her way at last – turn to **146**.

"Riddle me this, riddle me that," Alice says. "Why, that is a tricky riddle indeed."

She looks at the sundial again. "I suppose if I could work out the answer to the riddle I should spell it out by turning the gnomon to line up with each letter in turn, until I have spelt out the whole word."

Can you help Alice solve the riddle of the sundial? If so, turn each of the letters in the answer into a number using the code A=1, B=2... Z=26, add the numbers together and then turn to the paragraph with the same number. (If the paragraph makes no sense, you have failed to answer the riddle correctly and will have to return here.)

If you are unable to answer the riddle, Alice has no choice but to continue on her way (turn to **31**).

430

Alice remembers her Governess once telling her that Pliny's *Natural History* mentions four ancient labyrinths: the Cretan labyrinth, an Egyptian labyrinth, a Lemnian labyrinth, and an Italian labyrinth.

Coming to another junction, should Alice go:

East?   Turn to **420**.

South?   Turn to **490**.

West?   Turn to **470**.

431

Continuing to explore the Palace, Alice travels along torch-lit corridors and up and down flights of stairs until she climbs a broad set of stone steps and comes at last to the entrance to the throne room.

Standing in front of a set of double doors, painted gold and inset with rubies that form a myriad glittering hearts, is a huge, ogre-like figure. It is wearing a straining tabard that marks it out as the Ace of Clubs and its head is partially covered by a black hood.

The Guard stands with his hands resting on the haft of a huge axe, the heavy blade resting on the stone-flagged floor at his feet.

"I suppose you're the Royal Executioner!" Alice challenges the burly brute.

"You suppose right," says the Ace of Spades, "so I expect you can also guess what's coming next," he chuckles as he hefts the axe in his hands.

"Off with her head?" Alice hazards.

The Executioner just laughs and advances on the poor child, axe raised.

If she is still able to use *The Pen is Mightier* ability, and you want Alice to do so now, turn to **441**. If not, turn to **471**.

"You are old," says the child, "as I noticed before,
And have grown most uncommonly fat;
Yet you turned a back-somersault in at the door –
Pray, what is the reason of that?"

"In my youth," says the sage, as he shakes his grey locks,
"I kept all my limbs very supple
By the use of this ointment – one shilling the box –
Allow me to give you a couple!"

The old man offers Alice two boxes of 'Dr Lutwidge's Ligament Lubricator' and Alice pops them into the pocket of her pinafore dress. In the future, if Alice has to take an *Agility* test, you can cross off one of the boxes and Alice will automatically pass the test.

And now the curious old man is standing there balancing a writhing eel on the end of his nose.

"You are old," says the child, "one would hardly suppose
That your eye was as steady as ever;
Yet you balanced an eel on the end of your nose —
What made you so awfully clever?"

"I have answered your question, and that is enough,"
Says the old man; "don't give yourself airs!
Do you think I can listen all day to such stuff?
Be off, or I'll kick you down stairs!"

With that, the mists return until Alice can barely see her hand in front of her face. And then she opens her eyes…

Turn to **357**.

433

"You'd better not talk!" says Five, as Alice cautiously skirts the edge of the rose garden, trying to stay out of sight of the gardeners. "I heard the Queen say only yesterday you deserved to be beheaded!"

"What for?" says Two, the one who spoke first.

"That's none of your business, Two!" says Seven.

Take an Agility test and if Alice passes the test, turn to **443**, but if she fails, turn to **262**.

434

(Cross off one of the *Curiouser and Curiouser* boxes on Alice's Adventure Sheet.)

"Well this is a strange state of affairs, I must say," Alice says, furiously treading water in order to keep her head above the waves. "One minute I'm in an underground hallway, the next I'm in the middle of the sea with not a wall, or door, or rabbit-hole in sight. I suppose a ship will appear out of nowhere next."

Turn to **460**.

435

No matter how long she stares at the gate and its locks, Alice cannot see a pattern to their arrangement.

Can you help her? If you can solve the puzzle, turn to the number that is the same as the total you reach when you add up all of the numbers that the hour hands should be pointing to. If not (or if the paragraph you turn to doesn't make any sense, meaning you have got the answer wrong), turn to **455**.

436

Listening carefully as she manipulates her improvised picks in the lock, Alice finally hears a click and the door to her cell opens. Having checked that the way is clear, Alice heads off into the Palace without further delay.

Turn to **342**.

437

Alice carefully picks her way past the remaining puffballs and breathes a heartfelt – and spore-free – sigh of relief. Leaving the patch of puffballs behind, she finally emerges from the fungus forest.

She is standing at the top of a steep slope. Below her, at the bottom of the incline, to the north, on the other side of a rickety fence, she can see a curious house, with chimneys shaped like ears and its roof apparently thatched with fur. To the north-west there stands a grand house built in the Palladian style. Beyond the cottage Alice can see the towering yew hedge walls of a maze that appears to cover acres of ground.

In which direction should Alice go now? To head towards the grand house, turn to **319**. To make for the fur-thatched cottage, turn to **216**.

438

Pulling the jar from her pocket and unscrewing the lid, Alice empties its contents over the slimy bodies of the creatures. They hiss even louder but they also start to writhe about as if in pain, almost tying themselves in knots in the process. Repelled by the stinging pellets, the creatures slip back into their watery hole, leaving Alice free to pass by unmolested.

Turn to **286**.

439

The Wyvern is the first to lunge at Alice, but she manages to duck and instead the shrub-beast closes its prickle-filled jaws around the Unicorn's foreleg. In anger and pain, the Unicorn kicks out, catching the Lion in the face with its trimmed-hedge hooves.

Soon all three of the unreal monsters are fighting among themselves until all that is left of them are broken twigs and scattered leaves. With a sigh of relief, Alice sets off again along the garden path – turn to **146**.

440

"Help!" Alice shouts, as she furiously treads water, in order to keep her head above the waves. "Mayday! SOS! I appear to be all at sea without the aid of a lifebelt. Or even a lifeboat for that matter," she adds to herself. "Help!"

Turn to **460**.

441

With a mighty roar, the Executioner raises the enormous axe above his head, ready to bring it down on Alice's neck, but suddenly trips on an uneven flagstone at the top of the steps. Unbalancing, the brute tumbles forwards down the stairs, the axe tumbling after him.

By the time the Ace of Spades reaches the bottom of the steps, Executioner and axe have been reunited, although, admittedly, the axe is now buried in the Royal Executioner's head.

Turn to **456**.

442

"You are old," says the child, "and your jaws are too weak
For anything tougher than suet;
Yet you finished the goose, with the bones and the beak –
Pray how did you manage to do it?"

"In my youth," said the sage, "I took to the law,
And argued each case with my wife;
And the muscular strength, which it gave to my jaw,
Has lasted the rest of my life."

The old man starts to gnash his teeth, as if to prove the point, and then a hideous transformation overcomes him as the mists return. His features flatten and bright orange fur bursts from his face. His eyes turn yellow and his teeth become large fangs as he opens his mouth wider and wider and gives voice to a savage roar.

Turn to **452**.

443

Leaving the gardeners to their bickering, which way does Alice go as she leaves the rose garden? East (turn to **490**) or west (turn to **272**)?

444

Bending over backwards, Alice dodges the spinning pan as it hurtles past her head. Now turn to **384**.

Being only ten inches high, Alice doesn't have a hope of opening any of the other doors, whether they are unlocked or not. As she is gazing across the acres of tiled floor, wondering what to do next, something scuttles out from the darkness under a door.

Although she is, in general, a sensible child, Alice is not particularly fond of spiders. However, now that the spider is the size of an Alsatian, compared to her, the spinal-chill of dread fills her body and soul. Possibly considering the child a potential source of food, the eight-legged fiend stalks towards her, its long bristle-haired limbs moving in an eerily independent fashion. Fearing for her safety, Alice knows that she has to act decisively, and fast.

If you think she should prepare to defend herself, turn to **382**. If you would rather she used *The Pen is Mightier* ability, turn to **362**.

Alice gazes up at the grim-looking edifice before her. Despite the proliferation of hearts in its architecture – from its flying buttresses, to its crenulations, to its arrow-slits and stained glass windows – Alice has never seen a more sinister structure. The terracotta tiles of its sunken roofs are cracked, and entirely missing in some places, while black carrion birds circle its battlements having made their roosts atop the high walls.

The Palace is surrounded by a moat that is filled with brackish brown water, choked with waterweed and clogged with the bloated white bodies of dead fish and frogs. However, it will be no trouble for Alice to cross the disgusting morass that is the moat since the drawbridge is down, and, having done so, Alice discovers that the gates of the stronghold are open.

Warily Alice eases her way between the towering gates, convinced that she will run into a guard patrol, or maybe a guard dog, at any moment. But an eerie stillness hangs over the place, and Alice could almost believe that it is, in fact, deserted.

Alice heads off into the Palace… Turn to **342**.

447

A keening wail howls about the battlements of the stronghold, as if the place is haunted by the spirits of those stony sentinels who now keep their eternal vigil over the fortress.

Alice makes it to the entrance to the keep without meeting any opposition and, heaving open the age-worn door, weathered to the colour of old teeth, makes her way inside. Finding herself at the bottom of a spiral stone staircase, Alice begins her ascent, making her way up through the tower.

Upon reaching the top of the staircase Alice passes through an arched doorway and into an eerie mausoleum-like chamber. The room has a sepulchral air to it, which is hardly surprising considering that resting atop a plinth at its heart is a white stone tomb. Upon the lid is the carving of a knight, with a carved white beard. He is holding a stone sword and also wears a coronet atop his helm.

An inscription circles the white marble sarcophagus:

> To win the sword, speak loud my name,
> My title and my piece the same.
> Kneel now, my ring to kiss,
> And answer me, whose tomb is this?

Alice starts, hearing footsteps on the stair she has just ascended. Someone, or something, is coming.

Take a Logic test, and if Alice passes it, turn to **487**; but if she fails, turn to **497**.

448

Her fears prove perfectly justified when her foot catches one of the bloated fungi and a gust of choking spores puffs into Alice's face.

Roll one dice (or pick a card). If the number rolled is odd (or the card picked is black), turn to **458**. If the number rolled is even (or the card picked is red), turn to **468**.

449

Uncorking the bottle, Alice pours its contents over the slimy creatures, but the Patent Plant Provender doesn't seem to have any effect… At least, not on the slimy newt-like lizards.

The soft ground around Alice is pushed upwards as a host of knotty roots break through from beneath. These roots wrap themselves around Alice's feet and ankles, trapping her. Unable to escape the advancing horrors, she is forced to fight them, both at the same time. (The Slithy Toves have the initiative.)

	COMBAT	ENDURANCE
First SLITHY TOVE	6	6
Second SLITHY TOVE	6	5

If Alice slays the creatures, she can at last turn her attention to freeing herself from the ensnaring roots, and, having done so, sets off again through the swamp. Turn to **286**.

450

Unstoppering the bottle, Alice splashes what remains of its contents over the Snap-dragon-flies. However, her action does not have the desired effect. In fact, rather than causing the insects to shrink, the liquid only seems to encourage the brandy flames.

"I wonder what was in that!" Alice gasps. "A drop of Nanny's Ruin, I expect!"

The two Snap-dragon-flies buzz towards Alice with angry intent, and no sign of forgiving festive spirit. (Cross the Shrinking Potion off Alice's Adventure Sheet; she cannot use it again.)

If you want to use *The Pen is Mightier* ability to help Alice escape her fate, and you are still able to do so, turn to **393**. If not, turn to **404**.

451

Arming herself as best she can, Alice prepares to battle the bird, wondering if how she is feeling now was how St George felt when he fought the dragon. (The Jubjub Bird has the initiative in this fight.)

JUBJUB BIRD   COMBAT 10   ENDURANCE 12

If Alice defeats the Jubjub Bird, turn to **408**.

452

A huge tiger leaps at Alice from out of the mist but this is no ordinary tiger; it appears to have been formed from folded paper.

If you want Alice to use *The Pen is Mightier* ability to save herself from the origami big cat, turn to **481**. If you want her to use the *Curiouser and Curiouser* ability to change the story in some way, turn to **467**. If you do not think Alice should use either of these abilities now, she will have to fight the Paper Tiger – turn to **492**.

"Would you mind telling me," says Alice, a little timidly, "why you are painting those roses?"

Five and Seven say nothing, but look at Two.

"Why the fact is, you see, Miss," Two begins, "this here ought to have been a red rose-tree, and we put a white one in by mistake; and if the Queen was to find it out, we should all have our heads cut off, you know. So you see, Miss, we're doing our best, afore she comes, to–"

At this moment Five, who has been looking at Alice suspiciously, calls out, "It's her! It's the one the Queen wanted dead or alive!"

"Well that doesn't sound very friendly," says Alice grumpily.

Whatever you think Alice should do next, she is going to have to do it quickly. Should she:

Run for it?	Turn to **46**.
Prepare to fight?	Turn to **503**.
Use something suitable she might have found lying around the maze?	Turn to **463**.

Opening the door at the end of the long passageway, Alice finds herself standing at the threshold to a large kitchen, which is full of smoke.

A baby is howling in its cradle, which has been left next to an empty three-legged stool beside the hearth. Leaning over the fire, stirring a large cauldron, is a scrawny, sour-faced Cook. The heat and smoke and noise make Alice wonder if she hasn't entered the hellish city of Pandemonium by mistake.

"There's certainly too much pepper in that soup!" Alice says to herself, walking into the kitchen and trying to see what's in the cauldron. There is certainly too much pepper in the air, and Alice can't help but sneeze.

The Cook spins round at the sound and glowers at Alice through the fug of smoke and steam filling the kitchen. Her eyes narrow as she peers at Alice along her hooked nose, and then glares at the crib as the baby alternates between sneezing and howling without a moment's pause.

"Shut up!" squawks the Cook, flinging a fire-iron in the direction of the cradle.

"Oh, please mind what you're doing!" cries Alice, jumping up and down in an agony of terror.

"Speak roughly to your little boy, and beat him when he sneezes," the Cook snaps back. "He only does it to annoy, because he knows it teases." And with that she picks up a saucepan and hurls it at Alice.

Take an Agility test. If Alice passes it, turn to **444**. If she fails the test, turn to **424**.

455

Unable to unlock the secret of the Clock Gate, Alice has no choice but to return to the last junction she passed and choose another way to go – turn to **370**.

Alice can take the Executioner's Axe with her, to be her own weapon, if you like. Every time she delivers a successful strike with the weapon, it will cause 3 *Endurance* points of damage; however, because the axe is so heavy and hard to wield, Alice must also reduce her *Combat* score by 1 point for as long as she is using the weapon.

With no other obstacles barring her way now, Alice pushes open the ornate double doors and enters the palatial room beyond.

The throne room is as splendid as one might expect of the Palace of the Queen of Hearts, with pillars running round the outside edge of the heart-shaped chamber, a grand chandelier hanging from the high, vaulted ceiling bedecked with cut-crystal hearts and, at the centre of the room, where the curves of the heart join, is a magnificent royal seat that continues the heart-theme in both form and decoration.

Seated upon the throne is a tall, thin woman, wearing an elegant crimson gown, its embroidered detailing making much use of a teardrop pattern, and with a delicate diadem upon her head set with a blood-red ruby. The woman's skin is as pale as porcelain and her hair is as fine as spun silver. The irises of her eyes as are black as obsidian, and she is possessed of an unearthly beauty.

Lying beside her, on the heart-patterned rug at her feet, is the body of a much shorter woman, wearing a dress decorated with all manner of hearts and stained red with blood. Apart from the fact that she is lying spread-eagled

on the floor, there is one obvious thing wrong with the woman's body; it is quite clearly missing its head.

The mysterious beauty sitting on the throne is holding the missing head in one hand, smiling at the ugly woman's rigor mortis-locked expression of horror and disbelief that have seized her sagging features. In the red-robed woman's other gory hand is a still gently pulsating fist-sized lump of meat.

"Off with her head!" the woman says, a cruel smile curling her rosebud lips. "That was her favourite expression, wasn't it? Well you know what they say, you should be careful what you wish for…"

Alice cannot move, she cannot even speak, so appalled is she by what has been revealed before her in the throne room. And it is then that she realises the woman's dress isn't decorated with teardrops but rather it is embroidered with droplets of blood.

"The Queen of Hearts," the woman goes on, fixing Alice with a soul-penetrating stare. "Well not anymore."

With that she takes the Queen's still beating heart and opening her mouth wide, dislocating her jaw as if she were a snake, swallows it whole.

"And I suppose you were sent here to do away with the insane tyrant," she adds, licking her fingertips clean with a long, snaking tongue.

The woman, smiles seductively at Alice. "Come here child," she says, her unblinking gaze never once faltering, and beckons to Alice with a still bloody finger.

Take an Insanity test. If Alice passes the test, turn to **486**. If she fails the test, turn to **476**.

457

Alice gulps down the rest of the tincture (cross the Shrinking Potion off Alice's Adventure Sheet) and immediately starts to shrink. Soon she is small enough to slip under the door of the cell.

Once she is on the other side, she sets off along the cavernous passageway into the Palace. Fortunately, before she can run into any elephant-sized vermin, the effects of the potion wear off and she returns to her normal size.

Turn to **342**.

458

Alice can't help but inhale a lungful of the mycetic spores and doubles up as her body is wracked by a terrible coughing fit.

Lose 2 *Endurance* points and reduce Alice's *Agility* score by 1. If Alice is still alive, turn to **437**.

459

Retreating a few paces, to give herself more of a run-up, Alice runs towards the creatures at full pelt. At the last possible moment, she launches herself into the air, hoping to flip herself over their heads. The question is, did she give herself enough of a run-up?

Take an Agility test, and if Alice is successful, turn to **489**. If she is unsuccessful, turn to **469**.

"Ahoy there!" comes a voice from somewhere nearby, and turning her head Alice sees a great sailing ship bearing down on her.

It is a most curious sight; it has the appearance of a square-rigged merchantman, except that a great funnel, pumping out billows of thick black smoke, emerges from the aft castle. As the ship draws alongside her, a lifeboat it lowered, accompanied by the clanking of esoteric machineries. Hauling herself on board, Alice waits as the lifeboat is raised on its hoist again so that she might disembark onto the deck of the peculiar galleon.

The crew immediately gather round her. There is a Boot-maker, a Bonnet-maker, a Barrister, a Broker, a Billiard-marker, a Banker, a Butcher, a Baker, and – most curiously of all – a Beaver.

"Welcome! Welcome!" declaims their Captain, a Bellman, ringing his bell enthusiastically as he does so. "Welcome aboard the *Snark-Hunter*!"

"*Snark-Hunter?* What's a Snark-Hunter?" asks Alice, staring about her in amazement at the strange ship and her curious crew.

"Why, we are," says the Bellman, looking uffish. "All of us. We are, after all, hunting the Snark."

"And what, pray tell, is a Snark?"

"Why, let me tell you," the Bellman says, conspiratorially. "Come, listen my men," he goes on, beckoning to his crew, "while I tell you again the five unmistakeable marks by which you may know, wheresoever you go, the warranted genuine Snarks."

His men lean in closer, with Alice caught up among their throng, as the Captain of the Snark-Hunter passes on his especial knowledge of the creature they are, apparently, hunting.

"Let us take them in order. The first is the taste,
Which is meagre and hollow, but crisp:
Like a coat that is rather too tight in the waist,
With a flavour of Will-o'-the-wisp.

"Its habit of getting up late you'll agree
That it carries too far, when I say
That it frequently breakfasts at five-o'clock tea,
And dines on the following day.

"The third is its slowness in taking a jest.
Should you happen to venture on one,
It will sigh like a thing that is deeply distressed:
And it always looks grave at a pun.

"The fourth is its fondness for bathing-machines,
Which is constantly carries about,
And believes that they add to the beauty of scenes--
A sentiment open to doubt.

"The fifth is ambition. It next will be right
To describe each particular batch:
Distinguishing those that have feathers, and bite,
From those that have whiskers, and scratch.

"For, although common Snarks do no manner of harm,
Yet, I feel it my duty to say,
Some are Boojums–"

The Bellman breaks off in alarm, for the Baker has fainted away.

Their Captain's speech concluded, the rest of the crew go about their business, making sure that Alice feels quite at home on board. They offer her muffins and tea, which Alice tucks into with gusto (add 4 to Alice's *Endurance* score), and the Beaver evens offers her his second-hand dagger-proof coat.

If you want Alice to take the coat, add the Dagger-Proof Coat to Alice's Adventure Sheet, and for as long as she is wearing it, in battle Alice may reduce any damage done to her by her enemies by 1 point.

"And now," says the Bellman, "navigation is always a difficult art, with only one ship and one bell, but where can we take you? Will you join us on our quest or can you drop you somewhere on our way?"

How should Alice reply?

"Please drop me at the first safe
harbour we come to." Turn to **475**.

"I would like to come with you." Turn to **495**.

461

Alice is fast, and on any other day such a run would win the village show sprint, but the airborne Snap-dragon-flies are faster and quickly catch up with her, one of them delivering her a nasty sting with its thorny tail.

Lose 2 *Endurance* points, and if Alice is still able to continue her adventure, turn to **112**.

462

The Red Knight dead, Alice turns her attention to recovering the Vorpal Sword. Carefully easing it from between the effigy's fingers, Alice weighs it in her hands. The blade is perfectly balanced and unbelievably feels as light as a feather.

If Alice uses the Vorpal Sword in combat, you may add 1 point to her *Combat* score and any successful strike she makes against an opponent will cause 4 *Endurance* points of damage.

Hearing the clatter of armour and steel behind her, Alice turns in time to see the Red Knight rise from the floor and throw himself at her in one sudden, fluid movement.

At that same instant, the mausoleum echoes with the thundering sound of galloping hoof-beats and a phantasmal horse and rider emerge from the far wall, in a burst if ectoplasmic mist. The guardian of the tomb has come to Alice's rescue, now that she is mistress of the Vorpal Sword and its protector.

Ignoring Alice now, the Red Knight turns to meet the ghostly White Knight's charge. Swords clash and sparks fly.

"She's my prisoner, you know!" the Red Knight growls.

"Yes, but then I came and rescued her!" the White Knight replies.

"Well, we must fight for her, then," says the Red Knight.

"You will observe the Rules of Battle, of course?" the White Knight remarks.

"I always do," says the Red Knight.

It is all the distraction Alice needs. With one swing of the Vorpal Sword she takes the undead knight's head from his shoulders, as the keen-edged blade meets the stump of his bony neck.

As the knight's armoured head tumbles to the floor, the rest of the Red Queen's vampiric champion falls to his knees before poleaxing onto the floor, and remains motionless this time.

"You saved me!" Alice says as the ghostly White Knight dismounts from his phantasmal steed.

"It was a glorious victory, wasn't it?" says the ghost.

"Is it your body that lies within?" Alice asks, her eyes on the great stone sarcophagus.

"What does it matter where my body happens to be?" replies the knight. "What's done is done, but what still needs to be done must be done also. It is time you were gone from this place. Wonderland needs you."

If you have the word 'Portal' recorded on Alice's Adventure Sheet, then you will also have a number associated with it. If so, turn the section with the same number. If not, turn to **123**.

463

There are three things that Alice may have found whilst exploring the maze that might be of particular use to her now in her altercation with the gardeners.

If you want her to use a jar of Slug Pellets, turn to **473**. If you think she'd be better off using Bloom's Patent Plant Provender, turn to **493**. If you think she should arm herself with a Spade, turn to **66**.

If Alice has none of these items, or you don't want her to use any of them now, turn to **503**.

464

Putting her hands over her head, Alice runs for the library door as books continue to hammer her body. (Lose 1 more *Endurance* point.)

Back in the passageway, Alice slams the door behind her and is relieved to find that the Ghost does not follow her out into the corridor.

If she is still alive, turn to **454**.

465

The gravel path gives way to grass and Alice finds herself standing at the edge of what she supposes is a croquet-ground, although it is unlike any croquet-ground she has seen before, all ridges and furrows, with arches made of doubled-over playing cards larger than any she has ever seen… or has she?

If Alice has visited the Croquet-Ground before, turn to **248**. If his is her first visit, turn to **365**.

466

As the Red Queen throws herself at Alice, talon-like fingernails and fangs bared, an apparition materialises between them inside the throne room.

"Go!" the Ghost whispers to the child, and then turns to meet the shrieking vampire's onslaught.

Alice doesn't need to be told twice. The phantasm's appearance has bought her precious seconds that could mean the difference between life and death.

Turn to **245**.

467

No matter how she imagines events might differ from the path they seem set upon now, the Tiger continues to prowl towards her, despite Alice's best efforts to avert the inevitable. It would appear that this is one battle she is going to have to face up to.

Cross off one *Curiouser and Curiouser* box from Alice's Adventure Sheet and turn to **492**.

468

Before she can close her mouth and eyes against the toxic spore cloud, Alice begins to feel their ill-effects as her head starts to spin and she feels that she can no longer trust her own senses.

Add 1 point to Alice's *Insanity* score, reduce Alice's *Logic* score by 1 point, and then turn to **437**.

469

Just as Alice is thinking she has done it, one of the creatures arches backwards, almost bending itself in half, and a whip-like tongue shoots out of its mouth, its sticky tip catching her ankle, and pulls her out of the air.

She lands hard, grazing her knee against a stone. (Lose 1 *Endurance* point.) By the time she has picked herself up again, the newt-like lizards are on top of her.

Turn to **499**.

470

Alice finds herself standing before a faux classical temple in which stands the statue of a monstrous winged beast. Alice does not allow her gaze to linger too long upon the horror, lest it drive her mad!

From here Alice can only go east or west, so which is it to be?

East?   Turn to **430**.

West?   Turn to **480**.

471

The Executioner's laugh becomes a mighty roar, as he raises the axe above his head, ready to bring it down upon Alice's neck. (The Ace of Clubs has the initiative.)

ACE OF CLUBS   COMBAT 9   ENDURANCE 9

If Alice wins her epic battle with the Royal Executioner, turn to **456**.

472

Alice does not rejoice in insects at all, the truth being that she is rather afraid of them – especially the larger ones, like these Snap-dragon-flies. She runs like the wind and the fiery insects soon tire of the chase.

When she is sure she has lost them, she slows her pace to a walk once more. Turn to **146**.

473

Alice takes the jar of pellets from her pocket and hurls it at Two, only for the gardener to bat it away. The jar lands against another shrub, the glass shattering against the woody stem and scattering the pellets over the soil.

Cross the Slug Pellets off Alice's Adventure Sheet and turn to **503**.

474

Bravely Alice charges towards the Ghost, but she cannot cause any physical harm to its ethereal form. While Alice is trying to fight off the spectre she continues to be battered by heavy atlases and dry historical tomes. (Deduct another 2 *Endurance* points.)

If Alice is still conscious, turn to **464**.

475

"Steer to starboard, but keep her head larboard!" the Bellman cries to the helmsman, who does his best to comply, and soon Alice sees land ahead, and not long after that, she is disembarking by jolly boat, as the Beaver rows her to shore.

Exchanging farewells, the Beaver returns to the ship while Alice takes in her sandy surroundings.

Beyond the shore, the beach rises to a range of grass-topped dunes, and beyond those Alice can see the tops of trees interspersed with carefully-tended topiary. Looking left along the beach, Alice spies the entrance to a rocky cove, while to her right the shoreline curves round to a wide bay.

If you think Alice should investigate the rocky cove, turn to **138**. If you think she should head towards the sandy bay, turn to **258**. If you think she should just head into the dunes towards the well-tended topiary, turn to **312**.

476

Alice finds herself unable to resist as the Red Queen's mesmeric stare penetrates her soul. Her will no longer her own, the child climbs the steps of the dais and only stops when she is before the throne.

"Now then, my dear," says the Red Queen, smiling languidly, "I know what you'd like."

As she opens her jaws wide once more, Alice just stands there, not acting to protect herself, as the Red Queen sinks her cobra-like fangs into the child's jugular and starts to drink.

The part of Alice that is still Alice, thinks she hears the rumour of a voice carry to her on the wind, a voice that says, "Wake up, Alice dear!"

But Alice can't wake up. She is under the control of the Red Queen now. She will never wake up again.

THE END

477

Alice slumps to the ground, dejected and defeated.

Her melancholic reverie is disturbed by the arrival of another within the mausoleum chamber. Standing at the top of the stairs is a knight clad in a suit of blood-red armour, his face hidden behind the closed visor of his helm.

The Red Knight says nothing but drawing his black iron blade crosses the chamber, sword raised.

Without the Vorpal Sword, not only will Alice not be able to slay the fiend-like Red Queen, she will not be able to defend herself against the harridan's deathless servant either.

Alice's adventure ends here but her nightmare is only just beginning as the vampiric knights begins to feast...

THE END

Following the footpath, Alice comes to a clearing between the toadstool trees. Lying within it is a log that has been left hollow by rot. Being a naturally inquisitive child, Alice wonders what she might find inside.

If you want Alice to take a look, turn to **498**. If not, turn to **488**.

An eerie feeling comes over Alice as she explores the outer ward of the castle, as if a thousand eyes are fixed upon her. And yet, when she looks round, she sees nothing but the castle's petrified defenders.

In the far corner of the courtyard, at the base of a corner tower, Alice stumbles across all that is left of a huge broken egg.

"Humpty Dumpty sat on a wall: Humpty Dumpty had a great fall. All the King's horses and all the King's men, couldn't put Humpty Dumpty in his place again," Alice finds herself chanting under her breath.

The fractured shell is twice as tall as she is and it is empty. Alice can only wonder at what hatched from the enormous egg.

Deciding it best not to linger within the inner ward of the castle any longer, in case whatever hatched from the egg returns unexpectedly, she makes for the steps that lead to the entrance to the keep.

Turn to **447**.

480

It is not long before Alice reaches another right-angled turn in the leafy labyrinth. Should she go south (turn to **272**) or east (turn to **470**)?

481

No matter how hard she imagines the narrative of her story could differ from the path it seems set upon now, the Tiger continues to prowl towards the child, and there is nothing she can do to stop it. It would appear that this is one battle Alice is going to have to have to face up to.

Cross off one *The Pen is Mightier* box from Alice's Adventure Sheet and turn to **492**.

482

Opening the door Alice enters what can only be described as a small boudoir. Resting on a stand on a dressing table, in front of a mirror, is a grand, powdered wig, like something out of the history books her Governess made her read about the French Revolution.

The child can't help but lift the wig from its stand and try it on, imagining that she is Marie Antoinette as she regards herself in the mirror. (If you want Alice to keep the Wig on, make a note of it on Alice's Adventure Sheet.)

There is nothing else for Alice here so she eventually has to leave the boudoir through the same door she entered by.

Turn to **502**.

483

The handle turns, the door swings open, and stepping over the threshold Alice finds herself in the cool shade of a tiled entrance hall. Doors lead off from the hall ahead of her and to her left.

For Alice to try the door in front of her, turn to **166**. For Alice to open the door to her left, turn to **494**.

484

Alice feels exhausted after her battle with the Red Knight, but she has been victorious nonetheless.

If Alice previously solved a chess puzzle, double the answer to that puzzle and then subtract it from this paragraph, ultimately turning to the new paragraph.

If Alice has not previously comes across, or solved, such a puzzle, turn to **302**.

Alice's mind can barely comprehend what is happening to her, and with the appearance of the Spinebacks her spiralling descent into madness only worsens.

Add 1 to Alice's *Insanity* score and turn to **28**.

As the Red Queen's stare bores into her soul, Alice finds herself pacing across the throne room as if sleep-walking, a part of her screaming at her to break eye-contact with the blood-sucking leech and save herself.

"Now then, my dear," says the Red Queen, smiling languidly, "I know what you'd like."

It is then that Alice hears a voice carried as if from far, far away on a zephyr from a land beyond the borders of Wonderland: "Wake up, Alice dear!"

And as the Red Queen opens her mouth wide, to sink snake-like fangs into the child's neck, Alice succeeds at last in breaking free of the Red Queen's spell, and readies herself to fight back against the murderous witch.

"Very well!" hisses the harridan. "After all, it is better to be feared than loved."

If you think Alice should use *The Pen is Mightier* ability now, turn to **506**. If not, turn to **496**.

As Alice stands there, studying the inscription around the tomb, hearing the footsteps on the stairs coming closer with every passing second, she can't shake the thought that the stone soldiers in the courtyard reminded her of nothing more than chessmen...

If you think you know the answer to the riddle, convert the word into numbers using the code A=1, B=2... Z=26. Add the numbers together, and then turn to the paragraph with the same number as the total.

If upon reading the paragraph you turn to it makes no sense (meaning you have got the answer wrong) or you are unable to solve the riddle in the first place, turn to **477**.

Leaving the clearing by a path on the other side, Alice soon finds herself emerging from the towering toadstools and leaving the forest of fungi.

She is standing at the top of a steep slope. Below her, at the bottom of the incline, to the north, on the other side of a rickety fence, she can see a curious house, with chimneys shaped like ears and its roof apparently thatched with fur. To the north-west there stands a grand house built in the Palladian style. Beyond the cottage Alice can see the towering yew hedge walls of a maze that appears to cover acres of ground.

In which direction should Alice go now? To head towards the grand house, turn to **319**. To make for the fur-thatched cottage, turn to **216**.

489

Alice sails over the creatures and lands on the path behind them. Not waiting to judge their reaction, she races off again through the swamp. Turn to **286**.

490

Alice soon comes to another branching of the ways in the yew-hedge maze, but which way should she go?

North?   Turn to **430**.

East?   Turn to **134**.

West?   Turn to **413**.

Without a second thought, Alice gulps down the potion and, as she rapidly starts to shrink, leaps onto the back of the wasp. Grabbing hold of its antennae, Alice steers the insect back through the tulgey wood to the glade in which stands the mirror portal. And she arrives only just in time, for upon reaching the clearing, she starts to grow again.

Returning to her normal size, she steps up to the looking-glass. Alice closes her eyes and takes a step forward, the glass becoming a silvery mist before her as she does so. And then she is back in the palace… but the Red Queen is waiting for her.

Turn to **41**.

It may only be a Paper Tiger but the cat's card claws still look like they could cause Alice a nasty paper-cut. (Before you begin the battle, make a note of Alice's current *Endurance* score. Alice has the initiative.)

PAPER TIGER   COMBAT 8   ENDURANCE 8

If Alice is using a Pair of Scissors to fight the Paper Tiger, for every successful hit she makes against it, as well as causing 2 *Endurance* points damage, you can also deduct 1 from the Tiger's *Combat* score.

If Alice is victorious, turn to **517**, but if the Tiger wins the battle, turn to **507**.

493

Alice hurls the bottle of brown liquid at the gardeners but misses all three of them. The flask hits the roots of the rose-tree and smashes, splashing the strong-smelling liquid compost over the plant's roots. The effects are almost instantaneous.

Cross Bloom's Patent Plant Provender off Alice's Adventure Sheet and turn to **308**.

494

Passing through the door, Alice makes the transition from the tiled hall into a dusty, darkened room filled with glass cases containing displays of stuffed birds, animals and fish. They remind Alice of the collections at the University Museum of Natural History.

The drapes have been drawn across the window, allowing only a sliver of sunlight to enter the room, which illuminates the golden motes of dust spinning in the shaft of light, and the room's prize specimen, mounted on a perch of Madagascan rosewood, and, like the other specimens, behind glass.

It is a plump bird covered in bright blue-grey pigeon-like plumage. It has a tuft of tail feathers, short stout legs with bright yellow feet, and a large hooked bill, coloured from black through to green.

On the other side of the room is another door, this one a fine example of walnut-panelling.

If you want Alice to go through this door, turn to **516**. If you want her to examine the Dodo close-up first, turn to **505**.

495

"Capital! Capital!" the Bellman exclaims. Taking out a most curious map – it appears to have nothing drawn on it at all – the Captain of the *Snark-Hunter* sets about plotting a course.

"What's the good of Mercator's North Poles and Equators, Tropics, Zones, and Meridian Lines?" the Bellman cries, to which the crew reply, "They are merely conventional signs! Other maps are such shapes, with their islands and capes! But we've got our brave Captain to thank," so the crew does protest, "that he's bought us the best – a perfect and absolute blank!"

This is charming, no doubt, but they shortly find out that the Captain they've trusted so well, has only one notion for crossing the ocean, and that is to tingle his bell.

He is thoughtful and grave, but his orders, so brave, are enough to bewilder the crew. When he cries "Steer to starboard, but keep her head larboard!" what on earth is the helmsman to do?

But somehow they make it to their destination, a dark and gloomy island, and make land, unloading their boxes, portmanteaus and bags.

"Just the place for a Snark!" the Bellman cries. "You'd best be unpacking the things that you need to rig yourselves out for a fight," he tells the others.

Alice watches as the merry band busy themselves preparing for the quest ahead. When they are ready, they all set out in different directions, leaving Alice quite alone on the shore of this strange and sinister island. Seeing that she has little other choice, steeling herself, Alice sets off towards the island's interior.

Before very long, she finds herself negotiating the treacherous pathways of a terribly tangled forest. The grey-black trunks of the trees are contorted into shapes that speak of torment and pain, their branches clung with moss and snaking creepers. The air is redolent with the aroma of a compost heap and a sour yellow mist hangs in the air. Beads of moisture condense on Alice's skin, sucking the warmth from her body. Strange animal hoots and shrieks echo between the trees and have Alice looking all about her, wondering from where the next threat to her life might come.

"Beware the Jabberwock, my son! The jaws that bite, the claws that catch!" Alice mutters under her breath. "Beware the Jubjub bird, and shun the frumious Bandersnatch!"

And then the strange sounds of the forest are silenced by a blood-curdling howl that cuts through the tulgey wood, threatening to send an already anxious Alice over the edge.

Take an Insanity test and if Alice passes, turn to **367**. If she fails the test, turn to **347**.

The fiend-like queen's beautiful countenance twists into an ophidian hiss as the vampiric Red Queen launches herself at Alice, intent on drink her blood and sucking her very soul from her body. (The Red Queen has the initiative.)

RED QUEEN   COMBAT 11   ENDURANCE 12

If the Red Queen wins three consecutive Combat Rounds, she bites Alice's neck, draining an additional 2 *Endurance* points and 1 *Combat* point from the poor child. If Alice defeats the vampire, turn to **398**. If not, her adventure ends here, as a bloody prize for the usurper of the throne of Wonderland.

497

This riddle is taxing indeed. Nonetheless, if you think you know the answer convert the word into numbers using the code A=1, B=2... Z=26. Add the numbers together, and then turn to the paragraph with the same number as the total.

If upon reading the paragraph you turn to it makes no sense (meaning you have got the answer wrong) or you are unable to solve the riddle at all, turn to **477**.

Fascinated by what might have made the log its home, Alice bends down and peers inside. She jumps back again when she comes face to face with a larger than life Stag Beetle. Now aware of Alice's presence, and clearly considering her a potential meal, the beetle scuttles towards her, its huge jaws snapping in anticipation of devouring the wretched child.

Alice is either going to have to defend herself, once again (turn to **508**), or she will have to use *The Pen is Mightier* ability to save herself, if she can (turn to **518**).

The Slithy Toves try to snare Alice with their sticky tongues, bite her with their needle-sharp teeth, and claw her with their strange corkscrew talons. Manoeuvring herself cunningly upon the narrow path, she is able to make sure that she only has to fight them one at a time. (Alice has the initiative.)

	COMBAT	ENDURANCE
First SLITHY TOVE	6	6
Second SLITHY TOVE	6	5

If Alice slays the creatures, she hurries off again through the swamp. Turn to **286**.

500

Having given herself over to her bloodlust completely, the Red Queen starts to transform. Shedding her royal robes and her human skin, the vampire takes on the form of a monstrous blood-red serpent-woman. Hissing like a cobra, her sinuous body writhing with an almost hypnotic rhythm, the Gorgon strikes! (The Gorgon has the initiative in this battle.)

GORGON   COMBAT 12   ENDURANCE 14

If Alice somehow manages to slay the transformed Red Queen, turn to **125**.

501

Before anything untoward can befall her, Alice flees, running pell-mell through the tulgey wood, until she sees the battlements of an ancient fortress looming over the tops of the sickly trees.

Turn to **512**.

502

Leaving the hall she enters a long passageway that ends at a closed door. From beyond this door come the sounds of crying and screaming and a lot of sneezing. Every now and again, this cacophony is accompanied by a tremendous crash, as if a dish or kettle has been broken. Halfway down the corridor another door leads off to the left.

kevcrossley
-2015-

Should Alice make her way to the door at the end of the passageway (turn to **454**), open the door halfway down the corridor first (turn to **239**), or turn back and leave the house (turn to **249**)?

503

The gardeners run at Alice, dropping their paintbrushes and arming themselves with spade-shaped trowels and garden shears.

If Alice is still able to use *The Pen is Mightier* power, and you want her to now, turn to **13**. If Alice can still use the *Curiouser and Curiouser* ability, and you want her to use that instead, turn to **308**. If she is unable to use either of these abilities, or you do not want her to, turn to **26**.

504

Feeling a shiver of fear raising the hairs at the nape of her neck, Alice quickly closes the book, hoping that this will dispel the apparition. But the spectre remains there in the corner of the library.

As Alice watches, the ghost's mouth drops openly impossible wide and its features become the fleshless visage of a skull, as a blood-curdling scream rises from its fleshless throat.

Books start to fly off the shelves, battering Alice. (Lose 2 *Endurance* points and add 1 to Alice's *Insanity* score.)

What should Alice do now?

Flee from the haunted library?   Turn to **464**.

Try to drive the Ghost away?   Turn to **474**.

505

With a leathery creak the bird turns its glass-eyed stare on the child. "Ah, Alice, it is good to see you again."

"Again?" Alice says, in consternation.

"You mean you don't remember?" the Dodo says, crestfallen.

"I am quite sure that if I had a met such a curious bird before I would be able to recall the occasion," says the child, primly. "What I mean to say is that you are, quite clearly, a Dodo–"

"Yes, that's right, a flightless bird of the pigeon family endemic to the island of Mauritius."

"–and seeing as how you are extinct, our meeting would have surely made an indelible mark upon my memory.

"Oh dear, oh dear, oh dear," mutters the bird. "A classic case of somnia-related amnesia. But then I suppose it was some time ago."

"What was?" asks Alice.

"Our meeting," replies the Dodo. "But never mind that now. Let us start again. Raphus Cucullatus at your service" – and then adds, almost as an aside – "but my friends call me Raph."

"Pleased to meet you," Alice says offering the bird her hand – but not feeling it proper to call the Dodo by his first name – the Dodo offering her his wing in return.

"Time is short and on the path ahead you will meet all manner of menaces."

"What do you mean?" says Alice, unnerved by the Dodo's words.

"The Queen of Hearts has issued a decree that if you return to Wonderland you are to be killed or captured, and taken to her palace in chains. But the truth of the matter is that now you are here you must enter her palace, unseen, and put an end to Her Majesty before she can put an end to you."

"But why does it have to be me?" Alice asks, baulking at the enormity of the task that has been set before her.

"Because this is your dream – your nightmare. But I can offer you some assistance, even if I can no longer leave this perch. "To reach the Queen's palace you will first have to pass through the maze. When you enter the maze, go south, then east, then north, then east, then south, then east, then north, to reach the heart of the labyrinth, for the quickest way through is via the middle."

(Add 1 point to Alice's *Logic* score for gaining this useful piece of information.)

"And what about after that?" asks Alice.

"I am afraid that after that you are on your own, for I have never been further than the middle myself."

"Oh," says Alice, feeling more anxious than ever before.

"Now you had better be on your way," says the Dodo, nodding towards the walnut-panelled door. "He is waiting for you."

Curious to know just who is waiting for her, Alice bids the Dodo goodbye and makes her way across the dusty room to the other door. Upon reaching it, she slowly turns the handle... Turn to **516**.

506

In fear of her very soul, Alice runs from the throne room. Behind her, the Red Queen launches herself into the air to land right behind the wretched child. And then suddenly the Executioner's huge axe is in her hands and, her muscles granted new strength by the adrenaline rushing through every fibre of her being, she swings it at the harridan. The gleaming blade describes a lethal arc through the air before hitting the Red Queen in the chest, sending her crashing to the marbled floor behind her.

Turn to **398**.

As the Paper Tiger lays the final killing blow against Alice, she feels as if she is coming apart at every wound the cat's card claws have opened in her pliant flesh.

As the parts of her body tumble away from each other through the mist, she sees a hideous face form amidst the clouds. It is that of an ugly woman, with a large pointed nose, and wobbly double chins, and she is wearing a crown. The eyes in the face are spheres of molten iron and fixed on Alice.

The woman begins to laugh – a booming, raucous sound that threatens to either deafen Alice or drive her mad. (Add 1 to Alice's *Insanity* score.)

Just as she is feeling that she cannot bear it anymore, everything fades to darkness and Alice opens her eyes…

Turn to **9**.

508

The Stag Beetle's jaws are as sharp and as strong as garden shears. (The Stag Beetle has the initiative.)

STAG BEETLE   COMBAT 7   ENDURANCE 6

If Alice wins the fight with the forest inhabitant, turn to **488**.

"'Twas brillig, and the slithy toves did gyre and gimble in the wabe," Alice whispers as she regards the strange newt-like creatures creeping towards her. "All mimsy were the borogoves…"

Her poetry recital is cut short by a sudden squawking sound, and a pair of thin and shabby-looking birds, their feathers sticking out all round, drop down from the branches of a gnarled tree onto the path. The strange-looking fowl pluck the Slithy Toves from the ground, one each, and gulp them down whole.

Just as Alice breathes a sigh of relief, thinking that she is free of the threat posed by the Slithy Toves, the Borogoves advance towards her with curious strutting steps, and she is forced to defend herself.

If Alice is able to use *The Pen is Mightier* ability to resolve this battle in her favour, turn to **519**. If not, or you do not want her to use that ability now, turn to **265**.

510

At a right-hand turn in the maze Alice finds a blackberry bush growing and scoffs a handful of its ripe fruit to keep her hunger at bay. (Add 2 *Endurance* points.)

Which way should she go now?

North?   Turn to **184**.

East?   Turn to **304**.

511

"Who are you to challenge Tweedle-dum –" says the left-hand head.

"And Tweedle-dee?" asks the head on the right.

"Queen Alice!" Alice declares with greater confidence than she is actually feeling.

Take a Logic test. If Alice passes, turn to **43**. If she fails the test, turn to **30**.

512

And so at last the trees part and Alice finds herself standing before the ruined walls of the ancient fortress. Cautiously she steps through the open gates of the crumbling gatehouse and surveys the tableau that awaits her within.

The castle is manned by stone statues of men in armour, some of them even on horseback; an entire army turned to stone. What could have petrified these warriors, leaving them as silent sentinels of this forgotten fortress?

On the other side of the courtyard stands the keep, its walls the colour of ivory.

If you want Alice to pass between the ranks of petrified warriors in order to climb the steps to the entrance to the keep, turn to **447**. If you think she should explore the courtyard first, turn to **479**.

The Alice-Jabberwock staggers back, under the concerted attacks of Alice's allies, coming dangerously close to the edge of the chessboard and the bottomless, lightless void beyond.

For a moment it looks like Alice might have won the battle without even having to lay a blow against the beast. But then the monster rallies, the child's face atop the serpentine neck and dragon-like body twisted into a hideous snarl. Alice shifts her grip on the Vorpal Sword and prepares to fight for her life one last time.

(Alice has the initiative in this battle, but the Vorpal Sword will only cause 3 *Endurance* points of damage to the monster's iron-hard scales, rather than the usual 4.)

JABBERWOCK   COMBAT 8   ENDURANCE 9

If Alice slays the Jabberwock, turn to **520**.

514

But presently the Thing began
To shiver and to sneeze:
On which I said "Come, come, my man!
That's a most inconsiderate plan.
Less noise there, if you please!"

"I've caught a cold," the Thing replied,
"Out there upon the landing."
I turned to look in some surprise,
And there, before my very eyes,
A little Ghost was standing!

He trembled when he caught my eye,
And got behind a chair.
"How came you here," I said, "and why?
I never saw a thing so shy.
Come out! Don't shiver there!"

He said, "I'd gladly tell you how,
And also tell you why;
But" (here he gave a little bow)
"You're in so bad a temper now,
You'd think it all a lie.

"And as to being in a fright,
Allow me to remark
That Ghosts have just as good a right
In every way, to fear the light,
As Men to fear the dark."

Alice closes the book and there, in the corner of the library, is a phantasmal presence.

"What are you?" the child asks the spectre, trying to keep the quiver from her voice. "Phantom, goblin, elf, sprite or ghoul?"

"Ghost will do," says the spirit, "and I should thank you."

"What for?" asks Alice.

"For freeing me from my bookish prison." The Ghost makes a small bow. "But now I must bid you *adieu*." And then it is gone.

Alice may now also use *The Pen is Mightier* ability a total of four times, rather than three. Make a note of this and write down 'Phantasm' on Alice's Adventure Sheet and the number '466' next to it.

As Alice closes the book, ready to slip it back onto the shelf, something slips out from its hiding place within the spine of the book. It is a complicated-looking Skeleton Key. (If you want Alice to take it, note it down on Alice's Adventure Sheet.)

Alice sees no reason in lingering within in the library any longer and so returns to the passageway.

Turn to **454**.

515

As the mutated humanoid hedgehogs bound towards her Alice has the presence of mind to arm herself, sprinting for the bench and snatching up the croquet mallet.

If Alice chooses to use the Mallet in battle she swings it like a mace. Every time she lands a successful blow with the Mallet, roll two dice (or pick a card). If you roll 2-10 (or you pick an Ace up to a Jack), Alice's strike causes 3 *Endurance* points of damage to her opponent. However, if you roll 11 or 12 (or pick a Queen or King), Alice's blow knocks out her opponent, removing them from the fight.

"Shall we play?" says Alice, Mallet at the ready.

Turn to **28**.

516

The door opens and Alice enters a snug study. Sitting behind a leather-topped writing desk is the master of the house – the White Rabbit, who looks up in surprise at her unexpected entrance. A Lizard, wearing the cap and clothes of a gardener, and a Mouse, dressed very smartly, after the fashion of a bank clerk, are just as startled to see her.

"In this house we knock before entering a room," the White Rabbit chides her, "but I suppose I should just be grateful that you're here at last."

Turn to **135**.

517

In defeating the Paper Tiger, Alice has gone a long way to overcoming her own fears and will be all the better prepared to tackle the nightmare that is consuming her dream world. As the Tiger dissolves back into the mist, the fog of confusion starts to clear…

Subtract 3 from Alice's *Insanity* score and turn to **9**.

518

As Alice is backing away from the advancing Stag Beetle she hears a cicada-like hissing behind her and spins round to see a second giant Stag Beetle approaching from behind. Darting out of the way, she watches as the two males begin to battle for possession of the clearing and the tasty meal that Alice might provide.

Not waiting to discover the outcome of the battle, Alice hurries on her way as fast as she can – turn to **488**.

519

"'Twas brillig, and the slithy toves did gyre and gimble in the wabe; all mimsy were the borogoves," Alice begins.

The shadows either side of the path take on a glutinous solidity and long-fingered hands snatch Alice's enemies from the trail.

"And the mome raths outgrabe!" finishes Alice.

And then they are gone again, and the path ahead is clear.

Turn to **286**.

520

Alice plunges the Vorpal Sword through the monster's soft underbelly, piercing the Jabberwock's chest cavity and the heart within. Withdrawing the blade again, she brings it round in a sweeping arc and lops off the monster's head. Decapitated, the Alice-Jabberwock's body immediately starts to dissolve into mist. And as it does so, Alice's mind is flooded with memories long suppressed, of a previous visit to Wonderland.

Panting for breath, feeling light-headed from the rush of recollections, Alice watches, mouth agape, as the last wisps of mist are dispersed by a breeze that seems to blow up from nowhere. At the same time, the circling mirror-portals fracture again and again, into a thousand-thousand fragments, which scatter to the depthless reaches of the void, where they become twinkling pinpricks of starlight.

Alice looks around her at the cracked and chequered plain, but she is utterly alone. "And what happens to me now?" she asks the wind.

"That depends a good deal on where you want to get to," comes a familiar voice, speaking from a grinning mouth that has materialised in mid-air in front of her.

"Cheshire Puss!" Alice exclaims, and the rest of the Cat quickly coalesces around its smile.

"So where is it you want to get to?" the floating feline asks.

"I don't much care where –" Alice begins.

"Then it doesn't matter which way you go," says the Cat.

"– so long as I get somewhere," Alice adds, by way of an explanation.

"Oh, you're sure to do that."

And then the Cat too is dissolving into mist, only this mist swells and roils like massing thunderclouds, and other faces appear before Alice's eyes, formed from coiling tendrils of vapour. She sees a serene blue face smoking a hookah pipe, the brightly-coloured beak and blue-grey plumage of a dodo, and the mechanically blinking eyes of a stuffed white rabbit – and a myriad voices seem to whisper to her on the breeze, "Thank you, Alice, and goodbye."

The nightmare is over, Wonderland is saved, and, most importantly of all, Alice has saved herself from oblivion.

She feels the stress and strain of her adventures ease, the weariness in her bones melting away, and a smile spreads slowly across her face as the fractured chessboard arena and the midnight gulf beyond fade to white...

In a Wonderland they lie,
Dreaming as the days go by,
Dreaming as the summers die:
Ever drifting down the stream —
Lingering in the golden gleam —
Life, what is it but a dream?

THE END

ACKNOWLEDGEMENTS

What started out as one person's crazed vision has, once again through the power of Kickstarter, become a crazed vision shared by a host of like-minded individuals – that in this day and age of digital apps and console RPGs, in the 150th anniversary year of the publication of *Alice's Adventures in Wonderland*, there is still room for one more pencil and paper adventure, published in the form of a traditional, processed-tree-carcass gamebook. (Although a zeroes-and-ones eBook edition is also available.)

There are, however, some individuals who have joined me at this Mad Tea Party that I would like to single out for particular attention and recognition.

First of all, Emma Barnes of Snowbooks, for being so open to this new model of producing gamebooks and supporting *Alice's Nightmare in Wonderland* from the start, and Anna Torborg for doing such an excellent job of laying it out.

Secondly, I must give special mention to Kev Crossley, for bravely following in the footsteps of Sir John Tenniel et al and helping to bring my warped vision of Wonderland to life – and at very short notice too! *Alice's Nightmare in*

Wonderland simply would not be what it is without his wonderful illustrations.

Thirdly, I must mention all of those people who helped with the Kickstarter rewards. So thank you to Jonathan Oliver, David Moore and Ben Smith of Abaddon Books for allowing me to offer my novella *Pax Britannia: White Rabbit* as a reward to backers; thank you to Lydia Matts of Broken Geek Designs for making the bespoke *Alice's Nightmare in Wonderland* necklaces; thank you to Fil Baldowski for making the All Rolled Up game rolls; and a special thank you to Saskia Powys, who designed the unique deck of *Alice's Nightmare in Wonderland*-themed playing cards.

But most of all, I would like to say a huge and heartfelt thank you everyone who pledged their support to this project. Without them, *Alice's Nightmare in Wonderland* could not have happened at all. So here's to you, all of you.

And just remember, in the immortal words of the Cheshire Cat, "We're all mad here."

KICKSTARTER BACKERS

GRYPHON

Martin Gooch • PJ Montgomery • Michael Hartley • Geoffrey Bertram • Michelle Edmunds • Dr Mike Reddy • Black Chicken Studios, Inc. • Pang Peow Yeong & Family • Tamsin Bryant • PD Dr Oliver M Traxel • Marc Thorpe • Michael Johnston • Kevin Abbotts • Rebecca Scott • Aaron Tyrone Utting • John Edward Kirk • Maria Walley • Ed Brenton • Rms

WHITE KNIGHT

Stephane Bechard • James Catchpole • Chris Trapp • Alice Cruickshank • Thomas Dan Nielsen • Alan Tannenbaum • Vin de Silva • Robert Schwartz • Jordan E Carey • Hayley Allen • Phillip Bailey • Andrew Wright • Kathryn Berghold • Louie Reynolds & Zoe Harrison • Vanessa Pare • Gwendlyn Drayton

UNICORN

Frans Buddelmeijer

DODO

Amy Winchester • 林立人 Lin Liren • Don Alsafi • Mark Myers • Nicki Gray • Steve Dean • Xymon "Awesome" Owain • Colin Oaten • Mr Smiler • James A Hirons • Raj Rijhwani • Steven Pannell • Tiago Vieira Perretto • James Aukett • Amy-Jayne McGarry-Thickitt • Fabrice Gatille • Paul Windmill • Felipe Espinoza Yentzen

QUEEN OF HEARTS

Anthony Myers • Jeremy R Haupt • Graham Hart • Franck Teixido • Meryne Gray • Judy Kashman • Keith Tollfree • Mark and Catherine Richards • Alexander Ballingall • Luke Niedner • María Ariza • Christopher Blakely • Rhel ná DecVandé • (Dave!) David Stringer Archer • Zwolfondu • Nicole Jane Mcleary • Mr Jay S Broda • Happy Xmas Mandy, Love Matt.

RED QUEEN

Y. K. Lee • Shyue Wen • Ong • Jonathan Caines • J J Malpas • Robin Horton

About the Author

Jonathan Green is a writer of speculative fiction, with more than sixty books to his name. Well known for his contributions to the Fighting Fantasy range of adventure gamebooks, he has also written fiction for such diverse properties as Doctor Who, Star Wars: The Clone Wars, Warhammer, Warhammer 40,000, Sonic the Hedgehog, Teenage Mutant Ninja Turtles, Moshi Monsters, LEGO and Judge Dredd.

He is the creator of the *Pax Britannia* series for Abaddon Books and has written eight novels set within this steampunk universe, featuring the debonair dandy adventurer Ulysses Quicksilver. He is also the author of an increasing number of non-fiction titles, including the award-winning *YOU ARE THE HERO – A History of Fighting Fantasy Gamebooks*.

He has recently taken to editing and compiling short story anthologies. Two of these, the critically-acclaimed *GAME OVER* and *SHARKPUNK*, are also published by Snowbooks.

To find out more about his current projects visit **www. JonathanGreenAuthor.com** and follow him on Twitter **@jonathangreen**.

ALICE'S ADVENTURE SHEET

AGILITY

LOGIC

INSANITY

COMBAT

THE PEN IS MIGHTIER

CURIOUSER AND CURIOUSER

ENDURANCE

EQUIPMENT

NIGHTMARE ENCOUNTER BOXES

COMBAT=

ENDURANCE=

COMBAT=

ENDURANCE=

COMBAT=

ENDURANCE=

COMBAT=

ENDURANCE=

COMBAT=

ENDURANCE=

COMBAT=

ENDURANCE=

COMBAT=

ENDURANCE=

COMBAT=

ENDURANCE=

COMBAT=

ENDURANCE=

COMBAT=

ENDURANCE=

ALICE'S ADVENTURE SHEET

AGILITY

LOGIC

INSANITY

COMBAT

ENDURANCE

EQUIPMENT

THE PEN IS MIGHTIER

CURIOUSER AND CURIOUSER

nightmare
encounter boxes

COMBAT=

ENDURANCE=

COMBAT=

ENDURANCE=

COMBAT=

ENDURANCE=

COMBAT=

ENDURANCE=

COMBAT=

ENDURANCE=

COMBAT=

ENDURANCE=

COMBAT=

ENDURANCE=

COMBAT=

ENDURANCE=

COMBAT=

ENDURANCE=

COMBAT=

ENDURANCE=

ALICE'S ADVENTURE SHEET

AGILITY

LOGIC

INSANITY

COMBAT

ENDURANCE

EQUIPMENT

THE PEN IS MIGHTIER

CURIOUSER AND CURIOUSER

NIGHTMARE ENCOUNTER BOXES

COMBAT=

ENDURANCE=

COMBAT=

ENDURANCE=

COMBAT=

ENDURANCE=

COMBAT=

ENDURANCE=

COMBAT=

ENDURANCE=

COMBAT=

ENDURANCE=

COMBAT=

ENDURANCE=

COMBAT=

ENDURANCE=

COMBAT=

ENDURANCE=

COMBAT=

ENDURANCE=

ALICE'S ADVENTURE SHEET

AGILITY

LOGIC

INSANITY

COMBAT

THE PEN IS MIGHTIER

CURIOUSER AND CURIOUSER

ENDURANCE

EQUIPMENT

NIGHTMARE
ENCOUNTER BOXES

COMBAT=

ENDURANCE=

COMBAT=

ENDURANCE=

COMBAT=

ENDURANCE=

COMBAT=

ENDURANCE=

COMBAT=

ENDURANCE=

COMBAT=

ENDURANCE=

COMBAT=

ENDURANCE=

COMBAT=

ENDURANCE=

COMBAT=

ENDURANCE=

COMBAT=

ENDURANCE=

ALICE'S ADVENTURE SHEET

AGILITY

LOGIC

INSANITY

COMBAT

THE PEN IS MIGHTIER

☐ ☐ ☐

CURIOUSER AND CURIOUSER

☐ ☐ ☐

ENDURANCE

EQUIPMENT

NIGHTMARE ENCOUNTER BOXES

COMBAT=

ENDURANCE=

COMBAT=

ENDURANCE=

COMBAT=

ENDURANCE=

COMBAT=

ENDURANCE=

COMBAT=

ENDURANCE=

COMBAT=

ENDURANCE=

COMBAT=

ENDURANCE=

COMBAT=

ENDURANCE=

COMBAT=

ENDURANCE=

COMBAT=

ENDURANCE=

ALICE'S ADVENTURE SHEET

AGILITY

LOGIC

INSANITY

COMBAT

THE PEN IS MIGHTIER

CURIOUSER AND CURIOUSER

ENDURANCE

EQUIPMENT

NIGHTMARE ENCOUNTER BOXES

COMBAT=

ENDURANCE=

COMBAT=

ENDURANCE=

COMBAT=

ENDURANCE=

COMBAT=

ENDURANCE=

COMBAT=

ENDURANCE=

COMBAT=

ENDURANCE=

COMBAT=

ENDURANCE=

COMBAT=

ENDURANCE=

COMBAT=

ENDURANCE=

COMBAT=

ENDURANCE=

ALICE'S ADVENTURE SHEET

AGILITY

LOGIC

INSANITY

COMBAT

ENDURANCE

EQUIPMENT

THE PEN IS MIGHTIER

CURIOUSER AND CURIOUSER

NIGHTMARE
ENCOUNTER BOXES

COMBAT=

ENDURANCE=

COMBAT=

ENDURANCE=

COMBAT=

ENDURANCE=

COMBAT=

ENDURANCE=

COMBAT=

ENDURANCE=

COMBAT=

ENDURANCE=

COMBAT=

ENDURANCE=

COMBAT=

ENDURANCE=

COMBAT=

ENDURANCE=

COMBAT=

ENDURANCE=

ALICE'S ADVENTURE SHEET

AGILITY

LOGIC

INSANITY

COMBAT

ENDURANCE

EQUIPMENT

THE PEN IS MIGHTIER

CURIOUSER AND CURIOUSER

NIGHTMARE ENCOUNTER BOXES

COMBAT=

ENDURANCE=

COMBAT=

ENDURANCE=

COMBAT=

ENDURANCE=

COMBAT=

ENDURANCE=

COMBAT=

ENDURANCE=

COMBAT=

ENDURANCE=

COMBAT=

ENDURANCE=

COMBAT=

ENDURANCE=

COMBAT=

ENDURANCE=

COMBAT=

ENDURANCE=

Also Available from
JONATHAN GREEN and SNOWBOOKS

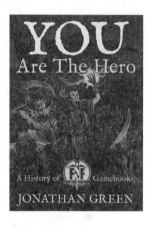

You Are the Hero
9781909679382

Sharkpunk
9781909679962

Game Over
9781909679573

Christmas Explained
9781909679375